ADVANCE

ADVANCE

ANIMUS™ BOOK FOUR

JOSHUA ANDERLE

MICHAEL ANDERLE

DISRUPTIVE IMAGINATION

LMBPN Publishing
PMB 196, 2540 South Maryland Pkwy
Las Vegas, NV 89109

First US edition, December 2018

THE ADVANCE TEAM

Thanks to the JIT Readers

Nicole Emens
James Caplan
Kelly O'Donnell
Crystal Wren
John Ashmore
Mary Morris
Joshua Ahles
Misty Roa
Kelly Ethan
Peter Manis
Terry Easom

If I've missed anyone, please let me know!

Editor
The Skyhunter Editing Team

*To Family, Friends and
Those Who Love
to Read.
May We All Enjoy Grace
to Live the Life We Are
Called.*

CHAPTER ONE

The dropship pierced through the Amazon's biosphere with a loud snap. A quick glance out the window revealed dark clouds as droplets of water began to smear across the screens. Clicks and hums indicated that the team had begun to prepare for their landing and tapped against their guns or activated them. One of the mercs moved his arm to one side to cram something in his pack and knocked a grenade off his vest. He grabbed at it quickly but was beaten to it by the bounty hunter across from him.

The man glared at him in annoyance from sharp, deep eyes framed by dark skin. He huffed an exasperated sigh as he handed the explosive to the merc. "I have no plans to die today," he murmured. "But if I have to, I would appreciate doing it with my boots on the ground rather than courtesy of a fool who doesn't know how clips work."

The man sneered and hooked the grenade on his vest. He slid against the wall of the dropship. "It wouldn't have gone off from a small drop. It ain't no Bouncing Betty."

The bounty hunter removed his brimmed hat and ran a hand through his cropped black hair. He replaced and lowered it as he snickered. In in a low tone, he said, "Considering the poor condition of your equipment, I wouldn't be surprised if those things blew up in your hand the first time you tried to use them."

The merc's sneer deepened and he looked at his two buddies on his left. "Do you believe this asshole? Mouthing off like this." He pointed a thumb at the cannon on his back. "You're gonna wish you were a little nicer when the shit goes down and you want the back-up of someone with some real firepower. What's your little rifle gonna do against mutants?"

The bounty hunter smiled and hefted his rifle. With a medium barrel and shortened stock, it had obviously seen a lot of use as the gray color had long since faded and long, dark spots dotted the barrel. "This is an old Medusa model rifle, so named because one shot could stop even heavily armored soldiers in their tracks. I like to call her 'Mary,' and this old girl's seen me through more fights than you've probably been in. She'll do the job just fine. I'm not sure I can count on you lot to do the same."

The three mercs scoffed and hissed their derision. One turned away while the one farthest away on the bench leaned forward and placed a hand on his knee. "Yer right, Hodder, this guy would do better to keep his lips shut than flap them at all." He growled and withdrew a small bottle from a pocket on his jacket. "Why would you talk all high and mighty like that? You're a bounty hunter and you're slumming it on a retrieval mission with guys like us. You must have fallen on some hard times to work with mercenaries rather than catching us." He unscrewed the top of his bottle, tilted it, and tapped the side until two pills fell into his waiting palm.

"I have my own reason for being here." The man shrugged and watched the merc pass the bottle across the silent team member to the big, grumpy one. He shook his head as he placed his rifle on his lap. "You're gonna pop some Jolts just before a mission?"

"Yeah? What about it?" the first, Hodder, barked. "Gets us all nice and peppy. We'll get this thing done in an hour and be back in time to find some ass on the night strip."

"Did you see the tits on the gig dealer back at the port?" his companion asked as he downed the pills. "I want to see if I can't find my way under that tight blouse of hers when we turn this thing in."

"I was too busy peeking at our little minx of a pilot." Hodder snickered. "I hope you don't get so amped that you can't fly, Kane. I wanna see if she and I can't have a little tumble in the cargo hold on the way back. I'll bet I can make that ass bounce like the ship's jets."

"Aren't you a romantic," another voice interjected. The three mercs and the bounty hunter looked at Kaiden, the fifth member of their team who sat in the dim, shoddy lighting near the back of the junker ship. "You said the same thing back when we took off. If you need a hole so badly, I'm sure the pinhole on that grenade you dropped would suffice."

"Another smartass?" Hodder growled. He aimed his cannon casually at the younger man with one large arm.

"I'm losing my patience with the two of you. You can stop with your little comedy routine. It ain't as funny as you think."

"I'm laughing." The bounty hunter chuckled and earned a quick glare from Hodder.

"Keep it up and I'll blow you away with this," he threatened.

"You might wanna mind your word choice there," Kaiden mused jovially and deliberately remained in the shadows. "And I don't think your little show is much better than ours. Your acting is terrible."

"What the hell are you talking about?" Hodder demanded. "This thing is primed and ready. I don't care if we're one—" He shot another questioning glare at the bounty hunter. "Or two men short. We can do this fine without you. It's dealing with punks like you that make chain gigs such a pain in the ass."

"For the first time so far, I agree with you," he said with a laugh.

Kaiden chuckled. He hadn't yet introduced himself, and no one had bothered to ask his name. "If it's one thing the Fire Riders are known for, it's accomplishing missions with impeccable grace and success rates." He pointed to the fireball and jackal tattoo on Hodder's shoulder. "And not being one of the bottom-rung gangs of the Midwest who are basically the bottom shelf hobo wine of gig fodder."

Hodder continued to seethe as Kane leaned forward to get a better look at the lone man. "Do you think you know what it means to be in a gang like ours? And you spout off like this bastard." He flicked a finger at the bounty hunter.

"All that hot air, but you're on this mission the same as us. Do you think you're any better?"

"First off, hell yes, I do." Kaiden nodded. "Secondly, let's answer that. How much are you getting paid for this?"

"Two hundred and fifty thousand credits." The skinny merc smiled.

"To split?" the bounty hunter asked. He tipped the brim of his hat up and revealed an amused look like he had a private joke only he knew about.

"It's called a deal—two hundred and fifty thousand credits for three members of the Fire Riders. That's a steal," he retorted. "I'd bet the two of you get maybe fifty thousand. We're the cleaners here."

"No. You are, as I've just explained, the fodder." Kaiden pointed to himself. "I'm getting two hundred and fifty thousand."

"What?" Kane yelled, and his gaze darted to the bounty hunter. "What are you raking in?"

"That's not a polite question to ask," he stated, and his smile became a cool smirk. "But something like four hundred, since you're prying."

"What the hell?" Kane hissed "That gig dealer screwed us!"

"Shut. Up," Hodder growled at his crony and shifted the cannon to aim at the bounty hunter. The target simply looked at it and frowned, his arms still folded. The merc traced a finger along the trigger. "Both of you, shut the hell up. I think I should maybe take you out now and collect your fees after this is done."

Boots thudded on the metal flooring and a pistol

pressed against the side of Hodder's head. "Like I said, your acting is terrible," Kaiden said. "You can't simply fire a cannon. It has to charge, unlike my pistol." He tapped the trigger threateningly. "And even if you were able to get a shot off, you would blow a hole in this ship and take everyone—you included—down with it. So either you're blowing smoke, or— Good Lord, did you not even consider that?"

"Hey, he's gotta worry about breathing, acting tough, and enunciating. He's taxed," the bounty hunter said as his smirk returned.

"Get away from him," Kane commanded and brandished a hand cannon. "You put that scrawny little peashooter away, or I'll give this ship an overdue paint job."

Kaiden glanced up, and the direct lighting revealed his tanned face with a scar to the right of his left eye and on the side of his neck. He studied Kane with piercing silver eyes, sighed, and tossed the pistol to his opposite hand. Kane smirked in triumph before a shot rang out. In an instant, his hand cannon was on the floor, and he held his hand in pain. Hodder looked at his friend before he realized that the pistol barrel now aimed between his eyes.

"You guys are not good at this intimidation thing, are you?" Kaiden asked. He seemed as deft with his left hand as he'd been with his right.

"Nice shot," the bounty hunter said approvingly. "Nice gun too. I don't think I've seen one like that."

The ace rotated the pistol to display the bronze frame and barrel with a black grip and small venting ports, and the weapon gleamed in the light. "Much obliged. It's called Debonair. It's a gift."

"Someone has good taste."

Kaiden smiled. "He's usually something of a bastard, but I put up with him—at least until I can take him down myself."

"How considerate of you."

"Get that thing out my face," Hodder demanded.

"Oh, found your voice again?" he asked but made no effort to remove the pistol. "And you managed not to piss yourself. Maybe you do have the backbone to go with all that bluster."

"I'll rip your damn—" the merc began, but a fist knocked his head back into the wall. The shooter raised the pistol and his eyebrows went up in surprise.

The fifth man had, up until this point, been silent. His shaven head and thin eyebrows gave his large, round face a boulder-like appearance. He folded his massive arms and returned the study. "Take a seat. There's no need for this. I'll make sure they shut up."

Kaiden looked at the merc, whom he assumed was the leader or head of their little party, then at Hodder who clutched the back of his head in pain. He shrugged and placed his pistol back into its holster. "It's nice to see at least one of you is civil."

"If all of us were like these jackasses, the Fire Riders wouldn't be any better than street punks," the man said solemnly. He unlatched a compartment on his belt and removed a pack of Sinner's Blend cigarettes. "Our rep may not be much better than you make it out to be, but we're doing some rebranding." He placed a cigarette in his mouth and raised his other hand to reveal a large gauntlet. The top part of the thumb

7

popped open and a small flame jetted out. He used it to light the cigarette.

"Surprising honesty," the bounty hunter said as Kaiden sat beside him, "We'll see if that pays off. I know the name of your two little caged pugs here, but I haven't got yours."

"Lazar," he stated and took a puff. "What about you, bounty hunter?"

"Magellan," he replied, and the merc looked at him in surprise.

"Magellan Desperaux?" Lazar asked and received a small nod in reply. "Well, I didn't think I'd run into someone with your pedigree on a gig like this." He took another drag and flicked the ash aside. "It makes me wonder what sort of trouble this gig has in store for us."

"I would say that this is clearly a hat-trick gig," Kaiden interjected. "Get in, get the payload, and get out. The guy who put me up to this suggested as much."

"I've had a few of those lately," Lazar muttered. "People grade the gig lower so they don't have to pay as much. They hide it behind easy objectives and hope that we do the actual job they want at half the price or less."

"You gotta admire the balls of the people who try that," Magellan mused. "Tricking anyone dangerous or crazy enough to take on a gig at a rogue port doesn't exactly lead to a long life."

"My source said this was supposedly requested by a corporation. You would think they could spare the creds," Kaiden protested.

Magellan chuckled. "Corps don't exactly have the best idea of what is fair." He looked at Kaiden. "You've been free with your info, but not your name. Tell us, youngblood, what are you called?"

"I'm not exactly a youngblood, not in this business, at least." He shrugged and grinned wryly. "But to keep up appearances and niceties and all that, I'm Kaiden—"

"Damn you." The three looked at Kane. His armor was cracked, and blood dripped from his hand. "Look what you did to my hand."

"I shot your gun and the explosion cracked your armor?" Kaiden asked in disbelief. "And your buddy made fun of this guy's rifle? How far are you gonna get with that clown suit?"

"I'll wring your damn neck," the merc vowed and shook his good fist.

"That would be impressive," Magellan commented.

"Settle down, Kane," Lazar ordered.

"But, boss…" the man whined and held his bleeding hand up again. "Look at what he—"

"Hey, partner." Chief appeared in front of Kane.

The skinny merc shielded his face, "My eyes!" he yelled as he winced and staggered back. He tripped and fell into the aisle and Lazar muttered under his breath in frustration.

Chief turned to look at the cowering merc. *"I should remember that not every peon can truly handle my shining magnificence. I should show more mercy and discretion."*

"You haven't adjusted your light display," Kaiden muttered and shielded his eyes as Magellan lowered his hat to cover his. "Turn the lights down already."

Chief sighed. *"It's a tragedy to have to lower myself to this level for the benefit of others. Life is unfair, I gotta say."* The EI's luminescence dimmed, and his golden glow faded to a sandy color as small blue and while lights raced around his form. His single eye scanned the dropship's cabin. *"You really brought out the A-team on this one, huh?"*

"You're quite a loud EI, aren't you?" Lazar mumbled as he finished his cigarette.

"I don't remember linking my oculars to see anyone else's EI," Magellan stated.

"He's a...special EI," Kaiden explained. "Well, I have a special EI device, but he's still unique in his own way."

"Yes, praise me," Chief declared.

"Goddammit, Chief." Kaiden sighed. "Is there any reason you needed to pop out?"

"I'm stretching my legs, partner," Chief said. Magellan looked beneath the floating orb and then at Kaiden with a questioning expression.

He waved a hand to tell him to forget about it. "Nothing else, then?"

"Well, we're gonna make landfall soon so you might wanna get the rest of your gear on."

Kaiden nodded in acknowledgment. "Good to know, but I think the pilot will tell us when—"

"Hey, jobbers in the back," a voice called over the intercom. "We'll land in five. Get ready because this will be a quick drop. Anyone who lags behind doesn't get a piece of the action, and that means they don't get their fee," she explained, and the intercom emitted a soft static whine as it clicked off.

"Well, it looks like it's time, gents." Magellan placed his rifle onto his back as he stood.

Kaiden smiled as he returned to his seat and grabbed

his helmet and rifle. "Let's earn some creds," he declared as he began to put on his helmet before he paused and turned back. "Oh, I forgot to fully answer your question. My name's Kaiden Jericho." He pulled the helmet on and locked it into place.

CHAPTER TWO

Kaiden watched as the dropship departed once the pilot stated that she would be back ten minutes after one of them activated their beacon. Kaiden looked at the small, square device. The instructions were simple enough—pop the safety glass and press the trigger for five seconds. He slid it into his supply case and joined the other members of the chain team.

Hodder bristled as he passed him and glared but said nothing, although he tapped his fingers on his cannon. Kane still fretted about his hand. He'd removed his almost destroyed glove and now applied a stitch cream. Kaiden winced as the man clenched his wounded hand. He had almost forgotten how the stuff felt considering the painless rejuvenation serum that he used back at Nexus. It repaired minor to moderate wounds quickly, but as the name implied, it felt like your hand was stitched with no anesthetic by a particularly new doctor.

He reached Magellan and Lazar on the cliffside of the hill where they had landed and looked over the ridge. In the distance and a little over a half-mile away, was their target—the now abandoned biodome belonging to the Axiom Corp. Even from this distance, Kaiden noticed breaches along the bottom lining of the dome and dents and tears in the top. According to the details they had been given, it had only been abandoned for twenty-two days, yet it appeared to have accrued a significant amount of damage in that short space of time.

"That big bastard has dealt with some shit while vacant, huh?" Kaiden commented, breaking the silence.

"No kidding. Biodomes are built quickly, but they aren't made of paper and string—especially one commissioned by a place like Axiom," Magellan noted. "Although why they decided to set up in this particular part of the Amazon... Mutants run the place. What do you think they could have been doing out here?"

Lazar huffed and tapped the ash from another cigarette. "Axiom is known for their blunders more than their successes. My guess is they were either searching for some sort of material out here or maybe working on the mutants themselves."

"I'd say the latter is the most likely," the bounty hunter agreed. "Maybe I'm getting more optimistic as I age, but perhaps they are looking into a way to reverse the effects or at least make them more docile."

"Hmm, not to be a killjoy, but I doubt they are that compassionate," Lazar stated. "If that were the case, sending in a team of heavily armed mercs and the like means they gave up on altruism rather quickly."

Kaiden retrieved an EI pad. "Chief, bring up the target," he ordered. The pad came to life and displayed a holographic image of a large silver tube with the Axiom AX logo embedded on it. "I have no idea what's in it, but they must want it badly to spend almost a million credits on its retrieval. You would think they would have their own teams to do that."

"They do," Magellan confirmed. "We'll probably run into whatever is left of them. Corporations and Zaibatsu's hate resorting to freelancers. My guess is that whatever is in there was too much for the guys whose usual day consists of guard duty and transferring projects from one base to the next with a full patrol of Hawk Jets and Outcast bombers."

"Not enough grit to get the job done," Lazar added and took another drag. "We'll see what we're dealing with once we get in, but from what I know, it'll be anything from venom leapers to those goddamn shriekers."

"Not to mention the mutated anacondas," Kaiden added. "What are they called? Nagas?"

Magellan nodded. "That's the Sanskrit word for serpent used in mythology to refer to a mythical race of snake people." He chuckled. "Viciss Labs really fucked up when they let that whole mess happen. Mutants are a worldwide problem now, but at least we know that the cryptos are the real deal now, even if they aren't nature's beasts."

"Oh, they are nature's now," Lazar grunted and readied his heavy machine gun. "Nature's abominations. Are you two ready back there?"

"Ready when you are, boss," Hodder acknowledged and turned toward him although his eyes glanced at Kane.

The weasely merc winced as he slipped his glove back on. "Yeah, we'll be right there."

"We're leaving in five. Take a final look in the crate and figure out what you're taking. Pile on as many explosives and grab as much ammo as you can. I wanna get this done quick, and I don't wanna hear your excuses if you run out," the merc captain commanded. He looked at Kaiden and Magellan. "We're the muscle here. I believe you about your rifle, Magellan, and you look or at least act like you can handle yourself, youngblood."

"I'm not a youngblood. That means I haven't done this before," Kaiden grumbled and drew his machine gun. The Tempest had camo casing over a black body with a short barrel and four vent ports on either side.

"Well, I can look at you and tell you're the youngest here. But I'll stick to Kaiden if you're that opposed." Lazar examined the gun quickly. "Is that a Tera Sovereign model?"

"Yes, sir," Kaiden said with a smile. "I bought and modified this one myself. It's energy based, so I added a mod to overcharge the core for stronger shots, another to reduce overheating to compensate for it, and improved stability. I've used it a few times already. Unless we run into any jumbos or hulks, I'll be fine."

"I doubt that'll be an issue," Lazar responded. "It's not really a place where Titan-class mutants live unless they're partial to taking vacations."

"Nagas have hides like steel, and they do live here," Magellan reminded them. "If we do run into one of them, we'll rely on you and your boys to take it down."

"Not a problem," Lazar promised. "Both Hodder and Kane have cannons and enough explosives to take down the big stuff, and if that doesn't work—" He tilted his head back, and Kaiden saw a collapsed grenade launcher attached to his belt. "I've got this. And plenty of special packages for anything that comes at us."

"That's considerate of you." Magellan studied the dome once more. "So, do either of you want to throw any plans out there before we head out?"

"It doesn't seem necessary. There aren't any human hostiles to worry about, and considering the weapons we have, sneaking doesn't seem to be a priority, right?" Kaiden looked at the others. Magellan shrugged and nodded, but Lazar remained stoic.

"Since you bring it up…" he began and eyed the bounty hunter. "You mentioned you were here for personal reasons. Can we expect you to run off at any point during the mission?"

"Perhaps, but it's unlikely," Magellan confessed. "You don't need to concern yourself with my personal objectives. I'll deal with my own problems."

"It's a concern if we are caught in the crossfire," Lazar pointed out and turned to scowl at the man with his arms folded. "You're a nearly top-level bounty hunter, Magellan—four-star class who command prices in the millions for their services. Why are you slumming it on something like this? Who or what are you looking for and are we in any danger of getting caught up in your mess?"

Kaiden was surprised. He looked cautiously at Magellan. The man certainly seemed to know what he was doing and was well armed, but from what he had seen back at the port and during the flight, he seemed rather aloof and laid back. He didn't look that old, and four stars was only one

rank away from the top. To achieve that rank at his age, he must be a damn good hunter.

"To be fair, it's only one to two million for a bounty. Millions is my count of bringing them in alive," he clarified with another casual shrug and smirk.

Good Lord. Kaiden hadn't run into many bounty hunters in his life besides Cameron and a few others at the Academy. Back in Texas, there had been the occasional Dead-Eye who pissed off the wrong person or earned a fierce reputation who had the occasional scrap with a hunter. Those were a much lower level—bronze to gold at the highest—and wanted more to make a name for themselves than anything else. A tingle of excitement coursed through him and he wanted to see what this guy could do.

"I suppose I can be more forthcoming. I doubt I'll have to worry about you trading info since if you did, you probably know rather well that I'll have no problem finding you." He spoke casually, but the menace was more in the calmness of the threat than in his tone. "The person I'm looking for… It's more of a personal hunt than a job. He's escaped me a couple of times and is damn hard to track. But he always finds opportunity in places like this." He nodded to the dome.

"He's a scavenger?" Kaiden asked.

"That's one of his professions. But he's also a murderer who's wanted in several countries, colonies, and stations. No clan, gang, or mercenary group backing. The last time he was in a merc group was the Starkillers, and he eliminated them."

"I've never heard of them. Did he kill their leader or something?" Lazar asked.

"Yes, along with the remaining fifty-six members of the group," Magellan revealed. "They almost lost a battle with a small team from the Omega Horde. He personally killed most of them in that fight. Apparently, he thought his mercenary group wasn't up to snuff, and instead of simply leaving, he felt the need to eliminate the entire gang. He killed those present and hunted down the others who weren't even there."

"So he's cold-blooded. A kind of guy who won't accept the weak?" Lazar questioned.

"Actually, he's a fairly nice guy and has a good sense of humor." Kaiden and Lazar gave him questioning looks. "He's certainly vile and tops my personal list of people who need a bullet in them, but he's not exactly the silent or chest-pounding type."

"A man who would kill off all his buddies for a single mistake doesn't strike me as a Mr. Personality," Kaiden retorted.

"Most serial killers don't think with the kind of logic we can necessarily understand," Magellan countered. "I don't agree with what he spouts, but I almost admire his commitment to his way of thinking. He's killed cops, guards, gang members, mercs, and other bounty hunters and even a couple of other killers and slavers. He has a 'live by the sword, die by the sword' mentality. If you pick up a weapon, your life is fair game. If you fail, it's forfeit."

"It sounds like he would be a bounty hunter for sport instead of creds," Lazar commented.

"He could have made a good hunter, in all honesty," Magellan agreed thoughtfully. "But I've trailed him for almost a year now. Like I said, he's damn slippery when he wants to be. At other times, he makes a scene and I can get to him in time, but he's been able to escape all four times." Magellan tapped his chest armor. "He uses a long-shot pistol he calls Whistle. My best guess is that it's a modified Specter, but he prefers a jagged blade he carries with him at all times. That blade of his has left me a few scars."

"You make him sound like some sort of phantom. Does he have a name?" Lazar asked.

Magellan nodded. "Gin Sonny."

The merc's eyes widened, and a cold chill chased up Kaiden's spine. He had heard the name in the news and on the lips of the people in rogue ports. He carried a bounty of almost sixty-five million credits and a body count in the hundreds and was known to mostly attack colonies and traveling vessels. Recently, he had slaughtered a dozen members of a gang and twenty guards, both on the Hughes Station.

"And you think he's here on Earth?" Lazar asked, his rumbling, serious tone sharpened by surprise. "Do you think he's here?" He gestured vaguely toward their destination.

Magellan nodded. "That's why I took this mission. It's easier to hide as a member of a chain team for a simple retrieval mission than to announce my presence by coming alone. If I took my own ship or even a commercial flight, that could potentially give me away." He palmed his pistol, a small silver weapon with a brighter sheen than his rifle. "This fires disrupter kinetic rounds and punches clean through armor and shields while barriers can't touch them," he explained. "Despite the fact that he seems to prefer more...visceral weapons, he has a talent for tech.

Part of the reason he keeps getting away is all the tech he scavenges and repurposes."

"That's a hell of a thing to keep hidden from us. It could mean our necks if he runs across us while trying to get to you," Lazar fumed.

"Or you could have taken this mission knowing nothing at all if I hadn't come," Magellan countered as he stowed his gun. "Besides, he has no vendetta with me, so it's not like he's stalking me and you're caught up in it. He may not be here, but it's a potential target. I searched every corner and tunnel of Hughes station and found no trace other than the pod ship he used to get there hiding in a bay. My guess is he boarded a supply ship to Earth, and the only ships that came through between his massacre and the time I arrived both came from South America—one from Chile and one from Brazil. The Brazilian one was larger and therefore provided more places to hide. Add this to the fact that the dome over there was abandoned by its team when it was attacked by mutants, and it seems the tastiest target for him. Unless, of course, he found another batch of victims, but I would have heard of that by now. He likes to show the corpses off."

Kaiden's heart raced and a prickle of something he hadn't felt in a long time left him oddly uneasy. Fear, he realized, but shrugged it off. He drew a deep breath and calmed himself while he checked his gear, grenades, salves, guns, blade, and armor. The routine activity restored his focus, and he reminded himself that everything was in place. Mutants were a bitch but weren't unconquerable. Essentially, they were only animals with enhanced capabilities and bloodlust, but they could still be defeated if you knew what you were doing—like mercs or most droids.

The enemies he had faced were more like an obstacle, not a threat. But potentially facing a killer like Gin Sonny —one who took joy in hunting you down and whose expertise was ending your life—somehow seemed immensely more potent.

Something infinitely more terrifying.

"Hey, boss, are we going? It's been more than five minutes," Hodder called.

Lazar looked at Magellan one last time before he turned to his lackeys. "Yeah, we're going, but I need to fill you two in on something first." He walked away from Kaiden and the bounty hunter.

"Don't worry about it, kid. If he is here, I'll take care of him," Magellan avowed and placed a hand briefly on Kaiden's shoulder before he walked away. The ace nodded, held up his weapon, and looked at the dome.

It was time to see if the Nexus training had paid off. If he fell on this trip, there were no lives to spare. This death would be final.

CHAPTER THREE

The group approached the doors of the biodome's entrance. One had been ripped off its hinges and laid damaged and rusting on the jungle floor. Hodder and Lazar took point, peered into the entrance, and signaled the others to move in. Kaiden entered first, his machine gun at the ready. They hadn't encountered anything thus far, but cries and growls echoed in the air and metallic crashes and thumps from within signaled that this wouldn't be a simple jaunt.

They proceeded into the building and a long passageway with a number of doors on either side that provided innumerable options.

"Should we split up?" Kaiden asked.

"Fuck that," Kane declared. The man clutched a cannon —smaller than Hodder's, but Kaiden was more worried about his than the big one, as Kane's finger's drummed nervously on the trigger. "We move as a group. I ain't walking around here alone, not with the possibility of running into that crazy killer. When we get through this, I'm demanding a raise in the pay."

"I'm beginning to miss all that bluster you had on the dropship." Kaiden activated the flashlight on his helmet. "Would you stop fidgeting with that thing? It makes me feel anxious because it seems more likely that you'll blow us apart than death by mutants."

"You'll hear him charge it up before he fires, remember?" Hodder sneered. He stepped up beside Kaiden and with a cocky smirk. "Besides, look at it like this. It'll be a quick death compared to having your limbs torn apart and eaten by shriekers."

Kaiden swung his gaze to the merc who raised a hand to block the light from his eyes. "If we run into any of them, they'll hopefully drown out his welching."

"How can you guys be so calm about this?" Kane hissed. "Dealing with a killer with a sixty-five million credit bounty? That's over the line."

"Quiet, Kane," Lazar instructed and pushed past the trio to peer down the hall. "If you're too chickenshit to continue, go back to the rendezvous point and wait there. We'll take care of this, and Hodder and I will split your cut."

Kane stiffened and a frown crossed his features. His breathing still hitched but the finger stopped tapping the trigger. "Fuck that too. I want my share."

"Good. Focus on that. We aren't here for anyone's head. We're here to retrieve that storage container and get out of here," Lazar reminded them. "This bastard might not even be here, and if he is, he's Magellan's problem, not ours."

"Let's get moving, boss," Hodder requested as he raised his cannon over his head and rolled his shoulders. "I want to find something to shoot. If there isn't anything here, then I wanna get back and get some liquor. There's too much blood in my alcohol stream."

"Is the Jolt finally kicking in?" Kaiden asked and earned a toothy smile from the grunt.

"Kane's still got some if you're looking for a lift," he offered.

Kaiden released a single sarcastic laugh. "Nah, I'm good. I'll drink like a fish, but I need my shooting hand to remain solid. It won't do any good if my shots keep spasming."

"Lightweight." The merc chuckled and continued down the hall.

"Where are you going? Do you know where this thing is?"

"I'll start kicking doors in. I'm bound to find it sooner or later," he called back and poised at the first door to do exactly that.

"Hodder, calm down," Lazar demanded. "You'll get your fix, but it's better to not bring this whole jungle down on top of us."

"Bring on whatever," the mouthy merc retorted. "I can take it. Maybe I'll even haul a few of the mutant carcasses back and earn some creds from the labs back home." He shrugged. "You're the boss, but make sure we find something. I gotta fever, you know?"

"No kidding," his leader grumbled.

Kaiden shifted his machine gun into a more comfortable grip. "At least he seems in better spirits than before."

"He's got a party going on in his head, only no brain cells were invited," Lazar muttered which prompted a snicker from Kaiden. "Hey, kid, so you think you can use that fancy EI of yours to get us a map?"

"I can, but I'll need a system to plug him into. I doubt Axiom has the layouts of their facilities on the extranet. Chief, do you have any ideas?"

"Check around. Fancy places like this usually have a directory or kiosk in the front. If it's still functional, I can download the map or schematics and get us a course," the EI suggested.

Kaiden nodded and exchanged a nod with Magellan. The bounty hunter walked past him and Kane and took his place beside Lazar. "The details said that it would be kept in some sort of storage unit in the cryo-bay," the merc leader informed them. "This place is running on minimal power, which makes me wonder if whatever they are looking for is even good anymore."

"The container itself is temperature-sealed and insulated, with coatings and protection well above what we're used to. I'll give Axiom and their ilk this—they're thorough." Magellan studied the cracked and dilapidated corridor. "Perhaps not wise, though. But I'm sure one of their suits is learning that hindsight comes at a high cost, even fiscally."

Lazar chuckled and fumbled for another cigarette. He offered one to Magellan, who nodded appreciatively. They lit up using Lazar's flame and watched as Kane walked past them to Hodder, who now did a little jig in place as his excitement built and the drugs coursed through his veins.

"You seemed to be stuck with rather interesting company," Magellan observed as Kane and Hodder jested with one another. "But you have their respect. It must have cost you a lot."

"Fire Riders are a simple bunch. I'll stay with them to the bitter end, but we're basically barbarians with laser guns and explosives," Lazar confessed. "The strongest comes out on top. I got my position through battle and killing a couple of my superiors. As for the cost..." He lifted the gauntlet on his arm "Let's just say that this isn't an accessory."

Magellan nodded and took a quick puff. "I noticed the attachment stitching along the rim. I figure you can at least make enough from this to get a regrowth treatment or perhaps nano-repair. I don't need the credits so I can throw some your way at the end of this. Think of it as hazard pay for getting caught up in my troubles."

"Nice of you," Lazar acknowledged and took a long drag, "I'll take you up on that. We'll discuss the incidentals on the ride back. But, from your tone, I'm guessing you really do think your target is here?"

Magellan placed the cigarette back to his lips. "There are still no guarantees, and my EI hasn't picked anything up but the scents and markings of mutants but... Call it a gut feeling."

"Then I'll keep watch. Gut feelings can be more useful than any radar or scanner," Lazar stated.

"Hey, I got a map." Magellan and Lazar stepped forward as Kaiden returned. "Good news and bad news. The cryo-bay is a straight shot from here." Kaiden had Chief bring up a large display of the biodome's interior. Seeing it,

Hodder and Kane walked over to join them. "The bad news is that it crosses right through this area." Kaiden pointed to a circular room at the end of the hall, "There are enough sensors left in this place to show life signs, and we have a fair number all in this room. The rest of the place is virtually clear, except for the occasional lifeform along the far side."

"They must have set up systems to repel the mutants, although they didn't do much good," Magellan mused.

"They still have a few emitters blasting those high-frequency sounds that drive away most mutants, along with others emitting smells," Chief explained. He assumed the form of a smaller version of himself on top of the map and looked at Kane and Hodder. "I'm surprised the two of you can stand being in here."

This earned the EI annoyed looks from the mercs as Kaiden smiled under his helmet. "Anyway," he continued as Kane leaned over and flicked the holographic sphere. "You can either push straight through or try to go around. There isn't a back entrance or anything, but there might be a damaged wall on the sides that you can blast through. But that would probably attract all the mutants in the dome to you anyway, not to mention anything else outside that can withstand the repellents—Would you quit that?" Chief yelled, and his brow furrowed angrily as he looked at Kane.

"It seems the mutants are adapting, as they are wont to do." Magellan sighed and flicked his finished cigarette away. "I agree that we should head straight there. There's little point in luring more potential problems here. Do we know what is waiting for us or is it merely vague lifeforms?"

"Shriekers, like we guessed. A small colony of them," Kaiden answered.

"Oh, they are gonna shriek all right," Hodder declared with a smile. "Come on, Kane. Let's go run out the squatters of this fine facility."

"But what about...you know?" Kane sounded worried, but Hodder waved his concerns aside.

"Pop another jolt or something, man. You're ruining my wave. Let's get a ruckus going."

Kane was still for a moment before he shook his head and ran off, clasping his cannon. Kaiden turned the map off as Lazar walked ahead. "You're with me, kid. The two jitter brothers will blow them up as soon as we open the doors, you and I will take out as many as we can while they charge, and Magellan... Watch our backs."

"Sounds good to me," the bounty hunter agreed and followed with his rifle at the ready.

Kaiden could feel his excitement build again. Mutant-slaying was a badge he had earned, and he was happy to be able to put it to use.

Hodder and Kane stood on either side of the doors to the lab. The larger man settled his finger on the trigger as he looked at Kane, his face grim but steady. They glanced at Lazar, who held his heavy machine gun beside Kaiden who held a thermal ready in his hand. The merc leader nodded at Kaiden and Magellan, who responded in the affirmative before he gave Hodder the go ahead.

The merc grinned broadly and pressed the trigger to

charge his cannon as he and Kane turned and kicked the doors open "Wakey, plasma bakey," he hollered as he and his partner fired two volleys of plasma charges from their cannons. A loud, piercing, carnal cry resounded as the charges connected and massive explosions scattered through the room.

Kaiden waited for the blowback to die down before he activated his thermal and threw it in. Lazar fired as Hodder and Kane moved in while their cannons charged again. Kaiden raised his machine gun and strafed the room as he and the merc leader followed. Magellan's rifle pounded from behind.

The room was dark, and if it weren't for the bright flashes of the cannon fire, he would have upped the light sensitivity in his visor. Instead, he traced along the floor and halls with the flashlight on his helmet as another shot of cannon fire erupted on the other side of the room. He spotted their targets. The shriekers stood between five and six feet tall and were covered in black fur tinged red with the dried blood of their prey. Long tails whipped behind them, and deep yellow eyes surrounded black irises. Two of them stared at Kaiden and bared their long, curved teeth. They emitted a high-pitched cry—the piercing shriek for which they were named—in an effort to frighten or stun them.

"Chief, activate sound dampeners," Kaiden ordered. Their cries were immediately muted, as were the shots from his gun. He eliminated the one on the left with ease as the other charged. Kaiden was able to fire two shots, one to the arm and the other to the shoulder. It swerved to the side and dashed along the ground before it leapt at the wall and used it to bounce off and tackle him. He landed and yanked out his blade quickly as the shrieker bit into his opposite shoulder. The armor cracked as it tried to sink its teeth into his flesh.

Kaiden dug the blade into the beast's back and dragged it down to its waist. The shrieker screamed and held on, but its head raised and gave him enough time to rip the knife out and drive it into its chest. They flipped, the shrieker now under him, and he drew Debonair and shoved the barrel on its forehead to fire three quick shots. He pushed off the body and scrambled to his feet to retrieve his Tempest.

"Help!"

Kane backed away from a group of four shriekers which stalked him, his cannon useless as it was venting. Kaiden spun and dropped to one knee. He fired at the group and dispatched two of them in a flurry of laser fire before his own weapon overheated. One of the shriekers hurdled over Kane and glowered at the ace, who began mentally counting down until his machine gun could be used again. The other shrieker continued its pursuit of the skinny merc. Lazar and Hodder were both too busy to lend their aid. Then, before the shrieker could pounce, a shot rang out and its head burst apart. The remains slumped to the floor. After a second shot, Kane's pursuer also dropped. Magellan stood in the corner and gave him a quick salute as he turned to fire at the remaining horde.

Before Kaiden could wave back, Chief yelled into his ear, *"Kaiden, above!"* He looked up as more shriekers descended. "Shit! Guys, look up."

"Hodder! Now!" Lazar ordered.

"Got it, boss," he responded as he turned a knob on one of the belts along his chest. "You guys have thirty seconds to get your asses out of here. This place is going to blow."

Kaiden continued to fire and a shrieker dropped dead out of the mid-air. The others simply jumped down instead of climbing.

"Kaiden, behind you is a room, and the doors still have power. I'll cast in and lock them." He looked back as the others retreated through the door they had come from. He was too far away to sprint to it, not with the number of mutants in his way. He nodded, ran into the small room, and smashed his hand on the console to close the doors behind him. Chief left his HUD for a moment before a click and shudder heralded heavy bars that crossed the doorway. The shriekers pounded and slammed against the doors as they emitted screams of rage. The frame warped against the assault. A large explosion all but shattered his eardrums, even with the dampeners on.

Smoke floated in through the cracks above the doors. He heard nothing but the ringing in his ears for a moment before it faded slightly. Pieces of debris crackled and thumped as they fell in the Lab room beyond.

"Crazy bastard," Kaiden muttered. "But at least we don't have to deal with those monsters anymore."

An arm wrapped around his shoulders. "You guys made a hell of a racket." Kaiden leapt instinctively aside and drew Debonair. He aimed it at the stranger in the room.

"You woke me up from my nap. Did you have to kill all of them? It seems like a waste. They make a good meal."

"Who the hell are you?" Kaiden demanded. The lights in

32

the room were fairly dim, but he could make out some details. The stranger was tall with tanned skin and a lanky physique and short blond hair. His long arms and legs suggested an athlete but his thin torso was noticeable even in his light armor which glimmered golden, indicating its shielding. He wore a visor or shades with pointed edges over his eyes and sported a lackadaisical grin on his face.

"Me? I'm merely a traveler, looking to see what I can find that tickles my fancy." He rubbed the back of his head and his neck cracked as he shifted it from side to side. He yawned before continuing, "I guess you guys are a retrieval team? Maybe not. You're too well-armed. Those pansies usually have stun guns and tracer rifles which aren't exactly built for mutant killing—or any killing, for that matter. For all the smarts those nerds in the labs are supposed to have, the muscle only helps the theory of Darwinism."

Kaiden, despite the friendly demeanor of the man, felt uneasy. For a moment, he wondered why he was apparently simply hanging out there. Then it dawned on him, and the chill returned. He raised Debonair to fire, but before he could pull the trigger, the stranger had closed in. His arm was forced behind his head and his shots went uselessly into the wall. His adversary slammed something into his chest and he heard a hum as surges of electricity danced along his armor. The barrier shattered, and he felt the full surge of electricity course through his body. The man flipped him, his thin physique belying his strength. He slammed Kaiden into the ground and followed by smashing his boot into his helmet.

"A little quick to the trigger there, Ace." He knelt and forced Kaiden's head to the ground. "But I guess that's what I get for losing my manners. My name is Gin Sonny." Kaiden's breath hitched.

"Tell me, kid…" He continued to push Kaiden's head against the floor. "How did ya get here?"

CHAPTER FOUR

Two Months Earlier

The gates to Nexus Academy's entrance opened, and the eager student body swarmed in. A cacophony of cheers and conversations created a jovial atmosphere. Students, wearing their Academy jackets that displayed their year and division, filed quickly into groups as friends met others in their new year and caught up.

Kaiden looked around and absorbed the pleasant feeling of familiarity as a returning student rather than being bussed in as a last-minute recruit like the previous year. Some students stared or gawked at him, and he allowed himself a small smile. He had wondered how many top scores and records he had to establish to make a name for himself around there. It was satisfying that he'd achieved a little celebrity status. Now, he simply had to keep it up.

He heard his name shouted. Even with all the voices

talking at once, this one was unmistakable, mostly because he called him "mate."

"Flynn, is that you?" he shouted, and his gaze swept the crowd. A shaggy blond waved his hand a dozen or so yards away. Kaiden returned the wave as Flynn and Amber made their way over.

"Hey, Kaiden, how was your break?" he asked.

"Good. I kept busy and could have used more than six weeks," he admitted. "It hardly feels like I left at all."

"At least you didn't have a chance to rust," Amber responded. "Unless you've been eating bonbons this entire time."

"He's more of a sucker kind of guy," Chief interjected as he popped into visibility.

"You'd better be talking about candy," Kaiden huffed and regarded the EI with playful anger.

"If that's the pet name you decided, sure," he chirped.

"That's a little low-brow for you," Kaiden sneered. "Are you already hitting the bottom of the barrel? You've only been active a year, shiny."

"If you didn't mess up so much, I wouldn't go through my A-material so quickly," Chief retorted and twirled for emphasis.

"Hello again to you too, Chief," Amber said.

"Howdy, Amber, Flynn. How y'all doing?" he asked.

"Better, now that we've actually arrived. Our flight was canceled and we only got to Seattle yesterday, then had to make the trip here a few hours after landing," Flynn mumbled. "But I guess I can't complain. Marlo had to drive all the way here. He stayed and worked with his uncle in

Arizona over the break. Apparently, he's in the World Council Military."

"Where is that big, lovable goof anyway? Y'all are usually tied at the hip," Kaiden asked.

"I don't know. He said he saw Luke and went to grab him but kinda got lost in the shuffle." Amber retrieved an EI pad from her pocket. "Hey, Luna?"

"Yes?" a light-blue nymph-like EI with wireframe wings appeared. *"Do you want me to look for Marlo on the network, miss?"*

"I might have mentioned it before, but that is a nauseously cute EI for what we usually do," Kaiden pointed out.

"Hey, I ain't complaining. Besides, not every EI can have my swagger," Chief stated.

"You are a damn ball." Kaiden deadpanned and stared in response to the EI's glare.

"It looks like you don't need to, Luna." Amber smiled and waved. "I see them. Hey, guys!"

"What's up?" Luke shouted. Cameron, Raul, and Marlo joined the group.

"Que Pasa," Cameron said and shook hands with Flynn. He gave Kaiden a brief, stern look that the ace returned before he smiled and offered a fist. Kaiden knocked his own against it in greeting. "It looks like the gang's back together—the good ones at least, except you, Kai."

"Keep talking that shit and see if I back you up the next time you have a team of droids after ya," he warned sarcastically,

"Good to see you all. Now, we're only missing Chiyo,

Silas, Izzy, and the Tsunas," Flynn remarked. "It should be easy enough to find them."

"Genos messaged me a few nights back. Apparently, the Tsuna report to the dorms first thing. They have some upgrades scheduled, and we'll have more than twice the number of Tsuna students this year. Evidently, they thought the first year was a great success."

"Well, if most of them are half as good as Genos and Jaxon, they'll make fine additions." Luke beamed and knocked his shoulder against Raul's head. "Would you quit messing with your hair?"

"Stop hitting me. This wind is messing up all my work," he grumbled and moved a few strands of hair back into place. "This is our first day as advanced students. I like to make a good impression."

"What? That you should be a hairdresser instead of a tracker?" Luke chuckled. "I worry that you're gonna bring a blow dryer as your sidearm."

"I have mods in my helmet for that," Raul stated and adjusted his jacket. "Style is half the battle. Once we're out of here and I make a name for myself, I'll be on the news and in fashion articles all the time."

"Heh, soldier chic. I'm sure it'll catch on," Cameron jeered.

"So, guys, what are we waiting for?" Marlo asked, and the group turned to him, "We should head to the theater before all the good seats are taken."

"Well, I had hoped we would all get together before going to the introduction ceremony," Flynn interjected. "Besides, there's one for every year. The initiates start first right?"

"No, last, at least this year. The initiates don't show up for another few days," Kaiden explained, and the others looked at him in surprise. "What? What did I say?"

"Nothing. But…I guess it's strange that you actually know what's going on with school events. After a year when you seemed to keep your head in the ground, it's a change of pace," Amber admitted.

"Yes. After a whole year, I learned enough to read the pamphlet," he quipped and rolled his eyes. "Nice of you to notice."

"Hey, Kaiden, what's up with the scars?" Marlo asked and pointed to his face and neck.

Kaiden rubbed the spot in question and hiked the collar of his shirt up. "Yeah, I got them while having a bit of fun. No worries."

"What kind of fun did you have?" Flynn asked mirthfully.

"The profitable kind," Kaiden answered and earned a puzzled look from Flynn and shrugs from a couple of the others.

"Hey, and hi," a voice called excitedly.

The group looked in the direction of the greeting. "Hey, Izzy! Silas!" Amber ran to hug her friend as Silas walked past.

The enforcer clasped Kaiden's hand and both showed a little force in the greeting. "Trying to show off there, Sy?"

"Nah, man, just greetin' ya." He smiled.

"It feels like your trying to snap my arm," Kaiden stated.

"I'm an enthusiastic greeter. Good to see everybody." He shook Flynn's and Cameron's hands. "It looks like we're only missing blues and purps."

"We probably won't see them until after the introduction. They have their own thing going on," Kaiden explained. "I guess with you and Izzy, that's all of us for now."

"What about Chiyo?" Izzy asked as she and Amber sauntered back into the group.

"She's already in there, saving us seats in the balcony, but I doubt she can hold that many for long." Kaiden looked at his list of messages from Chiyo on his oculars' HUD.

"Then let's make a move. There's no need to keep her waiting," Flynn declared. "Let's kick off the new year."

As Kaiden entered the side door that led onto the balcony, he took a moment to peer over the edge and saw several rows of Tsuna. It resembled a bizarre art project as various shades of blue moved and shifted in the seats. Their kelp-like hair in various designs and braids danced around with their movements. He looked for Genos and Jaxon and finally saw them at the far end.

He waved but they didn't seem to see him, and he wanted to shout but was pulled away by the others. As he followed the group, he sent Genos a quick message to tell him he had arrived and where he was and waited for him to read it. The Tsuna looked up. He wore some goggle-like headgear which Kaiden guessed were oculars for his EI.

The two friends exchanged gestures of greeting and Kaiden moved on to find Chiyo, who sat toward the end of her row. He wagged his fingers at her and grinned as he approached.

"It's good to see you, Kaiden." Chiyo greeted him with a smile as he sat beside her. "I hope your break went well."

"Just peachy," Kaiden replied as he kicked his feet up and rested them on the railing in front of him. The others took their seats along the row. "How about yours? We only talked a few times, but you said you went back home for a couple of weeks?"

"Yes, to see my father. It was nice to spend a little time with him, but I spent most of the break working."

"Yeah, I remember you telling me you shadowed Laurie." Kaiden snickered. "I haven't talked to him at all since last year ended and was surprised that he didn't fret about me and his precious device away from school grounds for more than a day. He's something of a trip, isn't he?"

"I only talked to him personally a few times. He was quite courteous for a man of his stature and whom most people believe to be a recluse."

The ace frowned and slouched in his chair. "Either he's taking pills, or I bring out the giddiness in him."

"He did speak about you, though, and said that you should pay him a visit. When he and I discussed the tests you and I did together, he said—and I quote—'Kaiden has been an awful handful, hasn't he?'"

"Did you remind him I was the MVP in those tests?" Kaiden responded but returned her gaze with a sheepish look. "No offense. You did damn good too."

"How kind of you." She said flatly and chuckled slightly

after a moment. "I made sure that your good name wasn't dragged through the muck, but it didn't take much. He seems rather enthralled with you."

"If only some of the women in my life were half as interested," Kaiden grumbled. "Still, I guess you're fit to burst with all that you learned. I can lend an ear until the ceremony starts."

"I've shared more than enough in our messages. Besides, the work I helped with cannot be freely discussed."

"You can tell me, but then you'll have to kill me?" Kaiden asked cheerfully.

"More like if I told you, you would be visited by several men who cannot be traced and you would vanish." Her tone held no joke or sarcasm.

"Yeah, maybe it's best you keep it to yourself." Kaiden coughed, folded his arms, and leaned back.

"I was joking, Kaiden." She smiled in response to his relieved sigh. "I haven't earned sufficient trust to work on something at that level yet. But I did work with a couple of the professor's personal infiltrators and learned a great deal. They've both been in the field for over two decades, and their skills and knowledge are tremendous."

"It's kinda surprising that there are hackers who are so good you seem in awe of them," Kaiden admitted.

"There is always room to grow and more to learn, particularly with how fast security adapts and programming changes. What they were able to do with their own skill alone I was only able to keep up with due to assistance from Kaitō."

He was openly impressed and wanted to ask what she'd learned and how they could use it in missions, but the lights dimmed as the stage was illuminated. Holoscreens materialized on the front of the balcony and Chancellor Durand's cheerful face appeared. Kaiden looked through the translucent screens to see the chancellor move to the podium on the stage.

"Good morning, students and now former initiates," he greeted them cheerfully. "Welcome to the first day of your second year at Nexus. You fought hard, learned much, and have paved your own road over the first year. Now, it is time to build on that determination and advance."

"Kinda sounds like he's ripping off Sasha's speech," Kaiden commented. Flynn shushed him with an elbow in his rib.

"This year will bring new challenges, and you will have new responsibilities and privileges," Durand continued. "You are now upperclassmen and other students will look up to you and follow your example. Your trials will be greater, and your courses will be deeper, but that's merely the start. And, if I were to guess, you would all be disappointed otherwise."

At the shouted agreements and chuckles, Durand nodded and raised a hand to quiet them as he continued. "This academy has earned its elite reputation for the kind of men and women we raise. If you were to balk or leave in fear, that would reflect poorly on us. We are your teachers, so your growth and failures fall on us, but the responsibility and achievements are yours." His face turned solemn for a moment but quickly relaxed. "There are also the benefits of continuing your studies—better classes, more choice and synapse points, and potentially free time which you can choose how you spend."

The chancellor looked off-stage and nodded at someone in the wings. "This year, we shall continue the focus and drive of your first year but will add a few surprises."

The chancellor's face faded from the holoscreens, which now displayed the profiles of the various students and scrolled through them.

"All three hundred of you passed last year—the first year we've ever had with no expulsions or failures. I'm proud of you all. But that means you may have grown comfortable in your status and standing here. Therefore, since you seem capable, we will increase the challenges immediately. I think I wish to see who among you took your vacation as a time of self-reflection or merely as an excuse to slack off."

"What's he on about?" Flynn wondered aloud. Kaiden knocked him in the ribs as payback. "Now you're simply being childish," the marksman huffed.

"You will leave this theater and immediately head to the Animus Center. Over the summer, we added two new wings to the building and increased the capacity by two hundred pods," Durand informed them. "You will find a pod, and once you sync, you will be sent on a training mission with two teammates chosen at random. Your objectives are unique and your map will be procedurally generated. Your success is dependent on you working together, and your score will determine your starting classes and privileges for the beginning of the year."

As the crowd erupted in surprised chatter, the holo-screens disappeared. Kaiden removed his legs from the rail and leaned over to look at Durand, who stood confidently in the center of the stage. "Welcome to the Advanced Class."

CHAPTER FIVE

"Hurry up, students. Find a pod and get in," an advisor yelled and herded the advanced class into the Animus hall.

"Best of luck to you guys," Luke called as they turned the corner. "Me and the guys want to check out the new wings and pods."

"Do you think they had a new paint job or something?" Kaiden joked. "Let me know how y'all do. Later!" His and Flynn's teams entered Hall Three.

"I didn't think we would be thrown in this quickly," Flynn admitted as they headed to the far end of the room and the remaining pods. "I'm not complaining. Back in the saddle, I suppose you would say."

"I would indeed. So, how random do you think this will be?" Kaiden asked and entered the first available pod.

"I'm not sure, but I did hear some things discussed during my time working with the Tech Department," Chiyo answered and selected the pod beside Kaiden.

"Oh? What has he brewed up now and how are we

suckered in?" Kaiden asked, his voice droll and gruff with displeasure.

"There's no need to worry about anything malicious. When I worked with the professor, he mentioned that he had updated aspects of the Animus, smoothed out the transition of the sync, and increased the ability of certain processes. The fact that the chancellor mentioned that the maps are procedurally generated and not crafted as usual must mean he's already implemented the features."

"And we'll probably be the Guinea pigs, joy," Kaiden muttered.

"You know, friend Kaiden, you talk about this professor in a rather disapproving tone, but isn't he the reason you have Chief and that unique device?" Genos asked from the pod across from him.

"You'll learn first impressions mean a hell of a lot on Earth, Genos." Kaiden sighed. "And he made a terrible one. Not that I say it to his face, but I sometimes wonder if there's some sort of self-destruct command in that thing he implanted."

"Get ready for sync, everyone," an advisor instructed as he walked down the hall and inspected the pods. "Are you all ready?" he asked the group.

"I feel right comfy, but I'm kinda surprised Akello isn't here. I usually end up with her," Kaiden noted.

"Advisor Faraji is working in the new east wing for the time being. She's overseeing the entire wing," the monitor stated.

"Akello got a promotion? I thought she had only been made an advisor last year," Chiyo commented.

"That's not how she sees it." The advisor chuckled. "But

she was a pod tech and Animus instructor before getting the advisor position, so she has the smarts and know-how to be an overseer. But it's not her official position at the moment. You can ask her once you get back. Closing the pods!" He shouted his last words as the Animus pods sealed.

The ace relaxed as the now familiar process began and he smiled to himself as he drifted off. He never would have thought that he would consider this almost nostalgic.

When Kaiden opened his eyes, he wore his normal coat and armor and the HUD of his visor activated as he looked at his surroundings. He was in a rec room—or, at least, what appeared to be a rather lonely one. Tables and chairs were neatly arranged and nondescript. The room had no windows and only a single door in the front.

A couple of flashes in his peripheral vision caught his attention. Two other advanced students appeared. One was a woman dressed in a dark-gray vest over a long-sleeved black shirt and dark pants with high-heeled shoes. Her short brown hair was cut in a bob with gold stripes on the left. She looked curiously at Kaiden with rounded hazel eyes before they both turned to the third member of their party, someone Kaiden recognized.

"Mack? Is that you?" he asked in surprise.

The vanguard spread his arms wide and almost slammed them into the girl. "Kaiden! What's happening, man?" he bellowed. "Show some love."

"I guess I don't have to worry about being dumped with

two scrubs. How have you been since the test?" he asked and raised a fist that the taller man bumped quickly.

"I've done all right. I spent the break working out with my brothers," he explained and folded his large arms across his even larger chest.

"Are they here in Nexus too?" Kaiden asked.

"Nah. Two of them serve in the American Guard, and the other is a Marine in the WCM. They put me through my paces, I can promise you that, but not enough to stop me getting a different kind of action during the break." He snickered.

"Has a big guy like you got yourself a big girl, then?" Kaiden inquired.

"Of a sort—a tourist chick from the east coast. She wanted to see Graceland and take a crawl through Beale Street and all that. I showed her around, and she showed me a good time," he boasted. "I didn't get her number or network info, but she found me on my social page before I came back and it seems she might be interested enough to make a return trip next year. Take another ride on the big Mack!"

Kaiden laughed and shook his head before turning to the girl again, "Sorry there, madame. He's not always such a dog."

"Unless you're talking hound dog," Mack jested.

"Who might you be?" the ace asked her and ignored his friend.

The girl composed herself quickly. She straightened and held her hands behind her back. "My name is Lancia Guðmundsdóttir, Logistics Division, Diplomat Class."

"Good Lord, that's a mouthful," Kaiden muttered. "I

haven't worked with a diplomat before, but I can already tell you that you're definitely ahead of me in that department if we aren't allowed to negotiate physically."

"That would usually be frowned upon," she stated and still stood at attention.

"I appreciate the show of courtesy, but you can relax. We're obviously not the biggest sticklers for conduct here," Kaiden told her and nodded at Mack who now sat on one of the tables. The top sagged under his massive weight.

She nodded and relaxed infinitesimally. "Thanks, but as a diplomat, the code of conduct is sacred. Soldiers keep up with weapons skills and conditions, so they are always at peak performance. We constantly practice etiquette and stature to keep our skills up to par."

"That's commendable, but it also sounds like a class I won't moonlight in anytime soon," Kaiden snarked. "Do you have any firearms skills or martial training?"

"I spend most of my points in my class tree and in general talents. I have the basic firearms training that every student learns in prep and in the initiate year," she explained.

"So you're here for something different, which is kinda obvious. I guess you and I will do the dirty work, Mack."

"That's the kind of work daddy likes." He nodded and punched a fist into his open palm.

"Simmer down, big guy. We don't even know what the hell we're supposed to do yet," Kaiden admonished and looked around the room. "I don't see a board or anything. Should we wait for instructions or something?"

A rapid beeping issued from a small console on a table in the corner. Kaiden glanced at his companions. Mack shrugged while Lancia stepped cautiously toward it. The console continued to beep and a small amber light flashed in sync with the noise. She clicked the answer button.

"Good evening lady and gentlemen," a voice greeted them in crisp tones. "This is your mission. You are to escort your team's diplomat to her shuttle through the terminal beyond the door of this room. Once inside, fly the shuttle to its destination, where you will disembark and the diplomat will meet her contacts. Her objectives will be transferred to her EI at the completion of this message, as will the soldiers'. Your final score will be tallied at the end and will comprise a mix of how many hostiles are eliminated, the number of objectives accomplished by the diplomat during her negotiation, and lives lost. The mission can continue if the soldiers die but if the diplomat falls, the test will end, and you will all fail."

"Nice of them to think of us," Kaiden grunted.

Mack shrugged. "It comes with the territory, right?"

"For how much I pay to come here, I would like to think we're worth more and are less expendable than a rental guard," Kaiden retorted.

Mack leaned his head back in thought before he raised a finger to the ceiling and looked at Kaiden. "To be fair, that's our contract. Someone else will pay for us and we work it off, so it's free, in a way."

Kaiden waved him off. "That's called indentured servitude, which isn't much better. And I'll be damned if I'll suck up to some fat cat who thinks I'll call him 'sir' for five years or something."

Mack laughed. "Maybe you should have given that more thought before signing up."

"My hindsight is exemplary, trust me. And I'm already dealing with it."

The large man cocked his head questioningly, but before he could say anything, Lancia held up a hand as the instructions came to an end. "You have your mission, the first of your advanced year. We wish you well. Hominum ultra." The message ended with a click and the console disappeared in white light.

A loadout screen appeared in front of Kaiden, and he scrolled through the options. "Will you go with heavy weapons, Mack?"

"I am the weapon," he stated. "As far as firearms are concerned, I'll go with a hand cannon. A Mark Two Buster, Sigma Munitions model. I'll add a caster attachment to my gauntlets to enable me to throw my barriers and some thermals— Wait, I guess that would be bad in enclosed spaces, huh?"

"It usually ends in lost body parts—for you and them. Better stick with shocks," Kaiden advised. "For your melee weapon, you should try a shock gauntlet. I hear there are some new models that will actually increase the power of shields around your hands."

"I already have one," he said with mirth in his voice. "The things pack a wallop. My brother Anthony let me test one over the break."

Kaiden nodded approvingly. "What are your options, Ms. Negotiator?"

"Mine are limited, as fighting isn't my field of expertise," she admitted. "Sidearm, melee, one gadget."

"Take a Servitor. It packs a punch that can shatter most low-level barriers and requires minimal charge-up. It can also fire a couple of dozen rounds before you need to vent it. As for melee, take whatever you're comfortable with, but we'll make sure they don't get close enough that you have to use it— Actually, change of thought. Grab a blade."

"Why?" she asked.

"From what the message hinted at, it doesn't look like our job ends when you start yours. Something may go down, so it would be better to have more offensive options just in case. Besides, it would be more intimidating when you do start negotiations," Kaiden offered.

"Threatening the people I'm supposed to haggle with isn't the friendliest display." She sighed. "But I'll take it into consideration."

"You should also grab a barrier projector and some armor," Kaiden said. "I'm not sure if that's normal for y'all. But in battlefields, an exposed body makes for an attractive target, particularly the head. If it's no trouble, it would make our job easier."

"I have a preload for armor for most of my normal missions, but fighting isn't usually involved," she explained. She tapped a button on her loadout screen and a set of light armor, white with blue accents, appeared around her. "I'll add a stealth mod." She pressed another button and her armor changed to black as the blue accents faded.

"Good idea. Let me finish up here." Kaiden looked through his options. He opted to go with his normal loadout but decided to add a machine gun and scanned quickly for one in particular. Once he found it, he smiled and selected it, then added a plasma blade, shock grenades, and a serum injector for his gadgets. He closed the screen out as his choices materialized on him, slid

Debonair into its holster, and checked his belt for his items.

To test the new addition to his usual gadgets, he flicked his wrist and the hilt of the plasma blade slid from his gauntlet and appeared in his hand. He pressed the trigger and the blade released. It was smaller than his normal blade but easier to retrieve in tight situations. He held the button down and it began to glow. Despite its size, it would still cut through almost anything.

"Nice choice, Kaiden." Mack complimented him and examined the machine gun. "Is that a Tempest?"

Kaiden nodded and held it up, "I've played around with some fun things too. I bought one for myself and a couple of mods to go with it. It cost me a lot in cred but made up for itself quickly."

"I would hope so." The vanguard chuckled. "There's no fun in dropping a lot of creds on something that you're only gonna use at the range." They looked at Lancia who finished making her choices.

She closed her screen out as a rounded helmet appeared on her head. "I'm ready to go when you two are."

"Let's get to it," Mack declared and thumped his chest. "Don't worry about a thing. Nothing will touch you before we get on that ship."

"Afterwards, however, it's completely possible," Kaiden scoffed as he moved to the door.

The large man rubbed the back of his head. "He's joking, of course."

"I know I'm in good hands. You seem rather confident and him…" She looked at Kaiden for a moment. "I know what he's capable of. Everyone from last year does by now."

"No kidding. You should have seen him during the Death Match," Mack confided and drew a deep breath. "Of course, I helped him out at the beginning and destroyed a Goliath class droid."

"Impressive." She smiled. "As much as I would like to see you in action, I'd be happy to not run into a Goliath during this mission."

"Shame. It could make for some good action." The vanguard sounded disappointed.

"As much as I would like to sit around and hear you two talk about how great I am, we should move. I didn't have much for breakfast because I didn't expect to get my happy ass tossed back in so quickly, so let's do this. I get grumpy when I'm peckish," Kaiden ordered.

Mack nodded, and he and Lancia joined him at the door. The ace pushed the switch to open the doors, his gun at the ready. A dark tunnel yawned ahead of them. They looked out in confusion before glow strips illuminated the ground and portions of the ceiling. The lights snaked through the tunnel and split into multiple paths as the rest of the room appeared. They stared at a winding trail of halls and paths across a vast space.

"I can barely see a thing," Lancia gasped.

"Have your EI adjust the light sensitivity in your visors," Kaiden suggested. "It'll make it easier, but I hope no one has any flashbangs."

"So we gotta make our way to the shuttle and take out potential hostiles without being able to see them coming?" Mack questioned.

"I'm sure they'll be as blind as we are. Plus, the glow strips will light our path," Kaiden stated and put his gun away. "What's wrong, Mack, scared of things that go bump in the dark?"

The vanguard slammed his fists together and his armor surged with energy as his barriers activated. "Heh, hell no. They're scared of me."

CHAPTER SIX

The group made their way along the illumined paths with the amber light of the glow strips their only means of navigation. They reached a split in the path where one direction continued ahead and the other led them to the left. Lancia stopped them, pointed down the left hallway, and beckoned them to follow.

"Do you have a map?" Kaiden whispered over their comm link.

"No, but I was given a compass that provides directions to the port," she explained. "It was loaded in with my objective."

"That's handy," Mack stated. "What exactly do you have to do once we get to this meeting place?"

"Right now, my only objectives are 'get to the shuttle' and 'don't die' once we arrive. I'll inform you of the rest when I get them," she promised. Kaiden looked around for enemies, cameras, turrets, or anything that could be a potential danger as they moved on. So far, nothing seemed remotely threatening. All he saw were the pathways and the low lights of the glow strips.

"I don't like this. I know it's cliché and everything, but it's too damn quiet," Chief grunted, and his eye looked around in Kaiden's HUD as if scanning the surroundings.

"Do you think they will port the hostiles in like they did during the Death Match?" Kaiden asked aloud.

"Maybe. At least it would be something," Mack huffed. "There's something creepy about walking around in an empty terminal. I guess I'm used to them being so busy that to see it this uninhabited is kind of unnerving."

Lancia lifted her hand to stroke the top of her opposite arm. "It's eerie, I'll admit, but it's better than laser fire and bullets coming at you from all sides."

"That's actually more of our native element," Mack jested.

They reached another break in the path, but Lancia continued directly ahead, and the others followed. "I can certainly appreciate your bravery, but the less of a mess this is, the quicker we can finish and the higher the score."

"While we're on the subject, what happens when we get to the shuttle?" Kaiden asked.

"What do you mean? It's pretty self-explanatory," Mack stated.

"Can either of you fly it?" he reasoned. "Unless there's an EI pilot on board, that's something we might wanna worry about now instead of later."

"I figured you could." Mack shrugged. "You seem like you would know how to work any number of vehicles."

"That's a potentially costly assumption." Kaiden chuckled. "I've flown a few ships, but nothing past basic level and certainly not in space."

"You think we're in space?" Mack questioned. "What makes you think that?"

"The window," Kaiden answered and pointed a finger to his left. Lancia and Mack walked to the side of the hallway and pressed against the glass. They peered out and looked into a darkened room. A line of windows directly below the ceiling showed a darker abyss outside, and the white light of distant stars shimmered in the void. "Either that's space or it's a damn dark night."

"Oh, well, that's different. I don't think I've done a mission in space yet," Mack said cheerfully. "A new first."

"If there is an auto-pilot feature on the ship, I can access it," Chief interjected. *"It'll at least get us out of here."*

"Most shuttles do have one, but what about after?" Kaiden asked.

"I hear humans like praying when no other options are available," the EI chirped.

"Aren't you helpful—"

"Relax. As long as there is auto-pilot I can get us to wherever...as long as we have a destination and as long as we don't get shot down," Chief promised.

"Well, I got us a pilot, with some caveats. But we should be good," Kaiden announced. "Let's keep mov— Mack, get ready."

"What is it?" the vanguard asked and grasped his hand cannon as his barriers flared.

Kaiden readied his machine gun. "A couple of stories up, I saw flickering along the glow strips like something moved past them. We have company headed our way."

"Should we run or wait to engage?" Mack asked. His cheerful and boisterous demeanor switched quickly to a serious one as his training kicked in.

"Let's leg it. We can cover more ground while we aren't under fire and make it as close to the shuttle as we can. If we have to fight the rest of the way there, so be it, but it's better to increase our chances as much as possible."

The vanguard nodded. "All right, I'll take point. Lancia, tell me the directions over comms."

"A-all right," she stammered, and her voice betrayed her lack of combat experience.

Kaiden placed a hand reassuringly on her shoulder. "We'll be fine. You made it through the Death Match so you'll make it through this."

"Truth be told, I didn't do much fighting during the test. My team and I were able to find a delegate station in the first few hours, and I spent most of my time away from the…violence."

"Well, that's a rather impressive feat on its own," the ace reminded her. He gripped his weapon in both hands and held it to his chest. "Double time!"

They raced down the hall. Mack moved much faster than his size suggested he would, and Lancia provided directions. Kaiden heard the boot stomps above them. Whoever or whatever they were seemed to be closing in. The team turned into another hall which led down and away from the approaching enemy. That, at least, seemed like a small blessing.

They reached a pair of doors and Mack slammed the switch to open them. When they found four Havoc droids on the other side, Kaiden felt that God was laughing.

"Get behind me!" Mack shouted. The droids' chain guns began to spin as the vanguard activated a large rectangular barrier. The bullets impacted the shield and ripples of energy surged across the surface.

"Can I fire through it?" Kaiden shouted.

"I have something better," the vanguard declared. "Watch this." He held his gauntlet up, which hummed with energy, and smashed his fist into the barrier. It hurtled forward and seemed to solidify as it moved to knock the droids back. They crashed into the far wall. "Now fire," Mack said and readied his hand cannon.

He laid down a barrage of ballistic rounds while Kaiden fired volleys of laser fire. One of the droids tried to stand but its head exploded with a shot from Mack. "Are we good?" he asked.

The ace heard the horde behind them closing in.

"Find them." The guttural command was followed quickly by, "Kill them!" as the enemy neared.

"It depends on your viewpoint, I guess," Kaiden muttered. "Keep going," he ordered and punched the console. Using Debonair, he shot the keypad as he slipped between the closing doors.

"How much farther?" he asked.

"I'm not sure. It doesn't give a total distance, only to the next path," Lancia clarified.

"How far to that?"

"Two hundred meters down the right hall."

"Then we'll take this section by section. Let's go!" he shouted. Speaking quietly over the comms seemed pointless now.

They continued their trek although it seemed they

constantly zig-zagged and made little progress. Kaiden wondered if the directions Lancia was given were corrupted or simply another part of the stupid test. They entered a hallway that now seemed to run alongside the enclosed areas.

"There," Mack called. The ace looked through the outer windows at a hangar bay below with a shuttle parked in the middle.

The craft was surrounded by mercs.

"Seriously? Is this normal in a diplomat's life?" he asked.

"Danger is expected, but normally, it's an assassination attempt and more subtle. This would cause a scene."

"You can't cause a scene in an empty terminal," the vanguard reasoned. "Kaiden, I have an idea."

"What are you thinking?" he asked, "And before you try any self-sacrifice bullshit, I can already tell you that there are other options."

"I ain't gonna kill myself with this. It's way too painful when I get out of the pod," Mack assured him, his voice eager yet ragged from their sprint. "Besides, why do something like that when I can do something cool."

"Out of curiosity, is this a proven method or are you winging it?" Kaiden asked. "Not that I have room to talk, but this doesn't seem like the time to try to do something you saw in a vid once."

"Trust me, this'll be good," he promised. "It probably won't take them all out, but it'll damn sure even the odds."

"What have you got?"

"You have shock grenades too, right?" he asked.

"Yeah."

"Let me have them."

Kaiden handed his container of shocks to Mack. "Do you still have yours? Are you gonna toss them all out?"

"That might work on the grunts and the lightly armored bastards, but it won't work on the heavies. I'm gonna give them some juice."

Kaiden cocked his head questioningly as Lancia pointed and shouted, "There's the elevator."

They stopped, and Kaiden eyed it warily. "That's basically boxing ourselves up and asking them to shoot us."

"We don't need to go down that way anyhow," Mack said, as he held up Kaiden's container of shock grenades in one hand and his own in the other. "Do me a couple of favors, would ya?"

"What do you need?"

"Take my gun and fire when I tell you to." He primed his shock gauntlet. "Hey, Buddy. Overcharge my barrier, I'm gonna nova!"

"What…what do I press?" Lancia asked.

"Huh? Oh, no, Buddy is my EI. But don't worry, we can be buddies too."

"You're going to nova? Doesn't that drain the rest of your barrier? You'll be exposed," Kaiden pointed out.

"Pshh, come on, man. I still have heavy armor here," he bellowed. "Besides, this'll be worth it."

Kaiden eyed him skeptically but took the hand cannon from the vanguard's holster. "Godspeed, you crazy bastard."

"You should check if you two are related sometime." Chief snickered. *"But I see what he's doing. This'll be a show."*

"Do you wanna fill me in? I have a crisis of faith here," the ace muttered.

"Well, he's about to take a leap of one. Watch, this'll be good."

Kaiden sighed as he heard a ding. Mack had punched the elevator button and the doors opened. "What are you doing?"

"Shoot out the back of the elevator," the vanguard demanded.

"What?"

"Shoot! Did you forget how?"

He grimaced, aimed, and fired a ballistic round. The rear shattered, and the lights dimmed. The large group of mercs below uttered surprised cries at the loud whirr as the elevator shut down.

"All right, you focus on getting her to the shuttle," Mack said. "When that's done, you can join the fun!" With that, he raced into the elevator and leapt through the new opening. The vanguard hurtled into the middle of the mercs. Some were caught by surprise while others fired on him. Many of the shots struck home but were useless against his super-powered barrier.

With another battle cry, he activated the two containers, threw them on the ground, and slammed his shock gauntlet on the floor as he landed. His barrier erupted and caught most of the mercs around him in a field as the grenades went off. Electricity flashed around the field, sparked, and sizzled through the mercs caught within. One or two were only tossed back, but the rest caught the brunt of the shock. Their barriers collapsed, and they convulsed and writhed on the ground from the streaks of electricity empowered by the barrier field.

"Damn, that was impressive." Kaiden whistled. "Come on. Let's get you in that shuttle. I don't want to miss this."

"How do we get down?" she asked.

"That armor of yours has absorbers, right?" Kaiden inquired. She nodded. "Then jump." He led by example and flung himself through the hole and down the three stories. He turned and looked up, waiting for her to follow. "Land with your feet slightly apart," he shouted as she jumped.

"What did you— Ah!" She yelped as her body tumbled. Kaiden sighed but chuckled, held his arms out, and caught her before she hit the ground. "That's another way of getting down," he joked.

"Oh, hell no! Sit your ass down. Be humble," Mack hollered. He tackled a heavy to the ground and landed hammer blows to his face as a merc grunt stood and aimed at him.

Kaiden aimed quickly with the hand cannon and fired. The blast opened his chest and knocked him away. "Heavy armor doesn't mean you can get careless," he shouted and received an unintelligible response from the vanguard.

"Go ahead and help him. I'll get on the shuttle and start it up," Lancia said. "See if you can find a way to open the bay doors."

"Gotcha." He nodded. "We'll be on board in a few minutes."

Mack now grappled with another heavy who clutched his chain gun and fired wildly into the air. Kaiden ejected the blade in his gauntlet as he approached a merc who struggled on the floor. He pressed the trigger to heat the blade before he swiped it along the man's neck. A few steps took him to Mack, and he hastily kicked the merc's legs out from under him. The combatant dropped his gun as he skidded back a few feet.

"Let's see how *you* like it," Mack growled. He snatched up the already wound chain gun and fired at his adversary, then swept it in a wide arc. The remaining mercs fell beneath the fusillade.

"You certainly have flair." Kaiden tossed him his pistol as the vanguard threw the chain gun to the ground.

"Grit and grind baby!" Mack hollered. "You know, we never got that drink after the test. We need to follow up on that."

"We don't need an excuse for that." The ace nodded. "I guess I know what I'll do with my first free time."

"Hell yeah." Kaiden froze as a narrow trace of blue glowed on the big man's armor.

"Mack, get back!" he shouted. He shoved the vanguard aside as a bullet skimmed past and drilled into the floor.

"Sharpshooter!" Mack hollered. "They got kinetic rounds."

"It looks like the other guys caught up," he responded as several mercs appeared in the hallway above. "We need to open the bay doors."

"Then do it," Mack shouted and fired at the oncoming group.

"Chief, can you find the console and access it?"

"I'm already on it. It's a good thing you put some points into it. Otherwise, this might have been a pickle," Chief stated. *"You two get on the shuttle. I'll take care of the backwash."*

"Mack, get to the shuttle," Kaiden ordered.

"Let's get out of here," the vanguard agreed and shot a few more rounds at their pursuers as he backed up to the entrance of the shuttle. The bay doors opened as the soldiers scrambled aboard.

The craft rattled as the mercs continued to fire on them. The ace hurried to the front. "Did you get this thing prepped?"

"It's ready. I can begin take off," Lancia said and primed the engines. Beeps and clicks sounded around the cockpit.

"Does this thing have auto-pilot?" Kaiden asked.

"It does, but I can't seem to access it."

"That won't be a problem. Chief, are you almost done? We need a pilot."

"I'm ready. Let's get going," he declared and appeared in the console screen. *"You might wanna hold on. I turned the hangar's barrier off."*

"Which means wha— *Ah!*" Kaiden shouted as he tumbled when the shuttle launched into space.

"Let's kick this pig," Chief cried. The thrusters activated and they rocketed forward. The ace scrambled to his feet. An image displayed on one of the screens of the mercs sucked out into space as the team left the terminal station behind.

CHAPTER SEVEN

Outside the Animus

"Would you care to repeat that?" Professor Alexander Laurie asked, his focus on the four screens, each of which showed the face of a member of the Academy board.

"We wanted to know if you are willing to cooperate with the World Council. They request access to the Academy's index and archives. We have provided what we can, but they seem to have a particular interest in your projects and knowledge." The response came from Victoria Molyneux. Laurie glanced at the far-left screen. Her dark blond hair had been pulled into a bun and her eyes were soft and appealing, seemingly in an effort to coax him into giving his approval.

It wasn't working, not even to calm him down.

"Ah, I see. My apologies for the confusion. Let me make it up to the lot of you by giving you a quick and simple response. No," Laurie stated flatly. He released the railing of the platform he stood on to turn and leave when another member of the board spoke.

"Come now, Laurie. This is a chance to build a better bridge with the council and earn their respect and admiration," a man with neatly groomed short hair and a thin white mustache admonished.

Laurie looked over his shoulder, reluctant to give them his full attention. "Along with access to their considerable coffers, Vincent?"

"I would see that as a pleasant outcome," he replied, "You say that with such a hostile tone, Laurie. You certainly don't seem to balk at the offers and expenses of the board on your behalf."

"Do you mean the ones that I'm contractually obliged to receive? The ones that are the major reason for me being here in the first place instead of running my company? Well, that and the opportunity to work on some truly great projects to test my skills and problems that would require every bit of knowledge and talent I had. And, of course, to lead a group of other exceptional technicians and engineers. Yes, these were all noble and exciting promises but have come to mean less and less over the years, particularly the last year. You've merely had me keep the Animus up to date and work on menial assignments. I've had to find my own interesting projects."

"Is that why you are being so difficult? Spite?" Vincent asked, and his eyes narrowed in annoyance.

"I can be very petulant when things don't go my way— being one of the greatest minds on and outside this planet allows me that. But in this case, no. I usually drown my frustrations with you in a pool of red wine or white if I've smothered my issues in fine meats as well. It's more difficult to complain when enjoying the advantages of your work, you see," Laurie explained. He looked casually at the screen on his wrist, more to show his indifference to the board rather than for any specific purpose. "But no, I'm uncooperative for the simple reason that I don't want to cooperate. The council has shown no interest in my work since the original creation of the Animus. I find their sudden change of heart rather offensive. If they want to work with a Laurie, their contracts with my father should suffice. He will still work on that 'Icarus' station for a couple more years."

"You really do have a way of making things all about you, Alexander," the aged and gruff Oswald Whitchurch replied. "Although I must say that I always get a kick out of your little rants—when I'm not specifically on the end of them, that is."

"You're usually the most agreeable of your colleagues, Oswald, at least without the commander present," Laurie confessed and finally turned to face them. "You've also been rather quiet for most of our little chat, so tell me your opinion of this mess."

"Hmph, very well," Oswald agreed. "I value this Academy's independence above almost everything else. I can understand the…appeal of extending olive branches to the council, but I don't like setting a precedent that we are willing to do things *for* them. We have created something wholly unique and powerful with the Ark Academy program, something so appealing that I have heard rumbles that the council will attempt to create their own in the near future, one that will be under their thumb."

"We were as well, at one point," Victoria reminded him.

"We were on lease, one that we've paid off," he countered.

"And now, at least one of you wants to crawl back into those oh so tempting claws." Laurie deadpanned and glanced at Vincent again. "Is it a sense of masochism or do they simply call you the right pet name to have you kowtow to them?"

Vincent glared at the professor. "You should be mindful of your tone."

Laurie scoffed. "I don't see how this will affect me in the slightest. Will you actually attempt to fire the man who designed and maintains the Animus? Even if you had the guts to do so, I'm only under contract while I retain my position here. Once I'm out, I'm sure one of the other five Ark Academies would be quite giddy at the prospect of acquiring my skills."

"That isn't a concern, Professor," Olivia Aoba, the final board member present, stated. Her auburn hair had been straightened, and small, hazel eyes looked down at him with ill-concealed impatience. The lenses of her optics brightened and appeared more translucent. "This isn't a matter of your standing. We simply wanted to inform you of an offer that the council—"

"Knew the answer to. Which is why, instead of asking me directly, they informed you and hoped you could use your combined influence to sway me." Laurie ran a hand through his long cream-colored tresses and took a moment to sigh and adjust his gloves. "This whole conversation makes me quite irate and is rather unbecoming, to be honest."

"Your sense of decorum is certainly still intact, at least," Vincent muttered. "If rather delayed."

Laurie grunted disdainfully. "It's been at least ten weeks since I've been able to see a therapist thanks to all the busywork you gave me at the end of last year and the Animus updates you simply had to have at the start of this year." He straightened his coat and stood with his hands clasped behind his back. "I've made do by relaxing to some delightful ambiance curated by Aurora along with a bottle of Acqua Armonia, both of which are calling to me. So, if I've answered your question well enough, I would like to get back to my domain. I'll be in touch with you with my report in three months."

He turned to leave, but his shoulders slumped and jaw clenched as Vincent called, "Wait a moment."

"Well, one of us is certainly acting spiteful," he grumbled and scowled over his shoulder. "What now?"

"I want to satisfy my curiosity by calling a board vote on the subject of Laurie giving the council access to his designs and technology," he explained. The professor raised an eyebrow and folded his arms.

"The chancellor isn't here, and you are missing your fifth member." Laurie looked at the empty screens. "It's not exactly official, is it?"

"That's why I said this was for my personal benefit," Vincent clarified. "I doubt the council will stop asking simply because the good professor is…disagreeable. I think we should see where we all stand in this regard considering the potential benefits a strengthened partnership with the council will bring us."

"More specifically, that of you being able to get your lips closer to their ass," Laurie muttered. "Well, you know my opinion, and I know yours, Vincent. What about the rest?"

Victoria was the first to speak. "Even considering that this is only a hypothetical hearing, I would still have to side with Vincent on this discussion. We have wanted to change the curriculum in this Academy and allow more applicants in. While we have seen a steady rise, we are still limited by resources and functions. A stronger partnership with the council would be a great benefit to us."

Laurie rolled his eyes. "How about the two of you?"

"I am against it," Olivia stated. "Considering your links to the council and previous mention of the desire to work closely with them, Vincent, you have an obvious bias. That said, I understand the hope you two have and the potential of what such a partnership could mean for the Academy. However, we have no guarantee that this would play out in our favor in any way. They simply made a request to see the professor's archives and to have more access to the Academy's database. It isn't inconceivable that they would merely get what they want and bid us a quick farewell."

"Agreed." Oswald nodded. "Even if this worked out for the best, the council isn't known for leaving the corporations and divisions under their wings autonomous. Our grand plans and hopes for the future shouldn't come at the cost of all we have built so far."

Laurie watched in amusement as Vincent's lips puckered and his eyes closed tightly but briefly in anger. He sighed, opened his eyes, and shook his head. "Then it's a stalemate, it seems."

"At least without the input of the chancellor or— Well, hello, Sasha." Laurie greeted the commander as he walked into the room and stood at the end of the walkway. Sasha nodded and approached. The professor moved to allow him to pass and stand on the central panel.

"I must admit, I'm surprised this meeting is still in progress." Sasha nodded acknowledgment to the other four board members. "When I read the report of the council's request, I assumed that this meeting would be quite brief and that Laurie would simply say no before he left in a huff."

"I did and tried," the professor confessed, irritation evident in his voice. "But they seemed to believe there was some sort of wiggle room there."

"We're covering all the potential bases, Alexander," Vincent huffed. "It's an interesting idea to have the World Council as a possible benefactor. I wanted to be sure you understood that. I'm certain that there would be plenty in it for you as well."

"I assure you, I'm fine," Laurie retorted. "Being able to go about my business without the high and mighty second-guessing everything I do is its own reward. For all my complaining about the pointless jobs you give me, I'll admit they are simple enough to complete and thus afford me more time to work on my own personal projects."

Sasha looked at the professor for a moment and rotated his hand to indicate that he would wrap things up. Laurie nodded and turned to leave. "As the professor previously stated, his contract with the Academy allows him a number of privileges, one of which is that he is allowed his privacy." No one questioned how the commander knew the gist of their conversation. Whether present or not, he had a knack of learning what he needed to know, and they had long since given up trying to work out how.

"If you wish to allow the council access to the academy's databases," he continued, "I'll allow that up to level three. That will provide some of the schematics and files on Laurie's work with the Animus and Nexus EI chips and devices which should sate their rather sudden curiosity. But unless the chancellor gives his blessing, it's a moot point." Sasha fixed the board members with a hard look. Oswald and Olivia nodded, and both seemed pleased with the solution. Victoria nodded but her eyes betrayed slight dissatisfaction, while Vincent merely sighed and agreed.

"Unless there was something else you wanted to discuss while we're all gathered here, I would say that this meeting is adjourned." There was silence for a moment, indicating that the board members agreed that they were finished for the day. "Very well. Hominum ultra."

They signed out with the same tag and the holoscreens disappeared. Sasha turned and walked down the path and through the doors of Laurie's conference room. The professor leaned against the wall, waiting for him.

"Good timing, Sasha. My patience had worn thin." Laurie sighed. "Oswald and Olivia try their best, but they seem stuck in the same officiate mindset most of the career-chasers have. Fortunately, they walk a different path than Vincent, although Victoria seems unfortunately swayed to his side."

"Vice-Chancellor Molyneux has relatives who work

within the world government. She was raised in that environment, so it makes sense that she would hold a more favorable view of them than others," Sasha reasoned and leaned against the opposite wall to Laurie. "As for Director Princeton... Well, he only took the position here as a means to make his way to the government proper. Now that he's been here for more than a decade, I'd imagine he's rather impatient."

"Speaking of which, I listened to your final words. Saying the council has a 'rather sudden interest' in my work is how I would put it myself. It makes me wonder if they have a true burgeoning interest in the applications of my work outside a defense context or if there's simply an interested party who wants a more intimate look at some of my personal projects."

"Do you think this could be linked to the Arbiter Organization?" Sasha asked. "You've been rather quiet on that front."

"So have you," Laurie pointed out, "Whatever happened to that 'friend' of yours who was supposed to investigate them."

"I've kept in touch with him, although he doesn't usually come to Earth that often. However, most of his findings had little merit," Sasha admitted. "There was little to be discovered beyond what we had already deduced, but he was able to find some odd transmissions."

"Honestly, I wondered if I made them a bigger boogeyman in my mind than they actually are. Between their pretentious messages and occasional sabotage that seemed to be more for personal amusement or theory, they

JOSHUA ANDERLE & MICHAEL ANDERLE

seem more along the lines of a Skull and Keys sort of secret society than a Machiavellian one."

"Has something changed your mind?" Sasha asked. "A sudden audit request couldn't have been all there was to make you suspicious, could it?"

"It's suspicious, but no. I'd rather not waste the time if this was nothing more than our paranoia," Laurie admitted. "I had two of my best infiltrators, Xavier and Mako, do some digging over the break."

"Digging into what? Have you been going into the council systems, Laurie?" Sasha asked. His voice got deeper and quieted. "That's dangerous and reckless, even for you. If you're caught, that will cause a huge scandal."

"Technically it's not me, although I was the one to give the command, so I suppose that makes me the ringleader or accomplice?" Laurie pondered and acted oblivious to Sasha's warning tone. "Don't worry about that. I wouldn't do anything to besmirch the name of our dear Academy, at least not publicly. My people are very good at what they do, as I'm sure you are aware."

"Even if you don't get caught and made an example of, no one is important enough to not be disappeared," Sasha warned.

Laurie smiled, leaned forward, and patted the commander on the shoulder. "It's nice to see that you do worry about me sometimes. But don't fret, dear Commander. I can take care of myself, and during the times I can't, I have more than enough robots and gadgets to make up for those pesky human deficiencies." He began to walk down the hall. "But if you are curious as to what I found, join me in my office. I can feel a headache coming on and must attend to it at once with some liquid stress relief."

"That, and the disruption commands you put on the cameras are about to shut off?" the commander asked.

"That too, but it's a lower priority," the professor admitted. "Come along. I think you'll find that our new friends are a rather interesting bunch of crazies."

CHAPTER EIGHT

Barrier Weaving: Increases knowledge of barrier manipulation and skills to achieve more use out of active barrier energy.

Rank: 2/4

"I might as well. It'll cost me all my points, though," Mack muttered. "Hey, Kaiden, do you think I should upgrade my barrier weaving?"

"What is that?" the ace asked as he skimmed through his own talent screen. "Do you use your barriers in home economics or something?"

Mack placed a heavy elbow on the table and rested his head on his clenched fist. "No, dumbass. It means I'll have more abilities and styles to use when my barrier is up."

"Then hell yeah, that sounds like it would be a vanguard's bread and butter." Kaiden turned his attention to his own screen and flipped quickly through the different trees. "Although shouldn't you learn stuff like that in your workshops?"

"We mostly focus on the best ways to use our barriers, conservation, and which forms to use and switch to for various situations. We'll probably get into more advanced stuff this year, but most vanguards don't exactly have a suit of armor and a high-level projector while growing up, you know? We gotta get the basics down first."

"I follow, but if you think you'll learn more stuff this year, maybe wait it out. It'll be more useful when you boost it after learning more."

Mack tapped a finger against his helmet. "I've got two ranks out of four and three points to spare. Ah, you're right. I'll see if I can't put it into something else. Do you have any suggestions?"

"Armor-smithing? That sounds useful for your class, and it's in the Soldier tree," Kaiden advised.

Mack switched to the Soldier tab and studied it. "I could go that way—maybe put a point in that and a point in grappling and heavy arms."

"You don't have any points in heavy arms? It seems like a no-brainer for a heavy, no pun intended."

"I've made do with my hand cannon and barriers. We're the most defensive heavy compared to the Titans and Demolitionists. I didn't see a reason to focus on weapons training during the first year, but considering the new tests they will throw at us, it might be safer to broaden my horizons."

"I'd say it's a safe bet but considering your stunt back at the terminal and watching you fight during the Death

Match, Squad Test, whatever, you seem able to crush heads just fine." Kaiden chortled.

"I grew up with three older brothers, and all of us trained in wrestling and boxing and picked up a few ranks in kick ass the natural way over the years," Mack explained and finished with a chuckle. "What are you going for?"

"I think I might put a point into the pilot talent," the ace replied. "Maybe it's time to get accustomed to flying on my own. I've usually had someone else on my team who could do it, but like you, I have to plan for whatever is gonna happen next. And actually being able to fly when we get caught in another situation like that will be important."

"Have I not done a good job?" Chief asked as his eye furrowed in the HUD.

"You're not even the one flying. You merely activated the auto-pilot," Kaiden retorted.

"I got us out of the hangar," Chief countered. *"Granted, it could have been smoother, but I was also taking care of business with those mercs at the same time."*

"I ain't dogging ya." Kaiden tried to quiet the EI. "But what if the ship didn't have an auto-pilot? Or it required a pilot to physically activate it in some way? We would have been up a creek. I'm a plenty good shooter, I think anyone would agree." He looked at Mack who waved his hand from side to side in a "so-so" manner. Kaiden opened his visor, glared at him, and raised a middle finger. The vanguard laughed. "Anyone who isn't trying to be a smartass would agree," he amended. "But I'm diversifying. We talked about this the other day when I spent most of my points."

"I still can't believe you put points into cooking," Chief

muttered. *"Do you think of yourself as more of a baker or grill master?"*

"I already told you I did that because of the gig. If I already had points in cooking, I could have sneaked into the kitchen to poison that guy instead of having to wait almost four hours in the alley for him to leave the damn place."

"You did a gig over break?" Mack asked and sounded impressed. "That much of a go-getter, huh?"

Kaiden smiled under his mask. "I did three, actually. Nothing too big but I got some good credits from them. The one I'm talking about is the one that actually left me with this scar." He removed his mask to reveal the scar along his eye and traced it carefully with his pointer finger. "I wish it was a cooler story, but the gig was a simple shakedown. One mob guy owed another some money and I played collector. I roughed up his two bodyguards while he was eating. I'd been told to leave all the parties alive, but they didn't have the same orders. One of them got me with a knife, but that was my own stupid fault. I was suckered into a bad situation with not a lot of room to maneuver. Still, I incapacitated them and waited for the target to come out so I could 'remind' him about a debt he owed. It turned out all right in the end. He paid on the spot and even tried to appeal to me by giving me something extra. It took my kind of 'diplomacy' to get that out of him, but it worked."

"That actually sounds more like enforcer work than something an ace would do," Mack commented.

"I'm starting out with a small list of clients while I build a rep. Fortunately, one of my contacts has been able to get me some good gigs, so I already have five to six-digit cred listings and jobs."

"Is your aim to stock up and be ready for when you get contracted?" Mack asked. "It's not a bad plan—it keeps your debt low, and you command higher prices and reputation so you access the good positions when you graduate."

"My aim is something a little different, to be honest," Kaiden admitted.

The vanguard tilted his head. "Like what?"

Before he could answer, Lancia spoke over the comm link. "Hey, guys, could you come to the cockpit?"

"On our way," Kaiden answered. He stood and curled a finger at Mack. "Let's go, jolly blue."

They entered the cockpit where Lancia sat in the co-pilot's chair. "What's up?"

"It looks like we're almost there," she said. "Or at least that there's something on the horizon."

"Considering this is deep space, I hope it's friendly." Kaiden took the pilot's seat. "That is…big."

In the distance, a massive dark ship floated directly ahead. It was almost hidden in the blackness of space but for the illumination of large lights along its hull.

"Is that a Dreadnought?" Mack asked.

"It looks like it," he replied. "It's not shooting at us so far, which makes it the nicest Dreadnought I've encountered so far in the Animus."

"We're being hailed," Lancia stated.

Kaiden folded his arms and his visor closed. "Chief, bring it onscreen."

A holoscreen appeared and displayed an older man with a salt-and-pepper beard in a black and gold uniform and hat. "This is the *Enyalius*. Identify yourself."

"Hmm… Do you wanna take the reins here, negotiator?" Kaiden offered Lancia.

She nodded and slid the screen to her side. "Greetings, I am Lancia Guðmundsdóttir, a negotiator here on behalf of the World Council to negotiate a ceasefire with the Io Marauders."

"Ah, splendid." The helmsman smiled. "We were worried that you wouldn't make it after reports of trouble at your last known location."

"There were some difficulties but nothing that my comrades couldn't handle."

"Very good. We will open a docking bay as soon as you send us your ship's information."

"Hop to it, Chief," Kaiden ordered.

"I can't. That requires pilot input."

"Seriously? You can fly the thing, but you can't transfer a file?"

"I'm not flying it, remember?" Chief reminded him. *"You simply have to click a few buttons unless you wanna go ahead and use that talent point."*

"Will it be enough?"

"To fly this jalopy? It'll be plenty. This isn't a bomber or fighter, merely a shuttle."

"Go ahead and load it in then," Kaiden requested. He leaned back and took a deep breath. A string of information and instructions appeared in his head as if it something he had grown familiar with over time came back to him in a rush. He exhaled, rolled his shoulders, and leaned forward to punch a few buttons on the screen. "Sending the ship's navpoint and model to you now, Helmsman. Which bay should we head to?"

"Usually, it would be on the lower decks, but the 'delegates' from the marauder band are already here, and some of my people say they have grown restless. We'll give you clearance to access the fighters' bay and will light the barrier green to make it easier to spot once we send you a navpoint."

"I appreciate it." Kaiden turned the shuttle's auto-pilot off and took control of the throttle. "We'll be there soon."

"Acknowledged. Prepare yourself, Negotiator. This may be…problematic for you."

"That's what we do, Helmsman. We solve problems," she said crisply. The man nodded as the screen disappeared. Kaiden guided the ship to the navpoint destination.

"Do you normally have long talks with moon mercs?" Mack asked and leaned against a console in the back to steady himself.

"Technically, marauders aren't mercs," Kaiden stated. "More like tribes or settlers that simply said 'fuck it' for one reason or another and became scavengers or hunters. They often go to war with other marauder clans and the WCM."

"But there have been over a dozen cases where peace was achieved between warring factions, so there is precedent that this can work," Lancia explained.

"Is that your mission? To bring peace between two marauder clans or something?" the vanguard inquired.

"My objective is to negotiate peace between the Io marauders and the WCM. Apparently, there aren't multiple marauder tribes on Io, only one large one. The others were wiped out."

"I suppose when you're the big dog, you get to say you own the planet." Mack chuckled.

Kaiden drifted the craft slowly to the side of the Dreadnought. "We actually studied some of their history in Ace strategy class. The Io marauders ain't as bad as some of the Phobos clans or even some of the merc groups in the area, but they make up for it by being crazy hostile, especially to the military. Apparently, they harbor a grudge due to the fact that the first settlers were stranded there for some time due to a mutiny that happened on one of the supply runs. That led to the creation of the Omega Horde, one of the only merc companies with an active line of battle-cruisers."

"Sheesh, I can't blame them for being a bit pissed but becoming a marauder tribe seems to be an extreme reaction. It's not like they did it on purpose."

"Hunger and disease on a lonely planet will drive you to some radical choices," Kaiden reasoned. "But hey, if they are here to bargain, it can't be all bad."

"There was an attempted negotiation with the actual Io marauders a few years ago, although that one ended poorly," she admitted. "I should also mention that 'stay alive' is still in my list of objectives."

The ace looked at Mack for a moment before he turned to her. "Yeah, that would be good to know. We're not in the homestretch just yet."

"Normally, these negotiations are for tests and trials to

see how to deal with situations where one party is less interested in peace than the other. This could end up as a disaster."

"It's time to flex your throat muscles," Mack quipped and went silent for a moment before he continued. "That sounds wrong—"

"I assume you'll be able to have a bodyguard with you?" Kaiden asked.

"Well, yes, but that could put the other party ill at ease."

"Not that I think these guys have a hell of a lot of common sense, but a little wariness is warranted when you have the reputation as a pack of raving lunatics from the stars."

"I can work something out. If I bring one of you, I could say that you represent the kind of soldier or technology we offer if they come back under the jurisdiction of the WCM," she suggested.

"If we're gonna go that route, take Mack. He's not packing like I am, and considering how big he is, he'll probably make them less likely to try anything stupid. Plus, his barriers will catch them off guard."

"I imagine that most of their weapons are energy based rather than kinetic. Even if they do attack, it'll be useless against me," Mack concurred.

"That sounds good." Lancia nodded and peered through the cockpit window. "Look above, Kaiden."

"I see it," Kaiden acknowledged and glided the ship easily into the docking bay. The green light of the barrier shimmered around them as they coasted in. He drifted to the left of the bay and followed the directions of large glow strip signals to an open space. Without conscious thought, he activated the landing gear, lowered the ship carefully into place, and set it down gently before giving the okay signal to his companions.

"Nice work. It's almost like you've done it all your life," Mack congratulated him.

"It kinda feels like it too," Kaiden said and flexed his fists. "I don't think I'll trade my guns for a pilot's license, but at least I have a fallback plan now."

"Please allow me a moment to change," Lancia requested as she stood and opened her loadout screen. She pressed one of the options, and her body was engulfed in white light. Once it faded, she was once again dressed in the dark formal suit she had worn when they first ported in.

"You still have your weapons, right?" the ace asked.

The negotiator nodded and moved her coat aside to show her Servitor attached to her upper thigh. She also revealed a bracer on her left hand that hadn't been there before, and she flicked it quickly. Her blade popped out, and Kaiden nodded approvingly.

"I had to ditch my gadgets, but this is better than nothing," she admitted. "For now, I'll rely on you two if this takes an unfortunate turn."

"We're always ready for that," Mack assured her. "But hey, take this as your moment to shine."

"I am quite confident in my talents, thank you. But I have seen how *you* fight, and it's not exactly subtle." This earned a shrug from Mack. "And I know about him—specifically that things tend to blow up around him."

Kaiden raised a hand in protest. "In my defense, something else generally makes the first move." He drew his

Tempest. "That noise we hear could be a merc with a chain gun or a Cleaning droid making weird noises."

"Well, this is a replication of a top-of-the-line WCM Dreadnought. I doubt we have to worry about the Cleaning droids rioting." She chuckled and pressed the button to open the exit on the side of the ship. "Ready, gentleman?"

Mack knocked his fists together. "Let's go negotiate the hell out of these guys."

CHAPTER NINE

The trio exited the shuttle. A group of Marines waited on the ground with the helmsman they had spoken to at the front of the group.

"Good day. Nice landing." He tipped his officer's cap. "Welcome aboard, but as much as I would like to go through all the proper pleasantries, we must get going."

"I understand." Lancia nodded. "Our apologies for the delay. Which way to the meeting?"

"These men will escort you." He looked at the group of six guards behind him. "It's up the hall, out of the bay. We can leave immedi—"

"Just a moment, Captain," one of the guards said and walked up to Kaiden and Mack.

"Captain? I guess we had that wrong." Kaiden shifted his attention to the guard, who seemed to assess him. The ace shifted slightly, and his finger slid closer to the Tempest's trigger. "Can I help you, or is this a greeting you guys do since you probably haven't seen anything this good-looking in a good few months?"

"Your weapons. Please relinquish them," the guard asked as two others stepped up behind him to help.

"Hell no." Kaiden balked and lowered the machine gun to point it at the guard's chest. "I don't remember any one of us agreeing to that."

The two other guards aimed at him while their leader raised his hands. "It's standard procedure. You're on a military vessel. It would be foolish of us to allow someone like you to walk around among the personnel with weapons on your person."

"And it would be foolish for someone like me to be stuck on a military vessel—which currently also houses murderous marauders—and not have my weapons on my person," Kaiden countered.

Although he couldn't see the guard's face behind his mask, he could hear his breathing speed up. "Will we have a problem here?" he growled.

"I thought we already had one. If so, what should we escalate this to?" he asked. "You know, I have to say I'm not impressed with your boarding party manners. I would have thought you would at least be as decent as the boy scouts, but you seem to be—ow! Hey!" The ace looked at Mack who had hit the back of his helmet with the broadside of his palm. He made a motion to tell Kaiden to quiet down as Lancia stepped forward.

"Please forgive my comrade, gentleman. It's been a long flight. He does raise an excellent point, however, considering the potential dangers inherent in having marauders aboard. Also, we are in unfamiliar territory and this vessel is in hostile space. Perhaps it is best that they retain their weapons. I'll surrender mine as I am here to negotiate, but they are both experienced soldiers and are only looking out for our team."

"This one's a soldier?" One of the guards snickered. "He's got shit discipline if that's the case."

Kaiden fought the urge to retaliate and held himself back. Instead, he shrugged and looked away from the guards as he raised the Tempest back into the air.

"Yes, I see your point negotiator." The captain nodded. "From my side, I should have advised you about our safety protocols, but I didn't think it would be an issue. I had no expectations that your teammates would surrender their weapons, and I should have explained that to the lieutenant," he muttered and glanced at the first guard. Kaiden noted two blue stripes on the side of the man's helmet as he turned away, something the others didn't have, and wondered if that was a symbol of rank or merely a personal touch.

"You may keep your weapons, but I assure you that nothing will go wrong," the captain promised. "Even if the marauders plan to betray us or cause harm, they only have five members on board—their leader, his assistant, and three bodyguards."

"That isn't too much to handle," Mack affirmed. "To eliminate five guys who probably have the equivalent of pointy sticks compared to what we have won't cause too much trouble."

"Again, I assure you that nothing of the sort will happen," The captain assured them. "It would be suicide for them to try anything on this craft. Not only is it crawling with over thirty-five hundred crewmen, even if they by some miracle escaped, they have no way to make it back to their planet."

"Why's that?" Kaiden asked.

"It's part of the negotiation agreement," Lancia explained. "The hostile party, in a show of trust, will either board the craft where the negotiations will take place or they will be taken to said location. In this situation, the marauders were taken aboard at another point and the *Enyalius* will jump to another point in space to evade any potential pursuers or ambush parties." She turned to the captain. "Correct?"

"Exactly." He nodded. "We frisked the marauders before allowing them on board and found no trace of any tracking equipment, and we are now well away from their home planet."

"Fine, fine, I getcha," Kaiden grumbled. "That means we're on the home stretch and we can get this done without a hitch." He turned to the negotiator. "Are you ready, Lancia?"

She nodded and looked at the guards. "Please take me to the meeting. I will attempt to complete this as quickly as possible."

One of the men nodded. "Please follow me." He turned to lead the group out of the bay. Kaiden stood beside the shuttle for a moment and glared at the insolent guard for a moment before he shrugged and followed.

The guard stirred an unease in Kaiden, an instinct he couldn't quite pin down. He wondered if he should let it go as he was simply an Animus creation, but the thought didn't settle him.

They approached the doors to the meeting room. Four guards stood at the end of the hall, while the remaining guard and the one Kaiden had argued with before turned and walked away. This second man had the same blue lines on his helmet as his teammate. Lancia removed her gun and handed it to Kaiden. "I'll let you hold on to this."

"It seems kinda pointless to give it away," Kaiden mused as he examined the pistol. "It's supposed to be for your safety. My pistol is more than enough for me."

"I know, but I want to make a good impression. That's difficult with a pistol strapped to my thigh."

"At least you'll know if they're paying attention or not," Mack pointed out and she flashed him a quick look. "Either way, she has me. And like they said in the dock, I doubt they are gonna try anything, not while they're at such a huge disadvantage. All we have to do now is make them sign on the dotted line or whatever and we're out."

"If you feel that confident, then by all means." Kaiden held Lancia's Servitor lazily in one hand as he leaned against the wall and slid down. "I'll keep watch."

"You can't even pretend to stand at attention before we go in?" Mack jeered.

The ace pointed at the guards. "They'll make up for me. Besides, it's not my gig. I'm an ace, sure, and starting to learn what it means to lead a team after a year of this. But that doesn't mean the old habits will go away all at once. I don't expect you to bow every time I walk into a room— although to be fair, that is mostly because I'm worried you'd fall over and crush me if I was too close."

"Where did all that come from?" Mack chuckled. "Being in a military vessel really has you on edge, huh?"

"I'm still grumpy from dealing with that guard." Kaiden sighed. "Don't mind me. I'm ready to be done with this. You do your thing, Lancia, and we'll be back to reality in no time."

"I'm not so sure. If it was that simple, I wouldn't need to go to a school as advanced as Nexus, would I?"

"What does that mean in terms of time?" he asked warily and craned his neck to look at her.

"Well, we could be done in short order—thirty minutes to an hour if this is mostly a formal affair—but I doubt that."

"Give me an estimate. How long do these things last on average?"

"Usually four to six hours. I've had higher level ones take days and have to save my progress and return to it several times," she explained and counted her fingers as if recalling her longer sessions.

Kaiden shook his head and glanced at Mack. "Maybe flex that muscle and pulse a little energy. It might speed things along."

"Unless lasers and explosives happen, our part is done, buddy." Mack shrugged. "It's all in her hands now."

"Great," Kaiden mumbled.

"I'm sorry for the delay," the captain apologized and hurried down the hall as the guards saluted. "I had to check in with the bridge before we entered. I'll act as both a witness and your advisor in the negotiations."

"I see. Thank you, Captain," Lancia acknowledged. "We are ready to begin."

"Very good. The marauders already await us." He approached the keypad beside the door and pressed four buttons in quick succession. The door unlocked and slid open. "Let us get this underway." He held a hand out, inviting Lancia and Mack inside.

Kaiden caught a small glimpse of one of the marauders before the doors closed. The man was dressed in tattered clothes, and his only armor was a chest plate and the top part of a helmet. His skin was an odd, ashen gray, and his eyes had bizarrely large pupils. Kaiden was unnerved by the thought that they were human.

The door closed and the ace looked at the guards who stood at attention a few yards away. They didn't seem to be a talkative bunch. He would have to find a way to entertain himself for the next few hours at least. That single brief sight of the marauder suggested that they wouldn't make Lancia's task easy.

"Hey, Chief, so you mind looking something up for me?" he asked.

"Whataya looking for exactly?" the EI asked. *"I should mention that certain sites aren't available during missions, at least not without getting into a lot of trouble."*

"I would imagine that they wouldn't see that as the most professional use of my time." Kaiden chuckled. "But that's not what I'm after. Do you still have that message from Julio saved?"

"Yeah. Do you want me to bring it up?"

"If you would." Kaiden nodded. The letter appeared in dim yellow letters across his HUD.

. . .

Hola, Kaiden,

It was good to see you. I wondered how things panned out after you left for that Academy. It's good to see how far you've come after all that, making something of yourself and showing some of those prissy bastards what a Dead-Eye can do. That's great, my friend.

However, considering what I've heard about the fees and such from that place, and the fact that you guys seem to do most of your training in virtual reality—is that for real?—I thought you could use an excuse or two to knock some heads and get paid while doing it.

I was gonna get this to you sooner but had to deal with a few things here at the lounge before I could. I chatted with the gig dealer here in Seattle and heard that you were already thinking the same thing I was and got a couple missions under your belt. A good thing. If you're interested in continuing your new practice, get in touch with me. I got access to a few higher paying gigs and some connections to rogue ports and guilds all through North and Central America. I'll have to set you up on one first considering how green you are in the eyes of some of these guys. Even your Dead-Eye credentials will only get you so far, but afterward, you'll have your pick, my friend.

Shoot me a message when you got the time and I'll get the order in. If you're not feeling it, you should still come down sometime. I have a new whiskey you got to try.

Regards,
Julio Alverez

P.S. Those punks you dealt with that day? Haven't seen them since, thanks for that.

"It looks promising," Kaiden said. "Although he never mentioned anything like this when I was bouncing for him over the summer. He must have wanted me to prove my mettle first."

"You gonna take him up on his offer?" Chief asked. *"It sounds like the potential for good money."*

"No doubt. I'll have to follow up with him. When do we get our first time off?"

"It all depends on how well we do here," the EI explained. *"If you pass with flying colors, you'll only have to take the minimum number of workshops. If you couple that with your training and Animus sessions, you'll be busy, but you have enough time to run a quick job every couple of weeks—nothing lasting longer than a few days, though."*

"And if we fail?

"That means make-up workshops, longer training sessions, and you'll probably have to do a few supervised Animus trials. You'll be swamped for at least the first part of the year."

Kaiden looked at the closed door of the meeting room and could hear nothing from within. "Tsk, I can't say I like sitting around here. At least in normal ops, I would have more of a hand in our outcome."

"Hey, you played your part. Now, it's her turn," Chief said consolingly. *"I'll boot up some games or something and we'll have to wait it— What the hell is that?"*

"What's what?" he asked and looked around quickly.

Nothing seemed unusual and even the guards hadn't moved. "Are you short-circuiting again or something?"

"Nah, not in here, you ass. I read something outside the ship, and it's gotta be something big for me to detect it considering we're in a dreadnought."

"Hey, there's something going on in the docking bays," one of the guards called. He looked at his tablet. "The barriers are being cleared. Wait, no, they are being deactivated!"

"What?" another asked, "Why would they— Lieutenant!" The guard who had confronted Kaiden earlier returned, flanked by three other guards. All had blue stripes on their armor. "There's something wrong with the systems in the docking bays. We need to inform the bridge that—"

The man's warning was silenced as the lieutenant fired a blaster into his chest. Scattered energy blasts punched their way through the guard's armor from close range. Those behind the lieutenant followed suit and killed the remaining guards who were too shocked to act quickly enough to defend themselves.

Kaiden scrambled to his feet and drew Debonair while he charged the Servitor, but a noise distracted him. Several shots from within the meeting room were muffled but evident, even with the doors closed. He cursed as he turned quickly to dispatch the hostile guards, only to be knocked to the ground by a blast from the lieutenant. The ace rose slightly, but his mask knocked against the barrel of the aggressor's blaster with a metal click. The man's finger eased back on the trigger.

CHAPTER TEN

Before the lieutenant could fire, both he and Kaiden lurched and fell when something crashed violently into the ship. The ace recovered quickly. He rolled and managed to halt his momentum enough to kneel on one leg and plant his other foot on the floor. He resumed charging the Servitor. Two of the guards turned to fire, and Kaiden used Debonair to shoot the rifle out of the hand of one of them. Three quick shots eliminated the second man. He fired the charged shot from the Servitor at the other guard. The blast erupted against his chest and pieces of his armor shattered and dropped from his body.

The last man helped the lieutenant up. Kaiden charged the Servitor again as he fired at them with Debonair. He wounded the guard twice in the shoulder, but the lieutenant scrambled out of the way and thrust his injured teammate into Kaiden's path. The ace grimaced but dispatched the guard with a few more shots before he stood. He aimed the Servitor at the escaping lieutenant and squeezed the trigger. The shot narrowly missed him and struck the wall as he spun around the corner. The discharge knocked him into the wall opposite him, but he simply bounced off and continued his retreat.

"Dammit," Kaiden grunted and took a moment to decide whether he should pursue him before another collision struck the Dreadnought. He stumbled and leaned against the wall to balance himself. "Chief! Do you have any idea what is going on?"

"It might not be obvious, but the Dreadnought is under attack," he snarked. *"That energy I detected was a warp gate. Something came out of it and attacked the ship."*

"Can you be any more vague?" Kaiden growled. "What's attacking?"

"I can't tell unless you can get me into an observation system or console to boost my scanner. Everything is muddled between the various energy outputs of the Dreadnought and whatever the hell is outside. The only thing I can say is that I pick up multiple readings—nothing too big so I assume that there might be a team of fighters and bombers out there."

"Trying to take on a Dreadnought with a handful of fighters? That's goddamn stupid." Kaiden slammed his hand against the wall in frustration. "I'll have to find a window to see what's going on, but first, get in that panel and open the door. I need to see if Mack and Lancia are all right."

"I'll try, but considering it's locked behind a code and you don't have proper clearance, I might take a while if I can do it at all."

"There anything I can do?"

"Check the bodies of the guards to see if they have ID chips or

key cards or something. Or hope that the captain is still alive and can get them out of there. I'll get to work in the meantime."

Kaiden hurried to check the bodies for anything that could help them open the door. A bright flash seen from the corner of his visor revealed that a fire had formed on the other side of the hall. Whatever had attacked had done significant damage in a short space of time. He mulled over the events as he searched. The guards who had murdered these four all had blue stripes like the lieutenant. The attack occurred incredibly quickly and the guards had mentioned the docking bays shields being deactivated. Common sense told him something wasn't right.

Did they get caught up in a mutiny? Was this intended to be a replication of the event that led to the creation of the Omega Horde? No, that didn't make sense. That had happened on a fleet of battleships, not on a Dreadnought, and the Io marauders didn't exist at that time. He recalled that the chancellor had made a big deal about these missions being procedurally generated. What they now faced seemed damn intricate for that. He might have to pay Laurie a visit after this was done and give him an earful about how successful his new updates were.

Another blast came from behind him, and Kaiden whirled with both pistols drawn. He lowered them and breathed a sigh of relief. Mack stood in the doorway, and the doors themselves lay in a shredded heap.

"Good to see you're all right, Kai— Damn, what happened here?" the vanguard asked. Lancia and the captain appeared behind him.

"Some of the guards—those ones over there with the blue stripes on their armor..." Kaiden used Debonair to point at a couple of the bodies. "They attacked and killed the others and were led by that lieutenant from the docking bay."

"What? Lieutenant Dirk? Are you sure?" the captain asked, his tone a mixture of disbelief and smoldering anger.

"I never got a look at his face," Kaiden admitted. "But he used the same weapon he was armed with at the dock and had the two stripes at the top of his helmet. All the other guys have different patterns on their armor." He pointed to one of the bodies that had three vertical lines on the left side of the helmet and another that started at the forehead and swirled to the neck. "I assume that's some sort of sign or designation."

"It was intended as a show of support for the Io marauders—the survivors, as we called them. It was an idea Dirk and a few other members of the security force suggested. This doesn't make any sense. Why would they betray the WCM? Why have they allied with the marauders?"

"I don't know everything, but my EI said he read a warp gate activation before we were attacked." Kaiden related.

"A warp gate? I never authorized—how did they even get their hands on one?"

"It would probably be helpful to know who they are," Kaiden pointed out. He turned to Mack and Lancia. "I heard shots in there. Did the marauders turn on you?"

"Well, kind of," Mack grunted and shrugged his shoulders. "One of them did."

"What do you mean?"

"The leader's advisor is the one who killed them and attacked us," Lancia explained. "He had an ocular in one eye. I saw it flash only a few minutes after we began our discussion and he drew a hidden pistol and shot the leader in the head. The bodyguards tried to return fire, but when they pulled the triggers, the guns erupted and killed them. He tried to shoot at us, but Mack blocked and shot his arm off. Then he...he had a bomb and activated it when we tried to question him."

"If it wasn't for this fellow's barrier, we would have been lost then and there," the captain stated. "We live, but we have no idea what is happening, and something has locked me out of the security systems. That's why we had to ask your vanguard friend to knock the door down."

"I have over a dozen uses, but battering ram is one of the most fun ones." Mack chuckled. "But now that we have a few moments to breathe, I assume we can safely say that ending this peacefully is no longer an option?"

"My objective is no longer listed," Lancia said. Her eyes lowered, and her face revealed uncertainty. "I now only have to survive again."

Kaiden looked at the despondent negotiator. "Now, I feel kind of bad. She didn't get a chance to do her thing before this all went to hell," he whispered to Chief but received no response. "Chief, are you there?"

"*Yeah... Yeah, give me...*" His response crackled with static.

"Again with that? Did something get into you?"

"*I was in the middle of trying to get into the systems to see if I could bypass the lock when your big ass friend there slammed through the doors. It caused a hard reboot. I'm fine or will be fine when I get all of me back together, but maybe we'll be more mindful of that in the future."*

"All right. I'm glad your back with us." Kaiden looked at Lancia "I'm sorry that this kinda turned more into our thing than yours," he apologized and gestured at himself and Mack. "I don't wanna sound like I'm dogging you, but I don't think diplomacy is really an option right now."

The look on her face quickly snapped from despondency to neutral understanding. "I've come to that conclusion myself," she agreed "What should we do now? I have no other priorities but survival. What about either of you?"

"Only to keep you alive," Mack said. "What about you, Kaiden?"

"Same, keep her— Wait, I have something new coming on. It says that I need to keep the negotiator alive and either escape the Dreadnought or take down the leader of the mutiny?"

"Who's that? The lieutenant guy?" Mack asked.

"It doesn't say. That's a hell of a lot to juggle right now," he muttered. "Where should we— Damn it!" He swore as the Dreadnought was rocked by another explosion. "That's starting to make me sick!"

"Wow, that's a lot of fire," Mack exclaimed. The ace turned, and his eyes widened when he saw that the small flicker he had seen before now engulfed nearly a third of the hallway behind them.

"Well, getting away from that seems to be the immediate priority," Kaiden stated dryly.

"I know it's a lot to ask…" The captain caught the trio's attention. "But can you escort me back to the bridge? I need to get control of the security systems and main weapons. Without those, we're compromised both outside and in."

"Your weapons are down?" Lancia asked.

"If they weren't, we would feel the aftershocks of the cannons firing. On top of that, our tracer guns are second to none. Whatever fighters or personal craft they may have wouldn't fly for very long."

Lancia nodded, but her eyes wandered to the side in thought. She turned to Kaiden. "If nothing else, helping the captain will stabilize the dreadnought. We can decide how to finish this from there."

"Sure, or we could simply find a batch of escape pods and be done with this," he retorted.

Though he couldn't see Mack's face, he imagined that he had a similar shocked expression to Lancia and the captain's.

"Uh, pardon my friend and me a minute," Mack mumbled. He gripped the ace's shoulder. "We'll be right back."

"Here, Lancia!" Kaiden tossed her the Servitor as Mack dragged him away. "Keep a lookout!"

The soldiers walked to the end of the hall where the fire raged. "Is this some sort of ruse or did you actually want to talk in front of the raging inferno?"

"I thought that maybe you were knocked on the head or something and the fire would snap you out of it," Mack countered.

"Don't go into therapy." Kaiden deadpanned. "Knock it off, would ya?"

The vanguard shook his head. He threw his arms back as his barrier energy sparked to life and clapped his hands together. The blast of energy smothered most of the fire, although a few small embers and flames remained.

"Nice trick."

"Quit it," Mack demanded. "What's with you?"

"What? About wanting to get the hell out of here? What's the matter with that? We've done the job, and now, they're goofing with us." He slid Debonair into its holster and his hands into his pockets. "It's not my fault my enthusiasm is waning."

"Still, I mean… I know we only worked together during the Death Match, but both there and in here you showed you liked to fight and to get things done. I respect that."

"I'm much obliged, but I don't see the problem here." Kaiden rolled his head like he was trying to get a stubborn crick out of it. "I'm not saying we should give up but that it would simply be easier to go with the escape route than run this little side mission and then find out who the 'leader' is… Although, if it is the lieutenant, I'll be pissed that I didn't kill him when he ran off."

"You let him go?" Mack inquired.

"I didn't think he was that important. Plus I was knocked off my feet by all the damn explosions, then you appeared and it slipped my mind," he said defensively.

They continued to bicker and argue. Lancia and the captain looked on, and the concern and impatience on the man's face became more evident.

"For someone who was so protective of his weapons, I would have never thought of him as a coward." The captain huffed his irritation.

"He's not," Lancia stated firmly. "Both of them got me here, and I know about other accomplishments of his.

Maybe he's simply annoyed about how things have turned out. He'll come around."

"And while he takes his sweet time finding his spine, the chaos onboard only grows worse," the captain muttered "I may have to go off on my own. I can't afford to stay here much longer."

"Leaving sooner won't matter if you die. If there are a lot of hostiles on board, they will be sure to try to stop you from reaching the bridge."

"There is that old saying, 'the captain goes down with the ship,' and if that does happen, I want to have tried my damnedest to stop this mutiny, not stand here twiddling my thumbs."

Lancia looked at the determination on the man's face and at her Servitor. "Then let's get you there."

"This is about free time?" Mack asked incredulously.

"It's about what I can do with it," Kaiden corrected "Either way, this test contributes to how the next few months will play out for us. We have a chance to end it now and pass. I think we should take it."

"Fair enough, but what about bonuses?"

"What bonuses? They never said anything about bonuses. Those are usually for the big tests."

"We only have one big test this year, and it's at the end of the year." Mack tapped the side of his helmet. "Things are different this year. Think about it, why would they give us two different ways to end it? One lets us pass, one hundred percent, A-grade, but the other goes a little beyond."

"Are you're saying you think we would get extra

points?" Kaiden considered this. "You must have talked to a few of my friends to know that appeals to me."

"I happened to talk to Silas and Izzy during the Death Match," he admitted. "They told me a few stories, specifically about your Division Test. But I also know you were rank three by the end of the year."

"Right, and?"

"You know that resets, right?"

Kaiden sighed. "Annoyingly, yes. I intended to find a way to get back up there. Those capsules aren't the same as a bunk or bed. They make me feel like I'm sleeping in a snack wrap."

"I can only guess, but maybe the more bonus points you collect, the more it contributes to your rank," Mack suggested.

"I see what you're saying… At least that means there's a possibility of doing it the hard way."

"Are you finally coming around?"

Kaiden chuckled, intertwined his fingers, and cracked them. "I guess I can't say no when you seem so giddy about it. Don't get me wrong, I usually like causing a ruckus. But I'm also usually in hostile headquarters or a jungle or something—places where I can be free to be me. I think they would dislike it if I shot up their precious ship." He looked down the hall to where some of the smaller flames flared once more. "Or maybe that's a moot point by now. Hey, captain! Do you mind if I—"

Lancia and the captain were gone.

CHAPTER ELEVEN

"Where the hell did they go?" Kaiden asked.

"Lancia? Lancia?!" Mack called into the comm link. "Where are you? Are you all right? You're where? With the captain? You couldn't have waited?"

Kaiden keyed into the conversation. "Lancia, you do realize that you are possibly the most important member of our little ragtag team at the moment and you are now where, exactly?"

"I'm escorting the captain to the bridge. We've been able to avoid hostiles so far and haven't seen any more of those guards with the blue stripes, but we've come across more marauders," she informed them. "My marker should be visible on the HUD."

"Wow, how long did we not pay attention?" Mack asked when he looked in the direction of Lancia's marker. "You're way faster than you look."

"I'm also not weighed down by a bunch of armor… although it looks like that could be useful right about now."

"Dammit. Hold on, we're coming," Kaiden ordered and

gestured at Mack to run. "Might I ask why you couldn't wait until we finished our little chat?"

"The captain said he needed to get to the bridge as quickly as possible. He didn't want to wait for you to finish your squabble and I didn't want to risk him going alone."

"You do know that it doesn't matter if he dies or not, right?"

She sighed over the mic. "I know it's not in our objectives, but I felt bad about—"

"Not that! I'm talking about the fact that he's an Animus creation. We're not actually losing a Dreadnought captain if he dies," he explained as they hurried left when they reached the end of the corridor.

"Well…yes, of course, it's just… We are supposed to take these missions seriously and go through them and make decisions like we actually would in reality," she pointed out. "We're closing in on the final—oh, my."

"Is something wrong?" Mack asked. "That sounded more shocked than worried."

"We-we are almost at the hallway leading to the bridge. We're at a window. Kaiden, it's horrible outside."

"What do you see—actually, hold that for a moment." A trio of marauders in the distance was better armored than the one he'd seen in the meeting room—probably because they were a boarding party and not there to talk things out. They were shielded by basic combat boots with leg and chest armor worn over more torn clothes and had basic machine guns slung around their shoulders. Whoever had supplied them didn't seem to spring for underlays or body suits. Which really was a pity, as they would have contained the mess resulting from what he was about to do much better.

Kaiden aimed his Tempest quickly, fired a volley of lasers at the trio, and eliminated them easily. He wondered if the plan was to overwhelm them with numbers or the chaos. If all them were so poorly armed, they wouldn't offer much of a fight for the properly armed military men and women on board.

Some of which were compromised, he reminded himself.

This truth was harshly confirmed a second after the marauder's bodies dropped when a squad of guards turned the corner. Kaiden hesitated briefly enough for them to take aim at him. He saw the lines, swore, and prepared to fire his Tempest as Mack dashed forward and created a wall of energy.

"We ain't got the time to deal with these fools," the vanguard hollered. Laser fire slammed into the shield and Kaiden heard a few clicks and dings from the vanguard's armor. At least one of the guards had kinetic rounds. "I'll make a hole. Shoot some on the way if you want but let's keep moving!"

Mack poured more energy into the barrier, and it sparked and solidified as it had at the terminal. He shoved it forward to crash it into the squad before it impacted with the wall ahead and shattered. Kaiden took point and fired on the guards, who were able to dodge. He dispatched one with a few quick shots, but the other activated a portable barrier. Kaiden flipped the knife in his gauntlet out quickly, took the blade end in his fingers, and tossed it at the guard as the man began to fire his rifle. The knife pierced the barrier and found its mark in the guard's shoulder between his neck and his shoulder pad. He swore in pain as the ace used the opportunity to rush forward and kick the grunt in the face.

The attacker fell, and Kaiden fired a few shots from his machine gun to make sure he stayed down. Mack fired his hand cannon at a huddle of adversaries who had been driven back by his energy wall.

"Double-tapping," he stated and put his weapon away. "We still have a few hundred yards to go."

"Let's get back to it," Kaiden ordered as they sprinted toward Lancia. "Hey, we were held up, but we're on our way again. What were you trying to tell us before?" There was silence on the other end. "Lancia? Are you still on comms?"

On his HUD, Kaiden saw a yellow light flash next to her name to indicate that she was in danger. "Shit. Mack do you have enough power to nova?"

"Just about, but I'll be at a minimum after."

"I guess we'll have to make do. They said they were almost there. Start priming!"

Although the ace didn't take the time to look back, he felt a pulse of energy behind him and a light flared. The vanguard had started the preparatory charge. As they closed in with only a few more turns and one hundred and ten yards to go, Kaiden slowed. Mack passed him, his entire body aglow in blue light that both coated him and trailed around his body. The ace heard shots and an explosion. When he remembered that Lancia no longer had a barrier projector, he began to worry.

Mack raced into the room and barreled into a group of

marauders and guards. His energy erupted, and Kaiden fired rapidly at all the enemies he could see. A few tried to retreat, but he refused to make the same mistake twice. He snapped to each target, pulled the trigger once, and held it only briefly before he switched to the next. The attackers retreated too slowly. They walked backward and returned fire when they should have turned and sprinted out of sight.

Their mistake.

The ace continued to execute all targets, and Mack added a few rounds from his hand cannon. Now, the enemy was in full retreat but was down to only three marauders. Kaiden shot two, one in the back of their head and the other in the stomach. The vanguard severed the final marauder's leg with one shot, but he made it into a room down the hall. The man's cries of pain muted as the doors closed.

"I wish we did earn points for all this," Kaiden mused and glanced at Mack. "I'd like to compare scores."

"I'd say you'd lag on this one." The large man chuckled.

"Only because you have large groups to use your nova on."

"Don't forget the thunderstorm effect I created on the terminal. Did that pay off or what?"

"I still think you did that mostly for flair."

"Of course. I gotta have a bit of fun now and then right?"

"I try to keep that to a max, but it's missions like these that bring out the worst in me." Kaiden sighed and took a moment to look around the room. "Lancia! Captain! You can come out now!"

"Kaiden, watch it!" the vanguard warned as a guard they hadn't seen aimed a sniper rifle at him. The ace flung himself aside as Mack turned to aim his hand cannon. Before he could fire, the attacker was shot in the back and thrown forward to land near Kaiden's boot. He groaned and tried to stand. Kaiden brought his leg down hard on his head and knocked him out to collapse spread-eagled on the floor.

"Are you all right?" Lancia asked as she scrambled from behind the crates she had used for cover.

"I thought we would be asking you that. Nice save," Kaiden quipped. "Where's the captain?"

"Right here!" he called and clambered from a pile of crates opposite Lancia's hiding place., "Nice of you to join us once again."

"It's good to see the two of you safe." Mack placed a hand on Lancia's shoulder. "Next time, stick with the group."

"Perhaps if you hadn't—" the Captain began but quieted when Kaiden stared at him and folded his arms. "Things could have been handled differently. I was possibly too hasty. But we are outside the bridge now and can bring this whole mutiny business to an end."

"Assuming that there isn't a horde of marauders and your traitorous guard waiting," Kaiden pointed out. "Are there any cameras or something we can use to see inside?"

"Here, let me look at the panel." The captain walked to a device on the side of the door. He pressed a switch on the side of the panel and a holoboard appeared on which he began to type furiously. "They locked me out of all the major functions and defense systems, but access to the monitor displays should still be accessible—ah ha!"

The three peered over the captain's shoulder. The lieutenant appeared on the screen. He paced in front of the captain's chair and yelled at the marauders.

"It doesn't look heavily defended," Lancia noted. "I assume most of the remaining traitors and marauders are fighting in other parts of the ship."

"The lieutenant seems rather pissed off." Kaiden snickered. "My guess is he thought you or I or both of us would hopefully be dead at this point."

"I wonder how long he's been in there," Mack pondered. "During a takeover, don't these guys usually pipe propaganda through the intercoms to lower moral or something?"

"Attention, crew of the *Enyalius,*" an angry voice barked over the speakers.

"There he goes."

"We have captured the bridge and assumed control of this dreadnought. If you wish to live, you will cease fighting, lay down your arms, and surrender to the Io marauders."

"I wonder why he would risk so much to help marauders. Do you think he's from there?"

The captain shook his head. "The lieut—Dirk is a colony boy, but he was raised on Luna. He's had an almost exemplary career—a few rough bouts and the occasional smartass retort—but always led those beneath him well and battled proudly for the military. I have no idea what is going on here."

"This is rather detailed for an Animus random scenario, don't you think, Chief?" Kaiden whispered to the EI.

"I wonder where Laurie got the backstory. Maybe from one of those war dramas?"

"Scan around the net. In the meantime, let's take care of this guy so we can—"

"Attention, crew of the *Enyalius*," the voice repeated.

Kaiden demolished the speaker directly above him with a single shot, although he could still hear an echo farther down the hall. "Great. He has it on loop. As I was saying, let's get in there and wrap this up."

"Do you think we can take it with a frontal assault?" Mack asked. "I'm with ya, but I still need a bit of time to charge."

"I thought maybe go with the whole 'cut the head of the snake off' strategy," Kaiden said and studied the panel. "Can you move the feed around, Captain?"

"Yes, of course, but only to the other active monitors." He pressed the left arrow key and shifted the view around the cabin. A handful of marauders and perhaps one other guard assured them of little resistance.

"Well, this is kind of an anti-climactic end." The ace sighed and stood back from the panel. "Captain, do you have the clearance to open this door still?"

"They've probably locked me out, but I know of a secondary way. If I issue an alarm through the panel it will force the door open, but then we won't—"

"That's all I needed to know," Kaiden interrupted. He stepped back and to the side with his head cocked as if he were looking through the closed door. "Mack, can I borrow your hand cannon?"

"Uh, sure." The vanguard handed him the large sidearm. "Can I ask what the plan is here or is that a secret for some reason?"

"It's more an action than a plan." Kaiden examined the weapon. "I need something with a lot more punching power than my Tempest or pistol. How many shots do I have before I need to vent? Did you vent it already?"

"Six shots and yeah, it's vented."

Kaiden nodded and held the gun with both hands. "Captain open the door if you would. Call it out right before it opens."

"Are you sure?" he asked warily.

"It'll be fine. The sooner we do this, the sooner you can stop whatever is going on outside."

"All right. I'm beginning to issue the alarm command."

Kaiden planted his feet firmly and lifted the gun. "Chief, activate battle suite."

The world shifted focus and Kaiden's vision enhanced. Some colors muted while others shimmered. He could feel his heart rate slow.

"Opening the door," the captain shouted.

The ace raised the hand cannon as Mack and Lancia stepped aside. The doors parted. The traitorous lieutenant stood a dozen yards away beside the captain's chair, and his head turned slowly as the doors continued to open. Kaiden fired, and the weapon bucked with the shot. The target's head burst apart from the impact. A few of the marauders jerked in surprise and the remaining guard turned to fire. After three more shots, the guard and marauders' bodies joined the lieutenant's on the floor.

Kaiden fired the last two shots at two marauders at the

front of the bridge. "Deactivate suite," he ordered and drew a deep breath as his vision returned to normal. "Thanks, Mack." He vented the hand cannon and tossed it to the vanguard before he retrieved his Tempest. "Hey, whoever is left in there," he called. "Let's reverse your once glorious leader's little declaration, huh? Unless you wanna end up like your pals, throw away your weapons and lay down on the floor."

Kaiden gave them a moment. Guns and blades clattered on the floor as per his instructions. He smiled under his mask and gestured at the captain. "The bridge is yours, good sir."

"Then the *Enyalius* has you all to thank for our salvation." The man bowed.

Another explosion rocked the ship. Kaiden and Lancia lowered to the ground to stabilize themselves while Mack simply stood firm. "That's gotta be adding up by this point."

"We will right it in a jiffy," the captain declared and rushed onto the bridge. "I can regain access to my commands from the captain's chair, then I can rearm the systems and take care of these ruffians." He took his seat and opened a holoscreen. His gaze darted to the trio as they approached and stopped near the remaining four marauders laying on the ground.

"Tracer guns online!" he shouted. "Main cannons online! Marking targets and returning fire!" He grinned at the group. "Care to watch?"

Before Kaiden could reply, the bridge began to fade and white light consumed his vision. He sighed lightly before he chuckled. "Damn. I could have done with a show." He gave his teammates a thumbs-up. "Good job, guys!"

No one was behind him. He looked around as the bridge disappeared into featureless light. He was alone. The light began to envelop him, but he didn't feel like he was de-syncing. He felt like he was waking up.

CHAPTER TWELVE

"Hey, kid, are you just going to keep lying there? Come on, now." Gin asked. The man's earring rattled as he moved his head around. "I'm sure you're having nice dreams or whatever, but it's rude to give me the silent treatment when I've asked you a question."

"What...what's going on? Who are you?" the ace groaned. He tried to stand, only to feel Gin's boot push him back down.

"Man, how high did I set that zapper?" the murderer pondered. "Come on, get those juices flowing. I don't want this scene of me with my foot on your chest to be misconstrued for something else, you know?"

Kaiden's memory returned slowly. He gripped his assailant's ankle and tried to lift the restraining foot, but to no avail. Gin watched him with an amused grin. "There's still some life in you, for however long that lasts." He knelt and peered into Kaiden's visor. "Tell me something, kid. Have you been doing this long?"

The ace continued to struggle. His strength returned

slowly and some of the muscles in his arm spasmed from the shocks. "I ask because I wanted a gauge of... Well, your stupidity for one, but also where I should rank you in my head," his captor continued. "You have some decent gear, you were quick on the draw—although that didn't really help when I think about it. I have a personal code when it comes to what I do, and I don't want people to think I'm all crazy, you know?"

"I...think you might be...a bit too late for that...you murderer," Kaiden growled, his voice hoarse and cracked.

"Now, let's not start with the name calling." Gin slammed a blade down beside Kaiden's head, and the tip sparked as it made contact with the metal floor. "I mean, that's a little hypocritical, wouldn't you say? You say that to try to hurt my feelings and yet I'm sure you've killed plenty in your time. Not to mention you killed all those poor, demented monkeys out there. That's gotta be on par with a few humans, right? We're pretty damn close on the evolution scale." The man ran a hand through his short hair and hummed to himself for a moment as he continued to slide the blade across the floor. "Mutation is another story, though. It's a nasty look, I gotta say. I prefer to modify myself with tech rather than get into the whole bio-freak crowd."

"Just...stab me!" Kaiden grunted and tried once again to push Gin's foot off as his faculties slowly restored. "Your constant...blathering is driving me...insane."

"Hey, there's that spirit. I like seeing that in the company I come across." The killer lifted the blade from the floor, grabbed the side of Kaiden's helmet, and lifted his head up for a moment as if to study him. He shrugged and dropped it, and the back of Kaiden's head smashed painfully into the ground. "I've developed the knack of reading people—had to, really," he mused as he now twirled the knife in his hand. "I haven't had a long relationship in the last few years, at least beyond a few where someone really wanted to kill me."

"You can add me to that list," Kaiden hissed. Gin looked at him, his eyes hidden behind shades but his lips pursed together. After a moment of silence, the man sighed, clutched the handle of the knife in his hand, and stabbed Kaiden quickly in his upper thigh before he ripped the weapon out almost as quickly.

For a moment, the ace didn't react. The killer had moved so fast he was almost unsure that it had actually happened. But in the same instant, the pain flared, and though his helmet muffled his cries of pain, his assailant still seemed impressed by the volume. "You know, I think it's moments like this that make me so...let's go with endearing to people," he mumbled.

Kaiden quieted. He sucked his teeth and growled from the pain as he tried to regain his calm. Now that he was fully awake, he needed to decide how the hell he could escape the creep.

"Kaiden, listen close. We've only got one shot at this," Chief ordered. *"You still have your blade, right?"*

"Tell me, kid, you got a name?" Gin asked and tapped the tip of the blade against the side of Kaiden's mask.

"Of course I do." He coughed and scowled at the man. "I don't see why I should tell you, though. I'll simply tell the clerk I turn your bounty in to."

Gin smiled in an almost unnervingly friendly way. "I

gotta admit, that's a new one. Most last words are something about me fucking myself or merely garbled noises."

"Black-out visor!" Kaiden shouted, and his visor turned almost opaque. His assailant raised a confused eyebrow as Chief popped up beside his head. "Do it, Chief!"

"Howdy!" he chirped and glowed as brightly as he could.

The killer grimaced. Even with his shades, the light was way too bright. He shielded his eyes with his arm and Kaiden used the distraction to retrieve his blade from his gauntlet and stab Gin's ankle. With a flick of the blade, he ripped through the back of the killer's leg. Gin didn't cry out as Kaiden was finally able to roll out from under his grasp. The ace snatched his Tempest that had been knocked to the floor and fell back against the wall but used it to steady himself as he fired. He held the trigger down until the gun overheated. Each shot struck the target in the chest or arms as he shielded his head. The man stumbled back and flipped over the table that he been on when Kaiden first entered. He vented the Tempest, threw it to the ground beside him, and retrieved Debonair.

He aimed above the table as if he expected Gin to hop back on top and lunge at him.

"What the hell was that?" A familiar shriek was easily recognizable as Kane's voice.

"Are you guys out there?" he called out.

"Is that you, Kaiden? So you are alive," Magellan responded. "We've got the device. You can come out of—"

"Magellan, you have to get in here. Gin is—"

"Nice moves, kid." A chill coursed through the ace and he turned slowly to the table. There was no way the man could survive nearly sixty shots to his body. "Good grouping too—a little erratic but it shows promise." The killer threw something over the table and it landed in front of him.

It was his boot, the one that Kaiden had driven his knife into, but the wound revealed no flesh and blood but metallic chunks and severed wires.

"It's a shame you didn't go for the other leg. That would have hurt like a bitch." He chuckled. "It would've been the first time anyone did any real damage to me since...Magellan, come to think of it. Speaking of that cheeky little devil, did I hear you call his name?"

"Chief, unlock the door," Kaiden demanded. He swept Tempest up in his free hand and used the wall for support to avoid putting weight on his wounded leg.

"I guess I should go and say hi. It's been a few months," Gin commented. "But I don't wanna run off if you still want to tussle. But I do gotta admit that I'm more interested in my buddy Magellan than you, so I'll make this quick."

He threw something else over the table—a black tube that glowed red.

Oh, no. Disintegration grenade.

"Chief!"

"Got it!"

The door slid open though it wobbled and creaked from the damage. Kaiden threw himself out and scrambled away on his hands and knees. He yelled at his team to get back as a blast of red energy erupted. Hands grabbed him and hauled him clear. Lazar and Magellan dragged him away from the blast while Hodder and Kane readied their cannons.

"What's going on, youngblood?" Hodder demanded. "Who's in there?"

"It's Gin," Kaiden called.

"That space kil—" Kane's voice stopped and he made a gurgling noise.

"Kane?" Hodder's voice was quiet and his tone disbelieving as he stared at the spike in his partner's throat. The wiry merc dropped his cannon as his hands clawed at his neck. His eyes went wide in shock and blood dripped from his mouth and the wound.

"Kane, what...what happened, man?" Hodder gasped. The surprise in his voice sharpened in pitch as he registered that his friend was mortally wounded. Kane slumped, and his knees struck the floor before his body followed.

"Kane?" Lazar muttered. He took a moment to look at his fallen comrade before he pushed his shock aside. "Hodder, get yourself together!"

"Who the hell did this?" the wild man snapped. He glared at the group with rage before he turned to the room Kaiden had left. Smoke and red dust, remnants of the disintegration grenade's energy, still billowed out of the room and swirled in the air. Hodder raised his cannon, charged it quickly, and fired three blasts. They pounded through the smoke and exploded inside the room. Silence followed with no cries of pain or surprise and no curses from within.

"Did he escape?" Lazar asked.

"There were no windows in there, and the only door is that one," Kaiden explained as he stood, removed a vial from his belt, and applied the thick substance it contained to his wound. He hissed at the burning sensation. The thick grey layer of the medication released an antibiotic and stretched over his wound to act as skin as it connected to the flesh around it and slowly drew it closed. He stood tentatively on the leg. It still hurt but the treatment did help. "I shot him with my Tempest—the entire charge before I had to vent it—and they all hit. He shouldn't have survived that."

"If he was that easy to kill, Kaiden, I wouldn't have had to hunt him as long as I have," Magellan muttered. "It's a barrier he stole from a lab on Luna. It was a prototype meant for elite vanguards and surrounds his entire body. Anything energy-based is useless."

"Get out here," Hodder bellowed and fired another charged shot into the room. "You coward. You bastard!"

"Hodder! Calm the hell down," Lazar ordered, but the merc ignored him and yelled a challenge as he charged another shot. Before he fired, something struck the barrel of his cannon. When he released the trigger, the gun exploded and knocked the man across the room. The other three stumbled and Kaiden almost fell, but Magellan caught him.

Hodder coughed and sputtered. Blood gushed from a wound on his forehead and his hands and arms were mangled from the blast, but his anger hadn't subsided. He stood and bared his teeth as a figure walked out of the smoking room. The merc screamed and charged although Lazar tried to grab him. "Stop, you're in no shape to fight."

Deaf to the warning, he tried to tackle Gin. "You took that explosion like a champ." The killer laughed. The merc bellowed again and slammed into his target who used the man's momentum against him and spun him violently.

"But I have other guys to play with," he said, his jagged blade in his hand.

Kaiden tried to shoot the knife from his hand, but in one quick movement, Gin drew the steel across Hodder's throat and dropped the body to the floor. The merc spluttered and twitched for a moment before he stilled in a pool of blood. Lazar winced, and his fist clenched as the killer stepped over the corpse.

"So, Kaiden, is that right?" Gin asked. He stepped fully out of the smoke and studied the remaining men. This time, he wore a helmet—white like the rest of his armor, with indented lines and slanted, rectangular visors in front of each eye. The lines also encircled his chest and arms. The helmet had an odd, black triangle design that encompassed the eyes and forehead.

"I'm happy to see you made it out of that. I have to admit, I felt guilty almost immediately. To take someone out with a grenade like that...well, it's too impersonal, you know?" Gin rotated his head and stretched it quickly from side to side. The bones snapped as if in warning. "Especially now considering you were nice enough to bring my friend Magellan along."

The bounty hunter's eyes were focused on the killer. Kaiden could almost see the wicked smile under Gin's helmet.

The killer raised a hand in greeting. "How have you been, Magellan?"

In response, Magellan raised his rifle and fired several shots. Light blossomed from Gin's hand, and the bullets struck it. Kaiden realized it was the same shield that he'd seen Mack and the other vanguards activate.

"Hard-light shielding," he explained. "It stops kinetic shots. Nifty, huh?"

"I'm not as amused with all the knick-knacks you've picked up every time we meet." Magellan reached into his coat, drew his pistol, and squeezed the trigger twice.

The killer dodged the shots, but they exploded behind him, thrust him away, and covered him in smoke.

"Ballistic rounds with a poison gas inside. It looks like you've picked up some fun things too."

Magellan donned a gas mask that covered his entire face while Lazar put one on that covered his mouth. Kaiden checked the seal of his helmet. He would be fine for now.

"Where did he go?" the merc asked. He aimed his grenade launcher at the poisonous cloud. The bounty hunter lowered the gun with a firm hand.

"That's a volatile concoction. I had it specially made to deal with some of his 'irregularities,'" he explained at a questioning look from Lazar.

"It's nice to know you think of me." Gin cackled. Kaiden whipped around in search of the voice and decided the killer had to be cloaked.

"Just be careful with your explosives. That poison is flammable," Magellan stated. He holstered the pistol and held his gun at the ready. "What are you waiting for, Gin? I know you like me to chase you all over the damn galaxy, but this cat-and-mouse shit is done. Come on out. I'll send my friends away, and you and I can finally settle this."

"It's tempting. Our meetings have been fun but I agree, they've grown a little stale." Gin's voice sounded like it came from everywhere at once. "I would take you up on that, but the more, the merrier and all that. I still want to finish my talk with Kaiden there."

"Oh, great, he's clingy." Kaiden chuckled, but his ease vanished when he saw Magellan glare at him. The man's eyes signaled that he needed to focus and that this wasn't something to joke about.

"Even if you did have the others hit the bricks, we wouldn't be alone. Not now, anyway."

"There!" Lazar shouted, and Magellan and Kaiden turned. The killer had somehow climbed the room and stood on a grate fifteen feet in the air in the corner of the room.

"They come to feed around this time." Gin looked at the corpses and parts of the shriekers. "And you've destroyed their dinner, which means they will have to find a different meal."

As Kaiden aimed and eased the trigger down, he heard a loud, breathy hiss. What should have been a quiet, subtle sound now echoed around the dome. He looked up, and his eyes widened.

Large white, grey, brown, and green scaly beasts slithered on the glass of the dome above, at least forty feet long and perhaps twenty in diameter with a frill around their heads. Large fangs protruded from their mouths.

Nagas. The mutant snakes descended into the building. They began to cover the ceiling, and one of the abominations leaped through the hole and released a loud hiss as it struck at Kaiden.

CHAPTER THIRTEEN

The ace's eyes widened as the great serpent flailed toward him. Its giant fangs, coated in an opaque liquid, were all he could focus on. Something slammed into his ribs and knocked him aside, followed by a reverberating *clunk* and a large blast.

"Get it together, kid!" Lazar yelled, as fleshy chunks of the naga splattered his armor and fell to the ground. His eyes were wild with anger and accented with drops of blood from the exploded mutant. "Or else you'll join the other two."

"They're swarming," Magellan warned. Kaiden, his leg still not properly healed, staggered to his feet and retrieved his Tempest. At least a half dozen nagas writhed down the walls.

"Well, this has certainly become a crowded party," Gin commented drily. Kaiden glanced at the killer who crouched on the catwalk above, his arms to the side and head tilted to observe the snakes. "They're magnificent creatures, but I've had my fill of them the last couple days."

He turned his attention to the trio, who now stood backed up against one another. "I'll be around, but I'd like to kick back and watch the festivities. I'll play with the survivors, all right?" Kaiden could envision an elongated, toothy smile under his helmet as he vanished from view.

"Dammit! He's gone ghost," Lazar growled and snapped his focus from Gin's previous position to the circling beasts. They were either more cautious than the first or simply understood to keep their distance after seeing it blown to bits.

"He won't run," Magellan stated calmly and aimed at one of the nagas. "Not when he has toys to play with."

"I stabbed him in the leg and tore through it," Kaiden muttered. "But he has a new one. Where did he get that? Can he regrow them or something?"

"No, nothing like that. Biologics aren't really his thing."

"Yeah, he told me." Kaiden pivoted slightly and took aim at a serpent that tried to slink closer. It coiled quickly to the side and hissed at him. "Is he a cyborg?"

"Technically, yes," the bounty hunter confessed. "But not the usual number of parts we typically associate with cyborgs. He still has a normal brain—well, as normal as a psychopath can have, anyway. He's augmented his left leg, both arms, part of his chest, and might have added more by now. He probably simply swapped them out after you gutted it."

"I don't want to babysit you two," Lazar interrupted as he slid another grenade into the chamber of his launcher. "We should focus on the immediate threat. This room isn't big enough to maneuver in with these things circling around like they are. If they get too close, you'll either be wrapped or bitten. The latter is probably the better option for a quick death."

"Then we'll have to take our leave," Magellan stated. "Although I assume there are more of these things in the facility, this isn't the normal amount for a cluster."

"Should we double back out the front?" Kaiden asked and fired a few rounds to keep the mutants at a distance.

"You should. I'm not leaving until I get another shot at Gin."

"What? That's—"

"Same here." Lazar agreed. Kaiden and Magellan looked at him with a mixture of shock and curiosity. "He killed my boys, dumbasses though they were." He sighed and glanced at the corpses of his fallen gang mates. "I already don't feel right knowing I'll probably have to leave them here to be food for the mutants or fertilizer, but I don't want to leave this place without a chance to avenge them. If there is an afterlife, I don't want to hear them bitchin' about it for eternity."

"It's honorable and even foolish, perhaps, but I suppose I can't condemn another person for their pride," Magellan acknowledged. At another round of loud hissing, they focused on four more nagas that slithered toward the hole in the dome above. "And out come the nagas. For now, let's focus on getting out of this room. Eventually, no amount of planning or scare tactics will stop them from getting a meal."

"Kid, do you still have that map of the place?" Lazar inquired. "Which direction has the most routes? Places we can run through and not get backed into a dead end?"

"Chief, bring it up," he ordered, and an isometric view

of the map appeared on his HUD. "It's the door in front of you, Magellan. It leads to a straight path that branches out to eight different paths. One leads back to the entrance too."

"Good to know, but we probably don't want to head directly back into the jungle," Magellan explained. "We've kicked the proverbial hornet's nest here. We can't slink through and avoid anything in the area like we did on our way in."

"Then how do we get out?"

"If we get out," Lazar corrected him. "Perhaps we can get to the roof or to a fire escape or something on the side of the building. We'll hit the beacon and have the pilot pick us up there. If she whines about it, I'll pay her from my share." He glanced at Hodder and Kane's corpses once more. "I'll have more to spare now."

"Then let us begin," Magellan ordered and drew his pistol. "We'll move down the halls and funnel them and eliminate them as they chase us." He aimed at the door in front of him. "Lazar, remember what I said about this gas being rather potent?"

"Yeah?"

"Be sure to step back a little but go ahead and shoot." Magellan fired an explosive shot, and the pressurized bullet erupted to release the gas around the nagas by the door. Lazar fired the explosive from his launcher. He dove forward and grabbed Kane's cannon as Kaiden and Magellan stepped back. The blast not only knocked the mutants around it away but also lit the gas to create a bigger explosion and set three of the snakes ablaze. The four above, who had begun their descent, crawled quickly away from the flames and to the other side of the room.

As the burning creatures hissed and writhed in an effort to extinguish the flames, the three men raced through the fire and the now wide-open doors. They entered the hall and Lazar charged the cannon. The merc fired at the furious nagas. The thin irises of their eyes had sharpened to knife-points, and their frills opened to reveal white webbing with dark lines crossing between them as they bared their fangs with unhinged jaws.

The energy shot from the cannon caught one directly in its throat. The snake bit down on the blast as if to swallow and it exploded internally. The mutant's eyes closed for a moment. Kaiden hoped it would collapse or shrivel in a death twitch, but its eyes snapped open again. It raised its head and glared at them. The mouth opened to reveal a substance pooled around the bottom of the jaw. It leaned its head back and spat the contents forward.

Kaiden grabbed the back of Lazar's neck and pulled him down. The glob of fluid arced over their heads and landed on the floor. It rolled for a few feet before the film around it gave way and the fluid drained. A large hole appeared as it burned the metal beneath it.

"Acid," Lazar stated and pushed himself up. "Or a really potent acidic toxin. Either way, you don't wanna get hit by it." He offered a hand to hoist the ace up. "These beasts seem more interested in a kill than a meal now. Thanks, kid."

"We can tally the 'thanks' and 'you're welcomes' when we get out of here," the ace responded. Two of the other nagas reared their heads. "Shit!" he cursed as each spat a glob of acid.

Two shots rang out, and the vile projectiles erupted in the mutants' faces. Magellan nodded, his expression serious. "Don't go dyin' when we just started the plan," he reprimanded them. "Keep in mind who else is stalking around. He might get bored waiting if we dawdle."

"Let him come," Lazar grunted and switched the cannon out for his grenade launcher. His face stony, he slid in another round. "If he had stuck around, we could have killed him back there with the snakes." He turned to fire and Kaiden stepped quickly out of the way as he pulled the trigger. The nagas in the back quickly sensed the approaching danger and retreated, but the three that launched their poison were caught in the blast. Kaiden held onto the wall as the explosion erupted and Lazar and Magellan took a step back as the force from the blast rocked the hall. The three nagas had left more guts and scales lining the walls and ceiling.

"I have one shot left," Lazar informed them and put the launcher away once again. "I'm gonna save it for when your buddy shows his face again."

Kaiden stepped away from the wall and observed the damage left by Lazar's blast. "Assuming he hasn't already left the building."

"He won't run, not now," Magellan said confidently. "He's found a new plaything."

"Do you really think he wants to kill me that badly?" Kaiden asked as he checked his gun. "Was it because of the leg? I'll buy him a new one."

"My guess is that it's pride," Lazar muttered. "A hunter doesn't like it when their prey sneaks away."

"I haven't figured out what makes him tick that way." Magellan popped the chamber of his pistol open, removed three shells, and loaded it. "If we don't take him out here and he doesn't take *you* out, I suggest you disappear for a while, Kaiden."

"I have to head back to school after this," he replied. "But it's crawling with former military personnel, security droids, and surrounded by one hell of a barrier. I think I'll be good."

"The hell? You going to a WC private or something?" Lazar questioned.

Kaiden shook his head. "Nexus Academy."

Lazar gave him a bewildered look while Magellan chuckled. "So you're an Ark kid? What are you doing running backworld gigs like this?"

"Well, besides making new friends and memories..." Kaiden swung as he heard another threatening hiss. The sharp exhale had almost begun to seem more like a demented screech. "I'm getting a head start on my tuition fees."

"I admire the effort, but let's hope your accumulated earnings don't end up paying for your funeral."

"Do you think there's a coffin that'll fit if I get swallowed by a naga?"

"Probably not, but they'll cut you out. The cleaning bills will be a bitch, though."

Kaiden laughed despite the situation. A little of the anxiety lifted and he began to feel that this was more like an Animus mission than the life and death scenario it was.

Lazar grabbed Kaiden's shoulder and dragged him forward. The ace looked at him in surprise before something combusted and sizzled behind him. He glanced back as another of the acidic orbs melted into the walls and dripped onto the floor.

So much for the moment of mirth.

"Shake it off and keep moving." Lazar pushed him away. "I've already lost two and don't care to lose anymore. Plus, you want another shot at that bastard, don't you?"

Kaiden nodded. "Right. Move down the hall and turn right at the end. That'll take us to another open room—a hangar or something—and give us room to maneuver."

"Are there ways to get out if things get worse?" Lazar asked. "We eliminated most of the shriekers, but you said there were still some hiding around the place."

"Yeah, but without getting Chief back into the systems, I only have the original print to work from," Kaiden explained. "There shouldn't be any there, but they may have migrated or—"

"Look out!" Magellan yelled and spun to fire down the hall at an attacking naga. The shots knocked it from the air, but it landed and raised its head. The liquid gathered around the sides of its mouth. He looked behind the serpent and his eyes widened.

"Move and talk," he shouted and turned to dash down the hall. "There's more of them."

"Did we invite the whole damn jungle's worth of these things in here?" Lazar hollered.

Kaiden spun and fired down the corridor as two other nagas advanced behind the one that had leapt at them. As the first reared its head back to spit, Magellan fired into the underside of its jaw. The impact knocked its head back, and some of the glob was expelled behind it while the rest drained down the sides of its mouth. One of the mutants twisted to avoid the acidic fluid and the acid spiraling behind it. Three other serpents that approached from behind darted away from the toxin quickly, and it landed in the burning room behind them.

"Did you see their scales?" Magellan asked as he caught up to the other two. "Dark green and bronze and heavier than the first batch."

"The big boys," Lazar muttered. "The ones we killed before must have been babes or only half-grown. These guys will be much harder to deal with."

As they turned down the hall, Kaiden fumbled for one of his grenades. "Not if I have...ah hell." He held up one of his shocks. "They've been short-circuited. It must have happened when Gin slammed that device into me. It felt like I was punched by lightning."

"Arc piston. I assume he learned how to adjust it." Magellan slid his rifle onto his back and quickened his pace. "The first few poor bastards he used it on were quite literally fried, so count your blessings, Kaiden."

"I'm on a baker's dozen so far," he replied. Double doors appeared directly ahead. "There! Chief, get the doors."

A green light flashed on the wall panel, and they slid open. Kaiden skidded to a halt, turned, and fired at the pursuing nagas. "Chief, lock it when I get in."

"Hurry up, Kaiden. We're clear," Lazar shouted. The ace continued to fire and ducked to dodge another venomous shot. He raced back to the doors as a stream of the fluid seeped toward the panel. "Now, Chief."

He ran in a second before the doors closed and locked behind him. A static snap indicated that the panel had been melted by the spit. He raised his weapon and expected the doors to open after the panel had been destroyed, but they held for now.

"I'm not sure how long those doors will hold, but we bought ourselves a little time to get some distance—" Someone tapped him on the shoulder. "What's... Oh."

At least a dozen shriekers stood above them and eyed them curiously, and a couple bared their fangs.

"Where exactly are the other doors in here, Kaiden?" Magellan asked.

"On the other side of the room."

"Fuckin' great," Magellan growled and aimed his cannon at one of the mutant beasts.

CHAPTER FOURTEEN

He perched on a ledge to the far right of the hangar. The dome wasn't as accommodating as some of the other squats he had stayed in. There weren't many ways to traverse the building—a few catwalks and a half-finished upper level. The few system ducts there were too small for him to crawl through, something he had noticed more and more throughout his misadventures. For a moment, he wondered if it was his gear or his girth. He slid a hand down the smooth path of his chest and stomach and snapped his teeth a couple of times before he opened them in a toothsome smile.

Nah, he was fine. You had to keep lean when your sport of choice could be so adaptable.

He watched as the party began to walk slowly around the edges of the hangar and kept a watchful eye on the shriekers. The door they had entered through wouldn't hold for long. It might have been made of sturdy stuff, but naga venom would eventually melt through it all the same—that is if they didn't simply sink their teeth into the metal and rip it from its frame. The nagas were tenacious and watching them hunt the shriekers and other mutants that had found refuge in the dome over the last couple of days had been a delight. He admired the way they coiled around their prey or attacked with quick, nearly silent bites. For such large creatures, they could be incredibly stealthy, just as they could be incredibly fearsome. The first time he saw one unhinge its jaw and swallow a whole echibara in one quick snap had been glorious.

They seemed to eat much more than their unmutated counterparts. The mutants always seemed to buck nature's role for them—or perhaps their previous role. They weren't quite right in the head, those freaks.

He took a moment to ponder whether he was a mutant and conceded that he hadn't run across too many others like him. Maybe a handful—six or seven—but the times that he had were certainly memorable. Their fill of lager and meat, chicks for a good time, moderate slaughter—these were almost mini-vacations from his personal journey, times when he didn't feel the need to kill, merely the desire.

Ah, dear Magellan. He focused on the bounty hunter. It was often said that a rivalry could feel like a warped friendship at some point and he'd begun to believe that a few months before. Magellan was the only constant in his life. They had conversations, and they met up at regular intervals and discussed the finer points of their respective careers. True, this was usually when he tried to rip the bounty hunter's throat out while Magellan attempted to blast holes in him. He'd succeeded at least a couple times, he conceded as he traced his bionic leg with his bionic arm, but it was all a part of the spirit of their little meet-ups.

He cast his doubts from his mind. He wasn't a mutant, merely spirited, unlike those bastards in the Star Killers. The generic name for a merc company should have been sufficient warning, but the Red Suns didn't align with his interests and the Omega Horde wasn't interested—which was ironic considering they had been the reason for his old company's downfall. No, it wasn't fair to put all the blame on them. The SK's weakness—that pitiful, infuriating weakness—was in their blood. That was why he had to get it out of them, even the ones who weren't there. It was obviously inherent, perhaps something in the bottled water they drank. He reminded himself that it was a good thing he never partook of the stuff.

Or was it partaked? Was that even a word? Partook—that sounded right. God, he was bored.

He looked at the gang once more as the youngblood, Kaiden, inched his way to the hallway door. Gin focused on the doors where cracks and melted surfaces appeared. What exactly was his plan here? Did he have one? Was he hoping the nagas would kill him faster than the shriekers? *You have a gun, kid. If you want a quick way out, you should go with that.*

Maybe he was broken. He could feel energy drain from him at the thought of one less person to play with, but the apathy left him quickly and was replaced by nonchalance. He didn't like playing with broken toys, and as upsetting as it was to see one that looked so shiny and promising fall apart like this, it meant he could focus on Magellan again.

Or, at least, that's what he wanted to think. The new

kid had shown promise. It wasn't like him to be wrong about something like that, and he didn't hand out gold stars on a whim. The last time he'd had a gut feeling like this was with Magellan and that officer on the Mars colony. He'd cut his arm off and left him to die as he cursed Gin's name...man, that one had fire. Soon after, he'd seen a news report that he had lived and instead of getting a regrown arm, he'd slapped a robotic arm in its place that transformed into a chain gun. That sounded like fun.

He really needed to pay him a visit again when he was done with his work here.

Two shriekers climbed along a grate above Kaiden. The boy saw them but didn't flinch or aim at them. Instead, he held something up in his hand as if beckoning them. This was new.

One of the shriekers froze and another tilted its head, plainly curious. It leapt off the grate and crawled to the boy. Kaiden gave it whatever was in his hand. It sniffed at it and tried to bite into it. Was it bait of some kind? The interaction was enough to persuade the other shrieker to climb down, and a few others above Magellan and the other merc watched the activity. Kaiden offered the second shrieker a piece of the food or bait and finally lured more to him.

He placed the last pieces of the lure on the ground and backed slowly toward his companions. The shriekers seemed oblivious to the scaled death that currently melted and bashed their way into the hangar. The plan finally clicked for Gin, and he smiled. Clever boys. If it worked, it looked like he would have an opportunity to play.

Magellan was held near and dear already. Kaiden was

still a wild card, but he had to give him his due, even though he would have been dead already if it weren't for that flashbang—was that an EI? One that could be seen without a link, obviously. He didn't remember hacking into the boy's systems, an oversight on his part. Still, it was a rather interesting piece of tech, and he made a note to see if he could scavenge it from the kid when he was done with him.

As for the last contestant, he hadn't quite made up his mind. The man seemed to have better survival instinct than the two he'd killed back in the observatory. He'd overheard him saying he wanted to avenge them, so Gin supposed they were his friends—or partners, at the very least. Maybe they were lackeys of his, and it was a bout of fool's pride. He looked stocky and well-built, a man who could take a beating. At least he would provide some challenge and perhaps even a thrill, but he would be the appetizer, the warm-up to the other two.

He activated his cloaking tech, leapt from the ledge to the top of a stack of crates, climbed down quickly, and sprinted to a dangling crane in the middle of the room. It was an easy task to climb up and balance the middle of his left foot on the point of the hook. It provided the perfect place from which to watch the gambit play out.

Sure enough, the door gave with a crash, and the small group of shriekers that had gathered nearby jumped in surprise. They growled and snapped their teeth as two of the nagas immediately surged into the room. One sank its fangs into the chest of one of the mutant monkeys. Two tried to pry it off as the other serpent launched a glob of toxin at the gathered group. As they moved out of the way, the remaining shriekers joined their brethren to attack the two nagas as six more appeared behind them. A clash between the two mutant species erupted in a chorus of furious hissing and demented shrieks.

The group used this opportunity to run behind and weave between the crates and tools around the hangar. Gin smiled and wondered which one of them had the idea. It spared them more battle, and there was now a good chance the mutants would be too busy to pursue them once again.

Now it was his turn.

The three ran beneath him, and Gin stood as motionless as possible. Without the proper equipment, they shouldn't be able to see him, but they were supposedly experienced mercenaries. An abandoned crane swinging in a room with no breeze would look suspicious, and maybe one of them was superstitious? Either way, the big one looked like he had an itchy trigger finger and it would be rather embarrassing for him to be discovered because of his own mistakes.

He looked at his hand. It was transparent, almost completely clear, and a slight haze was all that was visible. With a long energy span, no notable dip when moving, and no noticeable emissions, this generator was fantastic. When he'd heard about it at the Tokio Station, he knew he had to have it. It wasn't as hard to get an experimental piece as one would think, at least not there. A station focusing on scientific pursuits screened all their employees and all their onboard passengers. He made his way in on a distressed shuttle—one he had in fact distressed. The plan was simply to restock when they brought him in, but he'd found an even worthier catch. Things sometimes worked so beautifully in the great abyss.

What was he doing again?

Someone shouted above the rush of air as a door opened. Magellan hustled his two partners through the doors on the other side of the hangar. He waited for the bounty hunter to close them before he followed but as he turned, he could have sworn he saw the man's eyes narrow in his direction before he pressed the button to slide the doors shut. That Magellan...it was almost impossible for him to see him in this state, but he wouldn't put the possibility past him.

Gin leapt off the hook and ran to the door. It would be too obvious to use it, even if he waited, and there was a good chance it was booby trapped or they had locked the console. He studied the wall. There were no other entrances that he could see, but that didn't mean he couldn't make one, he realized as he jogged to the far left. The interior of these domes was mostly fixed paths and between the corridors and rooms were small pockets of nothing. Tent and metal surrounded everything, which meant that he could make up for the lack of extra paths by simply slipping between them.

He knocked on a couple walls and felt a metal surface on one and nothing but canvas on another. Quickly, he retrieved his blade, cut through the thin material, and slid into a large metal box that stretched up at least four floors and out for several hundred yards. He wouldn't be able to pursue them directly, but he could cut them off. They seemed as eager for a fight as he was, and he didn't want to disappoint them. That would be shockingly bad manners, and he wasn't so despicable.

He recalled that they'd discussed heading to the top of the dome to signal for a ship. Gin studied the metal fixture. They would have to climb stairs or ladders, but he wasn't so encumbered. He could beat them by a few floors and simply wait.

Aided by the jump jets in his boots, he leaned forward and jumped two stories, spun, and then released a pulse of barrier energy which boosted him up another ten feet. He flicked the fingers of his bionic arm. Small spikes emerged from the tips of his fingers and he used these to cling to the side of the building. He tested his knife against the metal, but it was too thick to cut through with his normal blade. Undeterred, he sheathed it and pressed a switch. Two clicks sounded and a plasma blade engaged. He drew it out again and activated the heated blade and forced it slowly into the metal plating.

When he was most of the way through, he moved the blade in a circle to create an entrance. That done, he tipped the knife up and forced the metal out and caught it between his thumb and palm. After sheathing the weapon, he climbed through and switched to his normal blade as his feet touched the ground. He slid the metal gingerly back into place. It wasn't perfect and jutted out a little, but he wasn't too concerned.

He could be stealthy, but that was when he was more interested in getting something done rather than enjoying himself.

His journey had brought him to a storage room of some sort. Unless they wanted to stock up on toiletries and cleaning supplies before their departure—he grinned at the stupidity of the thought—they probably wouldn't enter there.

A beep from his wrist indicated that his generator needed to recharge. So be it. He wanted to be sporting anyway. Gin deactivated his cloak as he walked to the storage room door, opened it casually, and poked his head out. It led to a much larger room with white tiles and a high ceiling. A few empty cages stood off to the side. It would probably have been used as a server or containment room had Axiom not been chased off so quickly.

He shut the door and wondered if they would come this way at all. They could have gone to the other side of the dome to try and find an exit at the edge. Would they risk it? There were probably more mutants that way. This place was absolutely lousy with them.

Then, the silence was broken by a tapping sound. Metal pounded below in an almost circular pattern. Gin smiled. They were coming—quickly, fervently, almost as if they raced to meet him.

Lovely.

CHAPTER FIFTEEN

"Of all the things they set up in this place, they didn't bother to install a working elevator?" Kaiden muttered heatedly as the group hastened up the steps.

"If you wanna take a break, you can go ahead and wait on the shriekers and nagas to catch up," Magellan suggested sarcastically.

"Or wait for the killer to show his face," Lazar added. "I haven't seen him since the nagas first showed up. Maybe Kaiden was right—he might have bolted."

"Hey, you used my real name. Are we getting along now?"

"He's not gone," Magellan interrupted before the gang leader could reply and he glared at him.

"Do you have some sort of psychic link with this guy?" he inquired. "You speak like he's some sort of boogeyman. He's a psycho with some shiny shit on his body—mortal like you and me."

"Do you know how many people I've killed, Lazar?"

Magellan retorted and headed up to another flight of stairs.

"I can guess, but I have a feeling that was rhetorical."

"Hundreds. I don't have an exact count as it isn't good manners to count your kills in the middle of firefights, but you know my hunter rank. That wasn't achieved by catching gutter scum and a few ex-mercs. I've never lost a bounty with the exception of Gin."

Kaiden paused and asked, "How many times have you run into him?"

Magellan stopped his ascent and Lazar almost knocked into him. "This makes nine, now," he answered without looking back. "Sometimes, he slips by without me having a good shot at him. Other times, I can take bits and pieces, but I have obviously never caught him. At this point, I feel much like the regretful owner of a feral dog."

"Yeah, you gave us the whole spiel before we came into the dome," Lazar said snidely. "You also said you would deal with him if we ran into him. That has left me with two dead teammates and the kid with PTSD."

"I'm not sure I would go that far," Kaiden muttered, mostly to himself. He had to admit he didn't feel as excited as he usually did to charge into danger and the realization shook him. But he had back-up this time and wouldn't face this guy alone. He checked his Tempest, examined the vents for damages or gunk, and brushed at a couple of scratches on the frame of the machine gun. It was routine to check his gear so it didn't jam in the middle of battle, but his fingers trembled a little this time.

"I'm aware of that," Magellan continued. Kaiden stopped his nervous cleaning. "I've gotten too...cocky, I suppose. The last three times I've run into him, ever since I blew his leg off, he hasn't really wanted to engage me directly, not like this. He's much more self-assured now, apparently."

"If that's how you want to put it," Lazar grunted and checked the cannon that Kane had carried. "We'll argue the details once we get on the dropship. But if you can at least keep the promise that I'll have a proper fight with him, that'll keep me cool for when this eventually hits me properly."

The bounty hunter looked up at the top floor as if he could see Gin through the walls above. "Despite what I've said, I know he won't run here. I didn't think he would attack so haphazardly, though."

"What would make you think he would stick around if he's run from you the past few times?" Kaiden asked.

Magellan drew a different pistol from the one that shot poisonous gas explosives. He twirled it once and inspected it. "His body count, the fact that he's been wanted for over three years, and that he's stolen tech from both official WC facilities and from top grade companies have placed him on the Revenant List. Do you know what that is?"

The merc leader propped the cannon against his shoulder and his gaze darted from one side to the other as he thought. "Supposedly, it's some unofficial wanted list that has guys with bounties worth fifty million creds or more."

"I can assure you it's quite real. The name comes from ancient times, and it means the reincarnated corpse of a violent or blasphemous person that would spread disease and generally make life miserable for people—an abomination to God and blight to man."

"That sounds about right for this guy." Kaiden nodded. "And the idea is to stick them back in the ground?"

"Dead man walking and all that." Magellan nodded. "Basically, anyone on the list is considered such a cancer on humanity that they have said fifty million-plus bounty on their heads, which can be turned in with no questions asked. But also, they regularly send out patrols of the WC's finest to try to catch one themselves."

"He's been able to avoid them all this time?" Lazar questioned.

The bounty hunter placed the pistol back into its holster. "I never said that. He's run into about four or five of them. Obviously, he's still around."

"Good Lord," Kaiden stammered. "This guy isn't…damn."

"We get it at this point, Magellan. Gin is a sick and deadly motherfucker who wouldn't spare your life if you gave him all your creds, a cupcake, and a bottle of something ridiculously expensive," Lazar growled. "Are you his hype man too?"

"My point is that this guy is hunted all over the galaxy. No matter how many Marines he has killed, coming to Earth—the home of the WC and tens of thousands of bounty hunters, trackers, soldiers, mercs, and gangs looking to make a name for themselves—is not the best place for a guy like him. He's as likely to have people hunting him as he is to be attacked by some crazy punk on the streets to make a scene," Magellan explained. "He's here for a reason, and it's likely that he will try to kill us as much for personal pleasure as for business. My guess is that he doesn't want witnesses, which is something he usually doesn't care about. It's one thing to fight someone who is insane, but it's another when they are insane and driven."

Lazar's head tilted as he thought for a moment before the realization hit him. He turned to look at Kaiden. "Gin can take out a group of WC Marines alone. This kid is still training for that shit. What do you think he can do against someone like that?"

"I don't expect him to do anything," Magellan stated and leaned against the stair railing. "On the next floor, there is a door that leads to the maintenance hall. Kaiden can take that to the outside of the building and hail the dropship."

"How do you know that?"

"Because I can see the sign on the door from here." The bounty hunter jerked a thumb behind him. "Since he hasn't already jumped us, he has to be waiting for us up above. I will engage him while the dropship makes its way back. You can obviously come too, Lazar."

"He could be right here," the merc pointed out. "He has that cloak so could be right beside us and we wouldn't be able to see—"

Magellan unclipped something from his belt and held up a blue cube. "This device emits pulses in an area and registers changes in energies in around a fifty-yard radius. It's mostly useless in normal circumstances—a heart or thermal scanner would do the same job it does but better. However, since no one really thinks of it when designing the latest stealth doodad, it's actually favored in my occupation. It is also one of the only things that can find someone with an eidolon grade or higher cloaking generator."

"You've tracked him this entire time?" Kaiden asked. "Has he been with us all the way through the entire facility?"

"He bolted when the nagas appeared but my EI told me he had a reading back at the hangar. We ran right beneath him."

"What?"

Gin sighed and knocked the back of his head impatiently against the wall. The steps he had heard had come to an abrupt stop. They no longer ascended the stairs, and he could occasionally hear murmured speech. Did they break for snacks?

They wouldn't leave without wishing him goodbye, would they? That would be incredibly rude. Magellan knew he didn't come to Earth very often, so this should be a special occasion.

Maybe they were creating an exit strategy? It was a wise move, he supposed, but also an annoying one. He sighed. As much as he was delighted to face Magellan again, he had the other two with him. Gin wanted to see what they could do, particularly the boy—or, at least, he wanted his shiny things. But if they weren't up to snuff, Magellan, big softy that he was, would probably prioritize their safety over facing him.

He wondered if he should record the fight.

The killer tapped his fingers together and considered his options. They had talked about a ship to take them away. This was a gig, which meant it was probably only a dropship and nothing with powerful weapons. Then again, they were rather fast and maneuverable, and for all his skills and gadgets, he had nothing that would enable him to tail them effectively. Worse, he'd arrived there in an escape pod, not exactly a multi-use vehicle.

Perhaps he should create a distraction? Something that wouldn't allow them to simply run off at their leisure? He checked the options on his suit. Most of his items were for personal use or use against human targets; he had nothing to destroy or disable ships. A little irritated, he fumbled through the compartments on his belt until he reached one on the back left. His fingers traced along something unfamiliar and he removed a glass vial filled with a brown liquid. It puzzled him for a moment until he remembered that he had found it at this very facility the day before. He smiled as he remembered its purpose. While it might not work as he intended, it would be something fun to add to the games.

He pushed himself off the wall and walked to the door to the roof. Hopefully, he would make it back in time to greet the party. If he didn't, it would be the height of rudeness.

"We walked right the hell past him and you said nothing?" Lazar growled. His face took on a heated shade of red and veins throbbed in his temples. "We could have taken him there."

"Yes, in a hangar bay full of mutants ripping each other apart that would come after us once they were finished. We would have faced both them and him."

"We could have killed him before that happened," Lazar rebutted. "*Or* we could have used more of that bait you have to distract the mutants."

"That's not how bait works. They usually don't care how good it smells when they are actively trying to kill you," Kaiden stated.

"Shut it, kid!" the merc barked. "Now is not the time to—"

"Lose your cool. I agree," Magellan interjected. Lazar's head whipped round to glare daggers at him. "Maybe that wasn't what you were going to say, but I must stress it."

The merc continued to draw in angry breaths and he clenched and unclenched his fists. "This is why I didn't say anything," the bounty hunter continued. "We have a chance to prepare for the fight right now, to plan for victory rather than simply hope for it. Gin doesn't seem to exactly understand what hubris is, and my guess is that he's underestimated you."

Lazar cocked an eyebrow. "He'll regret that if he has."

"That's my point," Magellan said. "I've mentioned that I feel some personal responsibility for him. Maybe that's foolish or self-centered, but I've never gone after him with anyone before. Perhaps that'll be enough for me to finally put an end to him. You screamed at Hodder to not let his anger make him do anything stupid, so take your own advice."

The other man shook his head. His breathing was still erratic, but his features no longer twisted in rage. "Good point. A jackass way to put it, but I follow." He heaved a sigh, opened his grenade launcher, and slowly slid the final grenade in before he turned to look at Kaiden. "Hey, Kaiden, hand me your shocks."

The ace opened his visor, clearly confused. "You can have them, but I already told you they are defective now."

"Getting hit in the head or chest by something as hard as a rock is still effective," the merc stated. He took the belt, unclipped it, and wrapped it around his massive arm while his eyes counted off all six. "At the very least, they can provide a distraction."

"Take the maintenance hallways out of here, Kaiden," Magellan said. "Use the map and find the fastest route. Have the pilot take you out of here, and we'll signal for her when we're done."

"I won't leave you two behind," Kaiden declared, his once shaking hand now balled into a fist. "How the hell would that sound? On my first chain mission, I left while two guys died and the other two got all the glory?"

Magellan shook his head while Lazar scoffed, "Don't be so pro—"

"I swear to God, if either of you tries to lecture me about pride, I'll kill you before you even find him."

After a minute of silence, Lazar and Magellan looked at each other as if asking whether they should debate it or simply club Kaiden on the head and leave him in the stairwell. Soon, Lazar turned and shrugged. "If he dies, I'm keeping his share."

"Fair enough." Magellan nodded. "I'll make sure your gig tag gets back to your loved ones."

"You won't have to make too many trips to do that." Kaiden slid his visor back into place "Who's going in first?"

Lazar, without saying a word, readied his cannon and grenade launcher and walked purposefully up the steps. Kaiden and Magellan followed as they prepped their weapons.

"This isn't smart, Kaiden," Chief warned.

"You're used to that already, aren't you?" Kaiden retorted. The EI uttered what sounded like a mix between a dejected laugh and an angry huff. "Besides, you're here to back me up right?"

"'Course I am, dumbass."

When they reached the top, Magellan and Kaiden stepped to either side of Lazar who stood in the center and one step down from the door. He lifted a leg and in one smooth motion, kicked the door in. He growled as he charged with Kaiden and Magellan behind him. They scanned the room, ready to fire at the barest hint of Gin, but found nothing.

Lazar snarled. "Seriously? Your intuition is shit, Magell—"

A creak from the far side of the room announced Gin's entrance. He closed the door behind him and raised a hand. "So you did come. I'm happy to see that."

Lazar fired his grenade at the killer. It exploded and engulfed him in flames.

CHAPTER SIXTEEN

Kaiden raised an arm to shield himself from the explosion. A part of him knew that was the purpose of his armor, but the blast was powerful enough to make the gesture instinctive.

"Do you think that got him?" Lazar asked as he slid one of Kaiden's defective shock grenades into the launcher and hooked it to his holster behind his waist.

"That would be surprisingly anti-climactic," Kaiden said. He raised his machine gun with both hands. "Not that I would mind."

Magellan said nothing as he fired ten shots into the flames. "He has that barrier, remember?" he muttered. "My rounds haven't hit anything, which means—" His eyes widened, and he shoved Kaiden and Lazar aside. Quickly, he drew his pistol, aimed upward, and fired. A jolt of electricity flared from the gun and the force of the shot knocked him to the floor.

His companions stared dumbfounded at the pistol's

power but clenched their eyes shut as the shot erupted in a shockwave on impact with something to create a shower of sparks. Kaiden rolled and retrieved his Tempest. His aim snapped from one side of the room to the other as he searched for their target.

"You came to play, I see," Gin shouted. The man used the cages in the room to pull himself up. Parts of his armor cloaked and decloaked at random. The barrier energy around his chest and arms fizzled and a loud hum emitted from the generator on his back. "All that sass from such a little gun. Is that a voltaic blaster, Magellan?"

Kaiden aimed and squeezed the trigger from his sitting position. The killer sprinted to remain ahead of the laser fire. He slid to his knees so the shots went over his head and flipped backward as he drew the Yokai.

The Tempest overheated and the ace vented it quickly. In a split second of shock, he realized that Gin's gun was one developed by Nexus technicians—how had he got his hands on one? The moment of speculation vanished as the killer aimed at his head. He pulled the trigger and the spike spun in the weapon, but he turned quickly and fired at Magellan. The missile barreled at the bounty hunter but collided with Lazar's metal gauntlet.

"A fellow aug—nice to meet you," Gin quipped. Lazar glared at him, lowered his arm, and raised his cannon with a shot already charged in the chamber. He fired the bolt and Gin spun to dodge the blast and threw several small orbs as the shot slammed into and destroyed the wall behind him.

"Flashbangs!" Magellan warned. He lowered his hat and looked away as Lazar shielded his eyes.

"Chief, darken visor," Kaiden ordered. The EI complied, and the ace looked away as the orbs erupted in several large flashes of light. His ears rang and he grimaced in frustration.

"Sorry, partner. I would have activated the dampeners, but the systems still aren't—Kaiden! Fall back and raise your gun!"

He did as Chief instructed and something thudded into his Tempest. The force of the impact knocked his weapon into his helmet and something scraped along the face of his mask.

A cry of pain was quickly suppressed and Magellan called Lazar's name. Kaiden regained his equilibrium and shook his head to clear it. Lazar had two more spikes in the gauntlet that shielded his face and one in his left arm. Magellan seemed unharmed, but two spikes pinned the bottom of his jacket and one of his sleeves to the ground.

Kaiden cursed at a barb embedded in his weapon. "Quick thinking, Chief, thanks." He tossed the machine gun to the side and drew Debonair as he scrambled to his feet. Gin now stood in front of the hole in the wall.

"It's a bit busy in here." He chuckled. "Let's open the floor up to keep this going." He stepped back through the hole and bent forward. The ace fired three quick shots as his target leapt up and out and the rounds sailed through the hole and ripped through the interior of the dome in the distance.

"Dammit!" Kaiden cursed. Something tore and Magellan rushed passed him, the bottom third and arm of his coat ripped. The bounty hunter vaulted through the hole and hurled a grappling hook up the side of the wall. The hook attached and yanked the man upward. Kaiden ran to Lazar, who tore the spike from his arm with a pained hiss. The ace plastered the remainder of his flesh adhesive on Lazar's wound. The merc leader's face twitched in pain for a moment, but as the liquid settled, he rolled his shoulder and yanked the spikes from his gauntlet.

"Go and assist him," he bellowed. Kaiden nodded and flung himself down beside the hole and rolled onto his back. Cautiously, he inched the top half of his body through and aimed Debonair upward. Magellan and Gin fought against the side of the structure. The killer had cut his adversary's hook wiring and the hunter was held in place only by what appeared to be a blade on one of his gauntlets. The murderer kicked at his rival and tried occasionally stab him with a jagged, curved blade. Kaiden couldn't get a clear shot. Magellan mostly dodged the attacks as his rifle was still slung over his shoulder. He blocked one of Gin's kicks with his knee and managed to draw his other pistol. A shot sounded, and the two combatants disappeared in a fog of poisonous gas.

The ace cursed again and scrambled to his feet. "I can't get a shot," he yelled to Lazar. "They are heading to the roof."

"Then let's get up there," the merc responded. He tried to close his fist a few times, and while his hand still worked, it responded slowly.

"Are you all right?" Kaiden asked as his companion retrieved his cannon and stomped to him.

"I'll make do," he grunted. "Up the stairs. I ain't losing this freak."

"Roger." Kaiden nodded as they sprinted to the top of the dome.

Gin grinned from ear to ear as he attempted another strike on his pursuer, this time aimed at his shoulder. Magellan released the blade on his gauntlet and disappeared under the poisoned smoke. The killer tried to deactivate the spines on his fingers but they wouldn't respond to his mental commands. "What exactly is in this little concoction, Magellan?" he asked. "My arm doesn't work properly, and my leg feels a little heavy... Oh, I guess there's a soft touch of chlorine?"

The bounty hunter responded with two bullets to the man's chest. The force was enough to dislodge his arm from the metal plating and impel him a few feet into the air. He slammed his artificial leg into the wall to keep himself from falling and ran his good hand over his chest. Pieces of his armor crumbled and fell and he felt the small layer of foam from the safety orbs within. He winced. "I see you're not in much of a mood to talk."

He dug his knife into the wall as another shot whistled past his ear. In a smooth motion, he used the knife to balance himself and pulled his leg free to thrust up the side and reach the edge of the roof. He pulled himself quickly to safety as Magellan fired three more rounds. Each chipped away the metal of the roof's edge.

"So damn feisty," Gin muttered. He flicked the fingers on his artificial arm, and after a few attempts, the spines finally receded. "That was a neat trick, Magellan, but you're

gonna need more than home remedies to keep me down…
although that stuff really fucked my filters up."

His barriers, thankfully, had regained some of their
energy. Lazar and Kaiden burst through the door onto the
roof. "And we'll keep it going, by the looks of things, " he
mused and turned his attention to them. "Keep me enter-
tained until Magellan gets here, would you?"

The ace fired Debonair, and the killer responded with a
small circular shield that absorbed the shots. "You gotta try
a little harder."

Lazar roared, raised his cannon, and charged a shot.
Gin cocked his head, closed his fist, and punched the
barrier toward them as the merc was about the release the
trigger.

"Lazar, don't!" Kaiden cried, but his warning came too
late. He jumped back as the bolt smashed into the barrier
only yards away from them. The blast blew the merc leader
back, and the cannon shattered as he slammed into the
rooftop. Kaiden was knocked to the edge and lost
Debonair as he flipped over the side of the roof. Franti-
cally, he managed to grab the ledge before he fell.

He hauled himself up and reached for Debonair but a
sharp pain stabbed through his hand. Blood dripped to the
metal floor from where a spike protruded through both the
top and bottom of his hand. Kaiden gasped and winced
and pushed the pain aside. He rolled to his pistol, snatched
it up, and raised it but was knocked onto his back by a boot
to his head.

"You're decent, kid—top one hundred, I can safely say."
Gin held his pistol aimed Kaiden's head as he stomped on
his chest. "But this is the second time I have you beaten and

under my boot. My guess is you're not as good at this as you like to believe you are."

The ace tried to respond, but the killer slammed his boot into his stomach. "Does your little EI have anything else up its cybernetic sleeve?" he asked and waved his pistol from side to side. "I want to see what it's capable of and what I can potentially do with it."

Something smashed into the man's hand and knocked the gun away. Gin gripped his hand in pain as one of Kaiden's shock grenades rolled along the ground.

"Fuck off and die, you creep," Lazar yelled and pounded a shoulder into the killer's back to thrust him away. Lazar dropped his launcher and hauled out his machine gun, but it wouldn't unfold. He slammed it against his leg. "Come on…activate, you piece of—" The weapon came to life and he hip-fired at Gin, who darted behind several of the generators and boxes lining the roof and flipped over the end of the roof across from them.

"You slimy, cowardly bitch," the merc roared. Kaiden grunted as he sat up and took a deep breath as he placed Debonair on the ground. His expression set with purpose; he wrapped his hand around the spike, clenched his teeth, and snarled in pain as he managed to pull the metal only partially out.

"Is this thing lined with barbs or something? It's barely budging." He groaned.

"You're thinking about it too much. It makes you hesitate," Lazar stated and grabbed the prong in one massive hand. "Just do it." He ripped the spike free, and the ace yelped in pain. "Hang on, kid. I can heal that quickly." He tossed Kaiden his machine gun and popped the thumb on his gauntlet which emitted a small flame. The merc spun the segment beneath it and the fire gained intensity to become a jet flame. "I got some surge rejuv, but it requires me to heat the wound first. I gotta cauterize it."

"Go ahead." Kaiden raised his hand and peered over the side of the building. "But make it quick. I don't want this guy to get the drop on us again."

"Try not to bite your tongue off," Lazar warned. He held the wounded hand and ran the flame over the top. Kaiden tried to choke back his pained screams, but as Lazar turned his hand and applied the flame to the other side, a brief bellow escaped before he tried to calm himself with deep breaths. The merc flipped the top of his thumb shut and adjusted the setting to its original position. He retrieved a vial of silver-white liquid and applied it to the wound top and bottom. The relief was almost immediate—a similar sting to the adhesive Kaiden had applied to his leg, but it was certainly less than what he felt as the spike was ripped out from his flesh and the wound flambéed.

"Thanks," he said through clenched teeth. Lazar helped him to stand, and they both jumped at a crash behind them. Magellan limped up the steps to the roof.

"What happened to you?" Lazar asked.

"I blocked a kick from his metal leg which smashed mine to bits," he growled. "I was knocked back down, barely caught myself, and took some shots, but I think I only hit him once or twice. Where is he?"

"He disappeared over the side," Kaiden informed him. "We had to do some emergency surgery. He hasn't shown his face since them."

"He's baiting us," Magellan huffed. "Biding his time for

something." He staggered and his teammates helped him up the remaining few steps.

"Are you in any shape to fight?" Kaiden asked as he handed Lazar his machine gun.

Magellan pointed to his leg which was wrapped in some sort of black cloth. "I'll be better in a few minutes. It needs to set. We will finish this."

"What do you think he's waiting for?" the merc asked and looked around. "His barrier has come back. Do you think his cloak is back on too?"

"Not good enough for us to not see him. He might be translucent, but the shot drains his systems' energy and staggers the recharge. If his barrier is already up, that thing is better than I was led to believe."

"It's not good enough to create big barriers, but he— Wait, that noise." A loud, ringing screech echoed on the wind—one Kaiden was familiar with. It made his blood run cold.

"Finally. I began to wonder if that stuff was useless." The trio turned as one. Gin sat on a large generator above them and seemed to ignore them as he looked up at the sky. As Kaiden retrieved Debonair and aimed at the killer, he noticed a brown liquid coating the generator he sat on.

"Chief, what is that?"

"Scanning... Oh, that's not good. That's a liquid constituted of mutant pheromones, Kaiden."

"For all mutants?"

"No, for—"

The wind kicked up as another cry rang out. Kaiden's eyes widened as he saw something that, until now, he was only familiar with in the Animus.

"Oh, two of them." Gin chuckled. "I wonder how many will gather in a few more minutes."

Two large creatures soared toward them, red and black in color, with beaks like scythes and hardened feathers that glinted in the light of the setting sun like scales.

Devil birds.

CHAPTER SEVENTEEN

Kaiden stood and stared, wide-eyed, as the flying mutants approached. Several shots rang out as his companions fired at Gin who flipped over the generator. The ace saw the Yokai still on the ground and ran to snatch it up. He shoved it haphazardly in Debonair's holster.

"You are not getting away," Lazar shouted and raced behind the generator, only to be knocked back by a kick from the killer.

"Oh, of course, I'm not. I have no intention of leaving. This is getting spirited," Gin quipped. Magellan raised his rifle and fired directly at him, but he blocked it with a hard-light shield barely bigger than the palm of his hand. "Tch, you're getting predictable Magellan."

The bounty hunter responded by launching two small spikes from his gauntlet which struck the man in the leg. They activated and shocked him, and he laughed and danced around. "Ah! Ow! Neat party trick."

Magellan removed the rifle's magazine and slotted in a new one before he drew the gas pistol and fired the remaining two shots at Gin. The shots exploded at his feet and again enveloped him in the gas.

"Kid, call the dropship," he ordered.

"What?" Kaiden balked. "Those devil birds will tear it out of the sky!"

"Not if we keep them distracted," the bounty hunter retorted. "Look, you lost your Tempest, Lazar lost his cannon, and his launcher has no ammo. My rifle is down to its last two mags which is twenty-four shots. We ain't got enough to take those things down ourselves and deal with Gin. The guns on the ship aren't exactly top-of-the-line, but they should be enough to at least take those big bastards out of the sky if not eliminate them completely."

"We can head back into the building," Kaiden said and pointed to the rooftop entrance. "Fight him where he doesn't have room to maneuver."

"Neither will we," Magellan countered. "He's already started to toy with the two of you. Do you really want to see what happens when he gets bored?"

"I thought you said we would finish this."

Magellan growled, grabbed Kaiden by his chest armor, and pulled him close. "Do you think I suggest this out of cowardice, kid?" he fumed. "As long as I can still walk and he keeps fighting, I won't leave unless he's dead or I am. But I won't ignore those flapping beasts. Now call the dropship. If she bitches, tell her I'll pay for the damages and ammo."

The ace looked at Lazar who now scrambled to his feet and muttered curses. Gin had still not emerged from the gas. Kaiden nodded silently and retrieved the small beacon device from the slot on his shoulder. "You should have kept this with you," he said as he broke the covering and pressed the button down until it blinked with a blue light.

"It was more important that one of you had it," Magellan stated. He opened his Volt pistol and removed one large, battery-like cartridge from it and slid in another. "This is meant to be used on droids or guys like Gin who use a lot of tech, but it has plenty of power behind it. It might be enough to make those devil birds think twice about—"

Something shimmered on a box behind the bounty hunter and a blurred shape appeared for a moment. "Magellan, move," Kaiden shouted. He pushed him aside as Gin leapt into the attack and aimed the killer's own pistol at him. Without conscious thought, he pressed the trigger to coil the shot.

The spike gouged into Gin, and he decloaked and tumbled to the surface. He flipped a couple of times before he managed to drag his metal hand along the roof to stop his slide.

"Shooting me with my own gun?" the killer inquired. He wrenched the spike from his rib, and a trail of blood spurted before it was covered by a foam-like substance released by his armor. "How rude." His voice had lowered and no longer held the delighted tone it had maintained up until now.

One of the devil birds landed on the edge of the roof as the other circled above the group. Gin looked at the mutant. "It's ironic. Now, I wish I hadn't called these things here." He glared at Kaiden and Magellan as his body became transparent again. "I want to take my time with you, kid."

The bounty hunter fired his pistol, the beam of electricity aimed directly at the killer. It struck the underside of the devil bird instead of the man and released another shockwave. The creature squawked in surprise and arcs of electricity danced up its body. The other screeched in the air and swooped down to dive-bomb the men on the roof.

Magellan aimed his rifle at the oncoming bird and fired four shots as it descended. Each struck the mutant's head, and it screeched again as it shook its head in pain. Kaiden and the bounty hunter used the moment to rush out of the way as the winged mutant slammed into the roof.

The rooftop gave way as cracks formed from the impact. A sudden shadow alerted the ace, and he looked up. The devil bird Magellan had shocked now stood above him, its sharp beak poised to strike.

Kaiden threw himself aside as it descended to impale itself only a few feet away. He scrambled to his feet as the mutant yanked its beak from the surface and released an angry hiss when it turned to swipe at him.

He spun clear and felt the wind of the beast's attack behind him. It continued its efforts to skewer him, and he weaved to avoid it. The speed of the attacks increased as the devil bird's strength quickly returned. Kaiden occasionally tried to fire at the creature, but neither his Debonair or Gin's Yokai did much to injure or slow the mutant down. The attacks certainly didn't calm it either.

Magellan and Lazar fought the other devil bird. The merc had jumped onto its back while it was down and now fired his machine gun directly into its skull.

The bounty hunter took aim as the beast violently thrashed. When it opened its beak to shriek, he delivered a volley of shots into the gaping maw. Smoke billowed from its mouth, and it continued to buck and flapped its wings to take flight once more. Finally, it managed to dislodge Lazar, who landed hard and vented his machine gun as his partner continued to shoot.

"We don't have the firepower to take them down!" the merc roared.

Magellan lowered his rifle as the devil bird took to the skies. "Maybe not conventionally. Do you still have your grenade launcher with you?"

"Yeah, but all I have are the kid's useless shockers."

"Not useless. Let me see one." Magellan took one of the grenades that Lazar tossed him, "Kaiden said they were short-circuited when Gin hit him with the arc piston, but my guess is that they deactivated the priming and activation switches. The energy still remains." He used a small knife to dig into the outer shell of the shock, tore off a piece, and studied the interior. "Yes, this will work, but there won't be a lot of room to mess up."

"Unfortunately, the only consistent thing we've done is fuck up." Kaiden ran from the other devil bird and created small tremors that they felt through their boots. "Hey, kid, would you keep it down?"

"Would you get off your ass and help?" Kaiden shouted and turned to fire Debonair as the devil bird opened its beak and tried to bite him. He dove to the ground as the two halves of the beak closed directly above him, pushed up, and continued his dash across the roof. His furious assailant continued the pursuit.

"It seems its wings are still paralyzed from the shock," Magellan observed. "But my guess is not for much longer."

Lazar sighed, readied his launcher, and unwound the belt of grenades from his arm. "Here, take these." He tossed them on the ground in front of the bounty hunter as he closed the vent of his machine gun. "I'll go help the kid. Finish doing whatever you plan to do with that, and don't let that freak catch you unawares."

"No need to worry about that," Magellan responded. "He'll show himself again soon but having his gadgets still not at their best seems to have shaken him slightly. If he was caught in that second blast, he's probably playing it cautious again."

"He can play this however he wants," the merc growled as he walked away. "I'll take him out the next time he decides to show his face."

"Would you piss off already?" Kaiden yelled and hurdled over a generator as the devil bird smashed it under its talons directly behind him. The ace had begun to tire. He'd been beaten, stabbed, shocked, and had run from mutants for the last few hours. All that now accumulated, and he wasn't sure how much longer he could maintain his current pace.

Rapid laser fire erupted behind him when Lazar blazed at the back of the mutant. "Over here, you ugly son of a bitch!" the merc howled. The creature turned and Kaiden could see its eye widen and its iris sharpen in anger. He saw an opening, spun, and pulled the trigger of the Yokai to direct a shot into its eye.

It struck home, and the mutant emitted a pained, angry screech.

"Nice shot," Lazar complimented him. "But now it looks more pissed off than before." The mutant flapped its wings. They were still too stiff for it to take off, but that didn't seem to be the goal. Instead, it whipped them around aimlessly as if attempting to hit them or toss them with the wind velocity.

Lazar continued his barrage until his gun overheated. Kaiden fired two more shots from the Yokai. One hit the devil bird in the head, and the other struck its throat. A small spray of blood erupted.

The Yokai was out of ammo, and Gin hadn't been kind enough to leave more. Kaiden grunted, slid Debonair into its holster, and shoved the Yokai into a compartment on his leg. He braced himself and ran toward the beast, ducked under its flailing wing, and jumped to wrap an arm around its throat. Clinging with one hand, he grabbed the spike with the other and tried to force it in a little farther.

"What are you doing, kid?" Lazar shouted. "That thing could take off any second."

"And we'll be easy pickings for the both of them," Kaiden responded and now climbed to the mutant's head. "We gotta keep it grounded as long as we can. Keep firing."

"You're in the way," Lazar said, although he snapped his gun closed and aimed at the beast.

"Then shoot anything that isn't me." The ace continued to climb until he was at the top of the devil bird's head. The merc's slugs tore into its body and it wiggled its head quickly to throw Kaiden off as he retrieved his blade and stabbed it into the other eye.

The mutant screamed and thrashed and stomped its feet into the roof in pain.

"Kaiden, jump off," Magellan ordered when he approached from behind Lazar with the launcher and aimed it at the mutant's open mouth. The ace placed his feet against the bird's neck and pushed himself off to land several yards away. The beast turned to snap at Lazar and gave the bounty hunter the perfect shot into its mouth.

He fired the launcher and a glowing orb arced from the weapon and down the creature's gullet. An explosive sound issued from within the devil bird. It reared back and screeched, and electric sparks erupted from its mouth before it collapsed.

"What did you do?" Lazar asked as he looked at the defeated mutant.

"I unlocked the safety mechanism on the bottom of the battery in the grenade, releasing the energy," the bounty hunter explained. "It supercharges the grenade and increases the energy output and blast radius, but you're as likely to get caught in the blast as whoever you're tossing it at, so I improvised."

"Heh, good work." Lazar kicked the mutant's head.

Kaiden approached it cautiously. "Is it dead?"

"I don't feel like checking for a pulse. But even if it isn't, I doubt it will recover in time for it to pose a problem for us."

At a shrill cry from above, the three turned their attention to the remaining creature. "Do you think you can pull a repeat performance?" Kaiden asked.

"Perhaps, but it doesn't look like that'll be necessary," Magellan stated and looked in the opposite direction.

"What do you—" Kaiden's question cut off when several explosive shots struck the mutant. It jerked, and the massive wings flapped less vigorously as its head snapped toward the north. The dropship approached with its cannons primed. It fired several more shots. The mutant managed to dodge a few, but the rest found their target. It didn't even cry out as it plummeted to the jungle below.

"That will cost you boys extra when we get back," the pilot's voice chastised from their comms. "That's for getting me involved in your mess. Have you found the thing you came here for?"

"We have," Magellan acknowledged and gestured with his thumb to the cylinder on his back. "But I recommend you stay at a safe distance for now. There's been a complication."

"Whatever. I'm hourly," she snorted. "But hurry the hell up. I'd prefer not to hang around here and deal with more bullshit than I have to."

The bounty hunter was silent for a moment, then removed the canister from his back and held it in his hand. "You guys should go ahead and head out."

Lazar spat a wad of saliva and blood to the ground. "We've already been through this," he growled. "I'm not leaving until I take out that chirpy asshole. His little party favors are dead, and he'll come back."

"He might have actually left this time," Magellan pointed out. "He didn't take any opportunity to attack us. If he didn't intend to—"

"Magellan!" Kaiden shouted and pointed behind the bounty hunter with one hand while the other reached for Debonair.

Gin stood with his arm raised and his blade firmly in his grasp. Magellan leapt back, tossed the canister aside, and slung his rifle into his hands. Lazar beat him to it and blasted his machine gun into the man's chest. The shots passed right through, and the killer didn't move. His body became transparent, and his head and arms shook with static.

"Hologram," Magellan shouted.

"Where is— Guh." Kaiden tasted blood. His helmet was still on, so nothing could have gotten in. Cold pain stabbed in his chest and he looked down at a jagged blade. A hand dropped on his shoulder, and Gin leaned forward with perverse glee. "I'm picking up where you and I left off, kid."

CHAPTER EIGHTEEN

"**K**aiden!" Magellan fired two shots at Gin's exposed helmet over Kaiden's shoulder. The killer leaned back and released Kaiden who fell to the floor with the blade still in his chest. The bounty hunter continued to fire until an empty click indicated that his rifle was out of ammo. Lazar took up the volley, but the killer simply created a barrier, this one bigger than those before.

"Dammit, his barriers are getting stronger," the merc shouted and rushed at their opponent. He swung his massive gauntlet, but Gin danced easily around his swings before he leapt back and tossed two more flashbangs.

Lazar and Magellan shielded their eyes. "Pilot, fire on him," Lazar ordered.

"Who is that?" she asked.

"Doesn't fucking matter. Shoot!"

The ship's cannons whirred and aimed at the killer, who serpentined across the roof as the blasts left craters in the dome. He created three holograms of him running to confuse the pilot.

"He's not getting away," Lazar challenged and raced after him. "Tend to the kid."

Magellan ran to Kaiden and knelt to inspect the wound. "EI, whatever the hell your name is, what are his vitals?"

His heart rate is slowing. He's lost blood, but the blade is stifling the flow. He's bleeding internally and has passed out from the shock. He was stabbed just above the solar plexus. For that kind of accuracy, you'd need to be a surgeon," Chief said. He appeared in the air and looked at his fallen partner. *"We can't remove the blade unless we have something to repair the damage or plug the hole. Kaiden used the rest of his adhesive on the merc. All he has is basic rejuv serum."*

"I have something." Magellan retrieved a small orb. "Glaze foam. It'll seal the wound and keep the blood from pouring out."

"Even with that, he won't last long. He needs medical attention or ultra-grade medicine," Chief advised. He turned to look at the bounty hunter. *"I know you want this Gin guy bad, but please don't abandon my partner."*

Magellan looked at the EI. "It's kinda odd to hear emotions from an EI, but I promise you, I won't."

"I'm almost out of shots," the pilot advised them. The ship's cannons tried to pin Gin's location down with little success. "I can't get a hit on this guy. How the hell is he able to avoid cannon fire?"

The killer and his holograms ran to where the devil bird had crashed. Lazar was in pursuit and maintained fire but only hit holograms that kept disappearing and reappearing. "Lazar! Stop," Magellan ordered.

Although he looked back in anger, the merc obeyed.

"Pilot, focus your fire on the large cracks in the roof.

Bring it down," the bounty hunter directed.

"Roger," she acknowledged. The cannons redirected to the target as Gin passed over it. She fired four rounds at the area and the explosions made the roof section gave way. The holograms vanished and the killer fell into the fissure that opened up.

"Good work! Come around." Magellan waved at the ship. The cannons folded into the sides as it coasted to the roof.

"This mission started with five of you. Are you the only ones left?" she asked.

"Yeah, and it'll be one less if we don't get this one back to a medical facility soon." Magellan beckoned to Lazar. The merc looked at the hole in the roof and grunted before he jogged quickly to him. "I need you to snap this blade so I can roll him over and take the rest of it out," he explained. He nodded, placed his gauntlet on the ace's chest, and gripped the blade firmly. He jerked his fist to the side and the metal snapped. The bounty hunter handed him the orb as he turned Kaiden. He placed one hand on his back and gripped the blade's hilt with the other. After a slow exhalation, he pulled the blade out in a single swift motion.

He flipped the still unconscious man again, took the orb from Lazar, and cracked it in his fingers before placing it on the puncture. Light-blue foam formed along the center of Kaiden's chest and seeped into his wound.

"Activating wound binding," Chief stated, and several strips emerged from the interior of the armor and wrapped Kaiden's chest. *"It'll have to do for now."*

"Help me get him on the ship." Magellan and Lazar lifted Kaiden and carried him to the dropship. The side door opened, and they moved him gently to one of the benches. The pilot, a woman in her twenties with dark cropped hair and tanned skin, approached with a red box. "I have basic medical training and some high-grade supplies," she explained. "What happened?"

"Stab wound—jagged blade to the chest," Lazar said and folded his arms.

"We've already removed the blade and applied glace foam. His armor was equipped with medical binding, but the internal damage is severe." Magellan walked to the back of the ship, opened a crate, and removed three magazines of ammo which he placed on his belt. He tossed a case of thermals to Lazar along with his grenade launcher.

"Take him to a medical center. We'll ring you when we're done." He prepared to walk out of the ship.

"I can't come back," she protested. "That's not how the gig licenses work. I can drop you off and retrieve you from a destination only once. After that, I become an unclassified aircraft and am liable to get shot down by the country's air force, not to mention all the mutants that will be flying around here because of all the ruckus."

"Then I guess we'll find our own way back," Lazar stated. He loaded a thermal into his launcher and closed it. "Go ahead and take the kid out of here."

She looked at Kaiden for a moment, then back at the merc and bounty hunter. "I can probably keep him stable enough for a while and buy you some time." She opened the medical box and removed a vial and injector. "I can keep the ship in a hover, but you have twenty minutes, tops. After that, I'll have to leave."

"Understood, but if he goes south, you leave immediately," Magellan ordered. She nodded in acknowledgment as he and Lazar stepped out of the ship. "Stay airborne in case he doubles back," he shouted to her. She nodded again and closed the door as they ran to the hole in the roof.

Lazar landed with a loud thud from the impact of the jump as Magellan slid down the side of a pillar, leapt off, and rolled onto the floor. They were in another hangar, this one more derelict than the last, but there was no sign of mutants in this one. Nor, it seemed, of Gin.

"Gin!" Magellan shouted and activated his pulse. "Come on out."

"Quite your hiding and skulking around," Lazar demanded. "You've been a bitch this entire time, so show some spine."

"I know you're bored with this," Magellan growled as he proceeded to aim his rifle at every nook and cranny of the hangar in turn. "I won't stop hunting you, and you won't be rid of me. I don't know why you thought coming to Earth was a good idea, but you have to realize how fucked you are when it gets out that you're here."

"With that bounty on your head, every gang on the planet will want a piece of you," Lazar threatened. "And the Fire Riders will be first in line. I'll see to that myself."

"You bring up excellent points." Lazar and Magellan spun quickly. Gin stood behind them with his arms folded and his head tilted nonchalantly. Lazar aimed his launcher, but Magellan raised a hand to block his firing line.

"Another hologram?" he asked. The bounty hunter

nodded and pointed to a shimmer along his arm.

"I'll admit to a little trepidation on my part. I lost my gun, I'm low on toys, and I only have one knife remaining. I unfortunately lost most of my stash when you blew up the room I used as my temporary living quarters." The hologram turned its head to face them. "I have to say, big man, you have been more sporting than I expected."

"Let me get hold of you and I'll change this to blood sport," he muttered.

"I believe that this has had plenty of blood. How's Kaiden?" he asked.

"You won't claim him," Magellan vowed. "He's out of your reach now."

The killer chuckled. "You know how persistent I can be when I set my mind to something, Magellan." The bounty hunter's eyes narrowed as the hologram tossed its hands up dramatically. "Although to be fair, I'll probably be far too busy to give him much time in the near future. I understand he's an Ark Academy student?"

"You overheard us?" Lazar questioned.

"I heard you mumbling in the stairwell. But it's rather easy to tell if you know what to look for—like that pistol of his, which has a schematic straight from the Nexus Academy and is similar to my pistol. I guess that makes us alumni."

"You went to Nexus?" Magellan asked, honestly surprised that he had never learned that detail.

"For a time. It wasn't a good fit, really." He chuckled. "I was in the Medic Division, if you can believe it, and swapped between surgeon and battle-medic. I ended up leaving after my third year. I bounced around, sharpened my skills and blades, and joined a gang or two before I settled with the Star Killers, but you know how that turned out."

Lazar shot a grenade to a floor above and the explosion knocked some debris to the ground. Magellan looked at him. "What the hell are you doing?"

"Getting impatient." He armed the launcher with another thermal. "Will you actually come out and fight, or merely prattle on? I'll level this entire place to find you."

"That would be quite an accomplishment with what I'm guessing is five thermals?" Gin inquired. "Take it from a seasoned vet, my big buddy, threats only work when they are both feasible and detailed."

"Enough, Gin," Magellan demanded and received another head-tilt from the killer. "I'm tired of this. Do you really want us to fight for the rest of our lives?"

"Considering our chosen professions, the 'rest of our lives' could be much closer than we think." He chuckled and looked at the floor. "I'm surprised you seem so forlorn, Magellan. You've always taken my little excursions personally, ever since the first time we met." He looked at the bounty hunter. "But this time, you didn't get to play hero, did you? You didn't show up in the nick of time to scare off big bad *moi* from harming any more innocents. It's not what I would call them, but it fits the scope better, I would say."

Magellan fired a shot through the hologram. The figure warped for a moment before resolving, and the static and haze became clearer.

"You need to find better company, Magellan," the killer mused. "This one's temper seems to rub off on you."

"I'm not picking anything up," Magellan told Lazar and now ignored the hologram's snide comments. "At least, not him. There's something along the edge of the hangar, though, and some signatures outside the dome to our left."

"Then let's ditch this glorified inflatable and see if we can find him. He can't have gone far," Lazar suggested. The partners turned to leave.

"Actually, I can," Gin interjected, and the two stopped momentarily. "As much fun as this has been, you were right, Magellan. I've grown a bit bored by it all. I've already left the building."

Lazar turned, and anger crept into his eyes. "You lying sack of—"

"I have many vices, big boy, but truth is one of my many virtues." He placed both hands on his chest. "Like I said, few options remain at my disposal, and as much fun as it would be to play a game of hide-and-go-slay with the two of you, I am a little late for my meeting already."

"Meeting?" Magellan asked, "Who reached out to you?"

"A gentleman never asks and a lady never tells," he chirped. "It's not how I would usually describe myself, but I can be prim and proper when the mood strikes me."

Lazar slammed his hand against his leg. "So we've been pissing time away," he muttered, "Maybe we can get the pilot to hunt him down if we get back to the ship."

"Sounds like a plan," Gin responded cheerfully. He held up his thumb and forefinger and scaled the gap down. "You may have one slight problem with that, however."

"Lazar, these readings are moving toward us. Multiple targets—more mutants."

"Because we haven't had enough of that," Lazar

growled. "We'll blow them to bits and make our way out. There's no point in sticking around."

"I think you might underestimate what is coming your way." The hologram ticked off its fingers. "Much like I underestimated the time it took those pheromones to activate."

"Pheromones?" Magellan spun around, "You had more?"

"Another vial." The hologram glanced downward. Magellan could scarcely make out the dark brown liquid which almost blended in with the dirt and grime on the floor. "Different blend but similar results, though. I was a little disappointed with my findings here, but I certainly got more use out of this stuff than I expected."

"Lazar, let's hurry and get out." Magellan froze as something ripped the dome's wall. A large beast with jet-black fur leapt into the hangar. It stood on all fours, with sharp claws and bloodied fangs, and stared at them with sharp black irises surrounded by muddy-green eyes.

Shriekers battered the door behind them, and their tell-tale screeches betrayed their bloodlust as they attempted to force it from its frame. Hisses sounded from the floor above, accompanied by the sizzle of naga venom sprayed against a wall or door as they tried to make their way in.

"A panzer, nagas, and shriekers." The killer laughed, and Magellan and Lazar readied their weapons. Their gazes scanned for a way out of the hangar as the panzer stalked slowly toward them.

The helmet of Gin's hologram faded to reveal a wide, devious grin on his face before the hologram began to shimmer out of existence. "Oh my."

CHAPTER NINETEEN

The panzer crept closer and closer to the men. Lazar scanned the upper level and flicked his gaze between the horde of shriekers that had almost battered their way in and the rapidly melting door that barely held the nagas at bay.

Magellan raised his rifle. The mutant cat flinched slightly and eyed his weapon with as much curiosity as hunger. It paced from left to right and watched to see the bounty hunter's next move while it considered whether to simply make its own.

"How do you wanna play this, Lazar?" Magellan asked, his voice calm but grim. "He's gone, and it would be point-less to chase him at this point."

"You would know best about that, right?" the merc grunted, and Magellan's hand tightened around his rifle's grip in annoyance. He forced himself to relax. Lazar wasn't wrong. The bounty hunter wanted to kill Gin more than he wanted anything else, but he was clear-headed enough to know that to rush into the dense jungle while low on supplies wouldn't achieve much. The killer had escaped again, and Magellan already felt that his reputation suffered each time it happened. He despised the way the merc taunted and mocked him, but he began to feel that he had simply pointed out facts than indulged in childish mockery.

"Are you going dark on me, Magellan?" the merc snorted. He lit up another cigarette— the last from the box, it would seem, as he crushed it in his hand and tossed it to the ground. "I didn't think a little ribbing would get you so ornery. I thought guys like you were more cool-headed than that."

Magellan remained silent. The panzer now moved to hide behind a fallen chunk of the dome. "This hasn't exactly been a great showing on my part."

"At least you didn't lose your men." Lazar looked at the level above. A couple of the shriekers grabbed onto the ledge, ready to drop down. He raised his launcher a few inches and warned them to back off. They replied with bared their teeth and smacked the floor in an angry display along with their piercing shrieks. The merc frowned and shook his head. "Dammit, that's annoying," he muttered and held one ear with his free hand. "I wish I had a fancy helmet like you and the kid to dampen that."

"How are your ears still functional?" Magellan asked as he patted his jacket to check his pistols.

"Years of going to metal shows and hanging out with a boisterous group of assholes gave me a tolerance for yelling and high-pitched shrilling." Lazar stuck his pinky casually into his earhole and twisted it. "Or it deafened me. I should probably have it checked at some point."

Magellan withdrew his volt pistol. "We don't have a lot of time left before the dropship leaves. We can fight the freaks off, but I don't wanna stay here while you fire your popgun. The scaffolding doesn't seem very stable."

"Well, you did have the pilot blow the ceiling apart." Nagas now slithered in through holes in the partially dissolved door. "I never liked snakes—the real things, mutants, or the metaphorical ones." Lazar gripped his machine gun in his other arm and looked over his shoulder. "Go ahead and get out of here, Magellan."

The bounty hunter looked at the gang captain in shock. "What are you—"

"I ain't dense and neither are you, so don't act like it," he retorted before Magellan could finish. "We can't both make it back to the ship and deal with this mess at the same time. It's better that one of us make it back than neither." His gaze darted to the approaching mutants. "And I probably look like the better slab of meat between the two of us."

"Lazar, I said I would take care of the situation if Gin showed up. I wasn't able to do that, but I can at least make sure you and Kaiden get out of here alive."

The merc laughed. "Jesus, do you think this is a suicide stand or something?" he demanded and aimed his grenade launcher at the nagas and his machine gun at the shriekers. "I guess I won't rely on you for moral support."

"And you think you can take them all? Madness leads to many things, suicide included."

"I'm mad, not insane," the merc clarified and shifted his

fingers on the triggers of each weapon. "You have a ship waiting back at the port, right? The pilot may be too much of a pansy to break protocol, but the least you can do is scoop me up once you get back. I'll make a smoke signal or something and cook a couple of these bastards while I wait for ya."

Magellan was taken aback by the man's sudden bravado. He studied the debris the panzer lurked behind. "I can scale up with my hook. I'll toss it back down and—"

"Don't start with that trash." Lazar snarled. "Get out of here. I need to kill some more. Come back if you feel like it, and if not, I guess I'll become one with the jungle or something. I don't look that far off from a gorilla so I'll blend right in."

Magellan pursed his lips and sighed as he pulled the brim of his hat down. "I'll come back for you. Don't die on me, ya hear?"

"Yeah, whatever."

"Lazar!"

"What? Do you want me to wrap my pinky in yours or something?" he barked, and a few of the shriekers above leapt back. "Get going."

Magellan placed his rifle on his back, switched the pistol to his other hand, and raised his free arm to fire his grappling hook to the top of the building. "Thanks, Lazar."

"Thank me by taking out that pissy pussycat before you head out," he grunted.

The panzer climbed on top of the debris and snarled at him as he ascended. "I didn't think you would simply let me waltz out of here," he sniped and aimed his pistol. The mutant cat roared and lunged at him. Magellan fired, and the force swung him away from the beast's claws as the electric bolt hit the panzer in the jugular. It sparked and the beast twitched and spasmed around a frazzled hiss as it was jettisoned back to the ground.

The shot released pandemonium. The shriekers cried and leapt from their platform, and the nagas spat their acidic venom at both men. Lazar dove quickly out of the way and fired a grenade that erupted in the middle of the coil of mutants.

Magellan used his body weight and twisted himself in the air to avoid the deadly spittle, but a small splash landed on the wire of his grappling hook a few feet above him. As he wound closer, he huffed and swung himself quickly to a ledge on his right. The wire snapped as he whipped himself onto the edge and the sudden disconnect enabled him to make the couple of extra feet it took to grab the ledge and hoist himself up. He readied his rifle and placed a few quick shots through the heads and chests of the shriekers before Lazar looked angrily at him. The bounty hunter raised his rifle and held up a hand before he turned to search for a staircase or ladder he could use to climb the rest of the way.

"This is bad," the pilot muttered as she examined the wounded soldier. An open holoscreen of his vitals hovered above her. "This kind of wound...getting stabbed by anything is horrible enough, sure, but such a precise strike? Who did this?"

"*A serial killer named Gin Sonny,*" Chief said. She looked

around for a moment before she saw the small orb in the corner the vitals screen.

"What are you?"

"I'm his EI," he explained. *"We can make proper introductions later. Right now, there isn't much we can do. We've treated the wound as best as we can physically, but he lost a lot of blood. Do you have any regen or hemoreplicant?"*

"I have replicant." She nodded, fished it out of the box, and grabbed an injector from the bench.

"Administer the entire vial. If you have any relaxant, administer a small dose of that as well."

"Right," she acknowledged and focused on his arm. "I need a place to inject him."

"Disengaging his armor locks." The buckles and grips on Kaiden's arm unlocked with a quick hiss and slid off. The pilot pried the armor along his arm off and left only his underlay, then cut a hole with a pair of snips so she could look for a vein. "It's so shallow," she whispered.

"Quickly, please," Chief instructed. She found a spot and administered the replicant.

"That should help with the blood loss, but everything else needs further treatment," she explained as she sorted through a collection of vials. "The wraps and the foam will keep him alive, but it's not a proper fix. Will this work?" She held up a small vial of purplish liquid.

Chief scanned it. *"That's too strong, at least to administer in full. A fifth of the vial."*

The pilot removed the empty vial of replicant, adjusted the injector knob to lower the injection pressure, and slid in the vial of relaxant. "I know I promised to wait, but seeing this...I'm not so sure I should wait for the other two. He needs help asap, and it's a long flight back to the port."

"They have a few more minutes," Chief stated. *"Give them that."*

"I thought you EIs had instructions to give your host's life precedence in situations like these."

"We do, but we also adapt to the desires and mindset of our hosts. He has his...faults, but he would tear himself up about leaving others behind for his sake, a point of stubbornness. I don't want him to die, but I don't want him bitching at me when he comes to, either. I can at least say we waited as long as we could."

She unlatched the bottom of Kaiden's helmet and removed it. He had paled dramatically, and his mouth was agape. Quickly, she traced her fingers along the neckline of his undersuit and moved it down his neck in search of a place to inject the relaxant.

"Then I hope they make it back in time."

Magellan raced up the steps and headed for the top. He wasn't sure if this would lead to the roof or not, but up was good enough for now. If he had to, he would blast his way through the ceiling.

A crunching sound stopped his ascent. A pair of shriekers munched on the corpse of another mutant or animal two stories up, too preoccupied with their meal to notice him. They must have been attracted by the pheromones but found the corpse more appealing than the smell. He leapt up the stairs and onto the platform of the next floor and steadied his rifle on the bars.

One of them turned as he fired and the top of its head exploded. The other, startled, jumped back and bit the bone in its mouth in half. It turned to the bounty hunter and bounded at him. The severed bone pierced its stomach and it screamed in anguish. Magellan moved aside, but it swung its long arms and knocked him down as it crashed to the wall. It grabbed the upper half of his leg and dragged him closer. He thudded the bottom of his boot into its head, raised his foot again, and brought it down into its eye. The shrieker yelled and swatted at the boot. The man rolled away and grabbed his rifle, fired a shot at the mutant, and silenced it as he continued to ascend the stairs.

When he reached the top, he found a hatch. He folded his rifle and slid it onto his back, gripped the lever, and pulled. The hatch clicked, and he pushed it open to the welcome hum of the dropship's engines as he hoisted himself in. He was on the opposite side of the roof and ran for the ship. As he passed the hole, he couldn't resist looking down to where Lazar still fought below. Another pang of guilt coursed through him. The merc was bathed in blood, and he grabbed a naga and smashed it into a wall while he forced the others back in a hail of gunfire.

He should have stayed.

"Hey!" a voice called. The pilot waved him over. "Hurry the hell up. We need to get this kid to the port."

The bounty hunter grimaced. He took one final look at the battle, then sprinted to the ship. As soon as he hopped in, the pilot closed the door and headed to the cockpit. "The other one didn't make it?"

"He stayed behind. I'm coming back for him later," he explained as he moved to look at Kaiden.

"I told you I can't come,"

"I said *I* would," Magellan snapped. "Don't worry about it. Take us back as fast as possible."

"Then strap yourself and the kid down," she ordered. He nodded and crossed the straps over Kaiden's body to fasten him in as the ship prepared for takeoff.

"You guys have trackers for us, right?" he asked and headed to the cockpit.

"Well, yeah, but nothing invasive," she muttered as she took the ship into the skies. "Merely a basic one, to keep a lookout. But we only use it when a long time has elapsed or with your permission—"

"It's fine," he interrupted and held out a hand. "Let me see it."

Blood dripped onto the floor with small plopping sounds and accompanied a few muttered groans and haggard breathing from the shriekers. Lazar sat on the crates that the Panzer had tried to hide behind. He looked at its unmoving corpse and decided he really had to get one of those guns if he made it back.

The merc scrabbled in the large pocket of his pants for another box of cigarettes. It was crushed, but he opened the lid and looked inside. Most of the cigarettes had either snapped or come undone, but a couple were still relatively intact. If he vaped, his device would have probably been destroyed in all the commotion, so he had the wiser vice.

He found one of the decent ones, lit up, and took a long, slow drag. The battle was over, and he had finished off the last of the mutants a few minutes before with his bare hands. He gazed at his metal arm, now coated in blood. Maybe bare wasn't the right word.

Lazar wondered how long it had taken. He was probably stuck there for a few more hours. He knew Magellan would return. Guys like that were the honorable sort, and it almost made him wish he had fallen in with that crowd earlier. But he still had a chance to make the boys back home into something like that.

A scraping sound like a boot sliding over dirt and gravel caught his attention. The merc inhaled deeply. Assuming he got back home, he reminded himself.

He scooped a glob of blood from the shrieker's corpse below him, stood, and looked around. The sun had set, but light still seeped through. A couple of minutes passed before he saw it—a slight haze, barely there, revealed in the low light of the sun arcing off the wall on the floor above.

He removed the cigarette from his mouth and spat on the floor before he heaved the blood at the figure. The blood impacted something well away from the wall and pillars.

"I thought so." He grunted and rolled his cigarette in his fingers. "Magellan usually only meets his bad guys once, but I've known plenty of bastards like you. You guys like to come back to see your handiwork."

The blood moved forward and dropped off the second floor. A small cloud of dust was kicked up as someone landed. Lazar placed the cigarette back in his mouth and folded his arms. The air shimmered before a figure in white appeared.

Gin reached up and removed his helmet to reveal a wide, cocky grin. "Well, you are much keener than you let on," he said approvingly and tilted his head as his smile faded to a rather unnerving blank look. "It's a great pity you aren't as wise."

CHAPTER TWENTY

Lazar eyed Gin cautiously. This was the first time he had seen him get... Mad wasn't right. Anything but annoyingly coy or whimsical. "Are you pissed that Magellan left or something?"

"Oh, extremely," the killer muttered. "But also that my little plan failed."

"Did you not notice it didn't exactly work the first time either?" Lazar growled through another long drag. The cigarette burned down to the end and he let the smoke trail out as he finished. "Did you think the second time would be the charm or something?"

"It makes me realize how pointless my stay here was." The killer sighed. "At least from a practical standpoint, I got to meet a couple of interesting people." His smile returned, though only as a small smirk along the lines of his mouth. "Although considering I've only killed two people in the last few hours, I feel I might have lost my touch or grown sluggish. Tell me, how's Kaiden doing?"

"I don't know. I haven't talked to anyone since Magellan

left. They are too far away to reach on comms at this point." Lazar's metal hand closed and opened a few times. "You should worry less about that, Gin. You still have me to deal with."

His adversary cocked an eyebrow. "I should keep a tally of people's last words. Or at least the clichés."

Lazar spat out the butt of his cigarette "Do you have a God complex too? You're as beaten and ragged as any of us were. You can play demon as much as you like, but you feel it. I'm made of tougher stuff than the poor bastards you typically get off on killin'."

"Which makes you slow," Gin pointed out. His hand snaked to the hilt of his blade and flipped a switch on its holster "Thick-skulled as well if I should take a guess. You seem to be out of weapons, gangbanger. For someone so sure I would return, you haven't prepared that well, have you?"

The merc smiled. "I may be out of ammo, but I held back a little." He retrieved two thermals from behind his back. "That blood I threw on you wasn't only to mark you but to make sure it wasn't another of those annoying holograms." He hit the activation buttons on the explosives and rolled his arm back. "You won't escape this time."

He threw the two grenades at Gin. As he moved to dodge, Lazar kicked his foot to knock his machine gun into the air. He grabbed it in one arm and fired the remaining rounds at the killer. A few knocked him back enough to keep him in place. The explosions surged forward in a hot wave of force and Lazar staggered back. He leaned down and steadied himself with a hand on the ground as the blasts engulfed the room. The entire structure trembled and debris crashed from the wall and floor above.

The shakes wore off, and he smiled proudly as he stood and looked at the smoke. "I guess I should have said almost out of ammo." He chuckled. "Magellan made this sound like it would be hard, but explosions have a way of making damn sure things end the way they are supposed to."

"With the target alive and well?"

Lazar narrowed his eyes and snarled. The dust and smoke cleared and Gin stood lazily amongst the debris, surrounded by a purple field "I'm not sure if you noticed, but my cloaking device was perfectly functional. Maybe you depended on my barriers to recharge slower? They do, but your deduction skills aren't as great as you seem to believe they are."

The merc tossed his now empty gun away. "Whatever. It'll be more fun like this. Besides, did you think it was such a smart idea to create a large hard-light barrier after a quick charge?"

The barrier dimmed before it evaporated. Gin looked around for a moment. "So you hoped it would kill me, but if not, it would drain my barrier's energy."

"It's always smart to keep up with your tech's maintenance," Lazar growled and took a few steps forward. "Without the power those vanguard shields supply, you don't look like you have the strength to do anything more than hit me with a few pansy slaps."

The killer drew his plasma cutter blade slowly out of its holster. "It's not my fists you should be worried about," he warned and tapped the weapon on his shoulder armor. His smile was now narrower, sharper, and more disturbed. "Whatever. It'll be more fun like this."

Lazar roared as he charged and swung his large metal fist in an arc to smash his adversary's skull. Gin leaned back to avoid the blow, and the fist struck the ground and smashed a rock nearby. The killer flipped the blade in his hand, pointed it at the man's neck, and stabbed at him. The merc blocked with his other hand and the blade cut into the side of his palm, but he caught his opponent's hand. He tightened his grip, turned, and threw Gin into a pillar which broke in two and thrust him to the ground. The floor above finally gave way as the middle section slid and crumbled into itself. Lazar walked out of its path and noticed a piece of long, twisted metal spiked into the floor. He seized it and held it like a lance as he ran at the other man.

Gin regained his feet and, as Lazar thrust the spike forward, he parried the attack and sliced at the metal to cut through it easily. The merc flipped it and held the other end in the air like a sword. He dodged two swipes from the killer and lunged at him with the back of his gauntlet. His adversary leaned back, and as the fist sailed over him, he placed his hands on the ground and flipped backward. Lazar howled, sprang forward, and attempted to chop him with the improvised weapon. Gin spun in place and when the attack failed, countered with his own. Lazar leaned away but felt a searing pain in his cheek.

His teeth clenched in anger, he shoved his boot into Gin's chest and knocked him back. He grabbed the metal in the center and threw it like a spear, but his opponent used his bionic arm to snatch it out of the air. With a smile, he closed his fist around it and snapped it in two and dropped the pieces to the floor. Lazar charged again and threw punches which the killer side-stepped before he grabbed the merc's artificial arm. Lazar pressed forward with all his strength, but Gin didn't budge. Instead, he leaned in with a cocky smile. "Yours is bigger, I'll admit." He snickered. "But quality over quantity and all that."

"You may have the latest model," Lazar snarled. "But I have something you don't."

"Rust?" his adversary questioned mockingly.

"Novelty," Lazar muttered and with his free hand, spun the dial under his thumb as far as it would go. The top opened, and a large jet of flames blew into the killer's face.

Gin cursed and stumbled back. His shades slid off his face as he tried to guard it with his free hand and his grip released. The merc grimaced at the indentions of the other man's claw in the side of his gauntlet. The flame stopped, completely tapped.

"Did I burn your pretty face, Gin?" he taunted. "Hold still and I'll make all that pain go away."

The killer straightened, his hand still pressed against the side of his face. He rubbed it for a moment before his hand lowered and he turned to look at Lazar, whose eyes widened in shock. His face was slightly seared, but his eyes were black and small circular dots glowed white where his irises should be. They widened slightly before they shrank once more like the shutter of a camera. The killer sighed when he saw that his shades had been trampled. "I was quite fond of that pair."

"You're much more of an aug than you let on." Lazar

held up his fist. "I guess I'll hear some static with the screams."

"It's only a few incidentals," Gin replied with a shrug. "You grow accustomed. Once you start, you can't stop." He pointed to his eyes "Although these were actually the first. But don't worry, I'm not some unfeeling cyborg."

"Yeah, right." Lazar dashed forward with his arm raised to strike. "Only a murderer."

Gin smirked and his bionic arm sparked with light as he raised it. When the merc closed in, he rammed it forward into his chest. Lazar's air expelled painfully and he was thrown across the room. He skidded a good distance and finally came to a halt in a pile of dirt and tile.

"I find the anger of the hypocrite to be one of the most humorous things in the galaxy," the killer mused as he slammed his metal foot down onto the large man's chest when he tried to stand. "Come now, a big guy like you in a big bad gang, I'm sure at least a few people had their lives cut short because of your actions? But I guess that doesn't matter to you. They weren't your buddies, were they?"

"Sure I have," Lazar admitted and spat a glob of blood from his mouth. "But they weren't human. That's a status you can lose if you fuck up enough."

Gin expression quickly changed from curious to amused. "It's not exactly a knight's code but I see the value in it." He straddled the merc. "It's close to mine, although yours has more wiggle room—unlike you at the moment."

Lazar stared coldly at him before he clamped his arm around Gin's leg. The killer tried to shake it off, but the man held firm and attempted to crush the bone. The killer muttered in irritation. A blade projected from the tip and the foot spun unnaturally to slice into the large man's arm. He roared and let go but managed to roll away from his assailant when the man slammed his foot into the ground to retract the blade.

"I am also quite fond of novelty," Gin stated. "I would have thought that was obvious, but whatever."

Lazar stood and inspected his arm. The blade had dug nearly halfway into his gauntlet. He tried to move his hand. The pinky and ring fingers jarred and moved slowly, but the rest seemed all right. He took a few steps forward, but pain thudded in his chest and his breathing was ragged. He couldn't keep the fight up much longer.

Gin folded his arms and observed the struggling gang leader. "Do you feel a little tired? Wanna take a big boy nap?"

"Shut the hell up," Lazar snapped. "I will kill you. That will be the last thing I do."

"That's what your life has come down to?" the killer asked glumly and raised his hands nonchalantly. "You didn't have many big dreams during your childhood, did you?

Lazar braced himself. "I bet that smart mouth of yours got you slapped around plenty during yours."

"Actually, mine was quite idyllic," Gin admitted. "I could have used a pony, maybe, but I can't complain too much."

The merc scowled and spat up another batch of blood. The sun had given way fully and the blood shimmered in the moonlight that seeped into the room. "So you're merely crazy then."

Gin shrugged and his smile remained in place. "I

couldn't quite say. Isn't the main problem of a crazy person that they don't know they are crazy?"

"That only makes you an idiot." Lazar lifted his metal arm. "I don't have time for idiots. We're going to end this now."

The killer spun his blade idly in his hand. "I said I don't keep a record of what people say during the last moments of their lives, but I can safely say that the last of that there…" He stopped twirling the knife and pointed it at Lazar. "Almost all the time, that is true. But it doesn't end well for the one who isn't me."

Lazar closed his fist, and his two end digits took a moment to fall into place. "Are you done gloating?"

"I could go on." Gin leaned forward and prepared to strike. "But you're right. This has been fun, but I didn't lie about having places to be. My honesty is a virtue that I take pride in. Do you have any actual last words? I'll make a note of them."

The gang leader didn't respond and simply stared at him. The killer lowered his head for a moment and when he looked up, the blank expression had returned. With the exception of the blood drops and the creak of the building, it was silent around them. Gin pressed a button on the hilt of his knife and the blade glowed with heat. Lazar tapped his fingers on his arm. He looked at his adversary, closed his eyes, and drew a deep breath as he slid a compartment in his wrist open and turned a dial.

He roared as he charged at the killer. His adversary's expression didn't change, and he didn't move as the merc barreled toward him. As Lazar closed in, Gin struck. His heated blade lashed out and quickly ripped into the merc's chest. He made three strikes, two on his chest and one across the throat. Blood sprayed, congealed in globs from the heat of the blade, and plopped onto the ground and Gin's face and arm. Lazar grabbed the killer's arm, but it was too late. He collapsed and gurgled and hissed from his wounds as his life fluid pooled around him. Somehow, he had hold of his opponent's arm, although the grip was weak.

Gin stared at him for a moment, deactivated his blade, and slid it into its holster. "If this was your dream, you should have learned what every kid does eventually," he muttered as Lazar gasped weak, pointless breaths and blood continued to pour from his wounds. "Don't dream so big."

He turned to leave but was held fast by the merc's grasp. He turned back with an annoyed look and shook his arm in an attempt to free himself, but the grip seemed to tighten. The killer twisted and turned his arm and used his free hand to try to pry the fingers off his wrist. A small light caught his eye. He turned the man's arm quickly. A panel glowed on the gauntlet's wrist and counted down from nine seconds.

Gin was confused for a moment before it dawned on him. He felt angry for a moment before it gave way to a chuckle when he looked at Lazar to see a bloody but wide and cocky smile.

"You really were more clever than you let on," the killer said appreciatively. The timer reached zero, and the gauntlet burst apart and engulfed them both in an explosion.

Magellan watched the vitals on the tracker screen, his only window to Lazar's condition. There was no image, but Lazar's heart rate had leveled before it spiked rapidly for some time. It had then evened out again and spiked once more, and now, it was dangerously low.

"Dammit, Lazar, this is why I wanted your promise," Magellan snapped as he slammed a fist down onto the bench. They were almost at the port. His ship was nearby and was significantly faster than this heap. If he headed back as soon as possible, he could be back in—

Lazar's vitals disappeared, and the word **deceased** appeared over his profile. The bounty hunter hung his head and slammed his fist again, albeit much more weakly, on the bench.

"You couldn't do that one damn thing, could you?"

CHAPTER TWENTY-ONE

His vision was a swirl of darkness and bright lights. He felt ill and sore, and a jagged pain seared his chest. The lights dominated his view, and the darkness crept away. Kaiden's eyes fluttered open. He took a moment to breathe deeply and tried to sit up but was hampered by a dull pain in his arms and a sharper one in his chest. He laid back on the bed, rolled his head from side to side to work out the stiffness, and looked around.

He was in an enclosed room with a sliding door at the far end, pale gray walls, and white floor tiles. Beige curtains were drawn closed on either side of his simple cot. A machine with an orb on top stood nearby—a biomonitor, he realized; a machine to monitor his physical well-being and administer vials of serum and drugs as needed. Obviously, he was in a hospital of some sort, but it seemed rather bare compared to the ones he was used to.

Steps behind the left curtain indicated that someone approached, and he turned his head to see who it was. The curtain was drawn back, and Magellan stared at him. His expression was grim, but a flicker of relief washed over him when he saw movement in Kaiden's eyes.

"Welcome back to the world of the living," he said and pulled a chair to the bedside. "How are you feeling? Are you all right?"

The ace tried to speak, but his throat was dry and itchy. He motioned with an arm for a glass of water. Magellan pulled a flask from his coat, undid the top, and handed it to him. Kaiden eyed him questioningly as he took it. "Although I imagine you'd like a shot of something strong after that. It's only water," he promised.

He nodded stiffly, then pressed his palm to his neck and rolled it for a moment before he took a swig from the flask. Cool water rushed down his throat a little too quickly. He coughed and the pain in his chest flared with each exhale.

"Easy now," Magellan warned and placed a hand on his chest to steady him. "Between the injury, physical exhaustion, drugs, and surgery, you're not up to snuff. Make smaller movements for now."

Kaiden's coughing softened and finally stopped and he nodded quickly before he took another small sip. "Where am I?" he asked.

"*A fixer station in the Los Angeles gig port,*" Chief explained. He appeared on Kaiden's right, his light dim, and his eye examined him. "*We were heading straight back to Seattle, but considering your condition, it was best to land here and fix the damage right away.*"

"How long?" he inquired and looked the bounty hunter and his EI in turn. "How long was I under?"

"Two days," Magellan replied.

He bit his lip. "I was supposed to be back at the Academy yesterday."

The bounty hunter's chuckle was low and almost muted. "That's what you're worried about after all this?" he asked and moved his hand to Kaiden's shoulder. "You're a tough bastard. After a stab like that, you should be dead. I was able to stabilize you and your EI got your armor's wrappings in place. The pilot gave you a little TLC but considering that was a strike meant to kill, you can at least count this as something of victory."

"I'm not saying I ain't used to taking a few hits for a win…" He trailed off for a moment, placed the flask against his leg, and tried to sit with help from Magellan. "But this doesn't feel like one."

The bounty hunter retrieved something from the ground. He showed Kaiden the cylinder containing the device they had been sent to retrieve. "You take what you can get sometimes and hope that the next one is more clear-cut." He placed it back on the ground and leaned back in his chair. "You're alive, finished the job, and you'll get paid once I turn this in. Take that for now."

"I'll spend most of my earnings paying for the painkillers and band-aids," he muttered. "It deflates the warm, fuzzy feeling a little."

"I'll foot the medical bills. Don't worry about that," Magellan assured the young man. "You need to rest for now. The rejuv should kick in soon, but it's diluted and on a slow release. They don't wanna flood your system considering everything else that went into you."

"I could probably choke a vampire," Kaiden muttered

and rubbed his neck once more. "I've had my fill of mutants for a while."

"True enough."

"Did Lazar take off already?" he asked and the smile on Magellan's face vanished. Kaiden lowered his hand, immediately understanding Magellan's grim visage. "He's gone too?"

His companion nodded slowly, removed his hat, and ran a hand through his hair. "He stayed behind so that I could leave and take you to get help. I intended to go back for him, but he died before we even landed."

"Was it Gin?" Kaiden asked, and anger crept into his voice. His heart speeded up and the pain in his chest throbbed. "The knife in my chest—that's the last thing I remember. Did he get Lazar after me?"

"I can't say for sure," the bounty hunter admitted. "He escaped after attacking you, led us into a trap, and attracted a group of mutants to us. I was only able to monitor Lazar using a basic vitals tracker the pilot had. I thought he'd made it, but after he had calmed down, his heart rate spiked again—like he'd got into another battle or was running from something. Then it slowed before it stopped altogether."

Kaiden leaned back with a deep sigh, "Dammit… Dammit!" he cursed and gripped his bed sheets. The movement jarred the flask against his leg and knocked it over. "What's the point of training for this kind of shit if I can't do something when it counts!?"

"Calm down, partner," Chief requested and floated almost in his face. *"You can't stress out like this."*

"You did more than almost anyone else could be asked

to at your age," Magellan said calmly and tried to quiet him.

"I'm training to be an ace," Kaiden huffed. "Not everything was easy in the Animus, but I beat it all despite that. I'm better than every other soldier in my division or in my year—hell, I've broken records from past years." The sharp pain surged again, and he ran his fingers over the bandages around his chest. "And when it gets real, I flake like this? I was a fucking Dead-Eye. I've dealt with people who tried to kill me and it wasn't a problem."

"There's a difference between dealing with someone who knows how to kill and dealing with a killer," Magellan pointed out. Kaiden turning his head to stare at him. "You might be the best in your class, and this mission should have been easy for you—for all of us. The old saying tells us to be prepared for anything,"

"Don't lecture me," he snapped, and the anger was immediately replaced with regret when Magellan simply stared at him. "Sorry."

"No worries." The bounty hunter shrugged. "I wasn't trying to lecture you, but I suppose it might come across that way. I intended to say that that old motto, while accurate, isn't something everyone can conceivably live up to. Running into a guy like Gin—that's a one in billions coincidence."

"Do you think that's all it was?" Kaiden asked. He released the bed sheets and picked up the flask.

Magellan's gaze darted away briefly before he looked at him. "Honestly, I can't say for sure. I don't have any reason or theories why he would be after anyone but me, and even then, he's never actively pursued me except for our second meeting. He wanted to finish me off, and I blew a chunk of his hand off." He shook his head. "I always looked down on him, but he talked a big game and had the skills to back it up. He got away from me, but he always ran and never finished me off. I dealt more damage to him than he did me. For all that cockiness I looked down on, I was becoming just like him in my own way. I took his arm, a leg, and gallons of blood. But I could never finish it. More people died, and I simply focused on the kill."

There was silence for a moment. Chief hovered and looked from one to the other to see who would speak first. The bounty hunter sighed and Kaiden looked at the ceiling. "I should call the Academy and tell them I'll be back soon."

"I already did," Magellan related.

"Did you have to pretend to be my guardian or something?" Kaiden asked. He lifted his arms and rested them on his legs.

"You're a twenty-one-year-old man. I don't need a consent form. I merely explained the situation. They said that you have grace days, but if you miss too many compulsory activities you'll be expelled. Although, since you are in a fixer station, get a report from the staff and they'll potentially not dock you anything."

"Maybe not the administration," Kaiden mumbled, "but a couple of my teachers might." Kaiden looked at the hospital smock he wore. "That reminds me, were you able to get my gear?"

"What remains is in a locker. When you're discharged, you'll get it back. Your pistol is fine, your armor and underlay... Well, you can salvage some of it, but the underlay was shredded and the chest plate is shattered, along with a number of the other pieces. I would recommend salvaging the mods and getting a new suit altogether."

"Along with a new machine gun," he muttered. "This lifestyle gets pretty pricey, huh?"

"Why do you think I haven't retired yet?" Magellan responded, and the moment of levity gave them both a sense of calm for a minute. The bounty hunter retrieved a scroll-stick and opened it into a tablet. "I'll be leaving in a minute," he declared. Kaiden, at a loss for words, simply looked at him as he stood. "I'll turn the device in and make sure you get paid. Then I'll collect the others' tags and get them to any friends in their hometown."

The ace nodded glumly and sighed as he fell back onto the pillows. "Thank you, Magellan." The bounty hunter glanced at him in surprise. "I know I would be dead now if it wasn't for you. If it helps at all, you're not the only one who let themselves get too cocky."

The man closed his eyes as he turned away. "You're a good soldier, Kaiden, don't doubt yourself there. But you're a student. Maybe you are one of the best or even the best, but you are still a student. You have more to learn." He walked to the sliding door, opened it, and looked back one more time. "Don't let him win, Kaiden. There is a more metaphorical reason guys like him are called revenants. Even if you kill them, they can haunt you and stop you from making your own choices. They can make you constantly doubt and question yourself. When they walk among us, they are horrible, but even in death, they can cost you your life. Don't let him do that."

Kaiden, although he didn't really understand what Magellan meant, nodded. The bounty hunter replaced his hat and tipped it to him before he stepped out and closed the door and left Kaiden to himself.

Julio Alvarez, the proprietor and bartender of the Emerald Lounge in Seattle, was in good spirits. There were plenty of patrons but not enough that it was a hassle. The rain outside tapped against the windows and roof and he always found it soothing—which was a good thing since it happened so often. The real stuff too, not the biosphere synthesized stuff. Most people said it sounded and felt the same, but he knew the rattle of real rain.

"Another round, Commander?" he asked his patron. Sasha nodded and slid his glass over. Julio filled it with the commander's preferred lager, Peacemaker Amber. "It's nice to catch up now and again. Kaiden barely writes or calls. I saw him a few times during the break, though."

"That was actually one of the things I wanted to discuss," Sasha explained. "He parlayed some of his early free time and left town. The statement on his form said it was personal, but I was told by one of my comrades that he was scheduled on a job."

"Kaiden's done gigs from time to time for extra credits and even worked as my doorman for a couple weeks." He passed the commander his drink. "It's kind of full circle in a way, don't you think?"

Sasha nodded and enjoyed a small sip of the lager before he set it back down. "The thing is, he hasn't returned. His classes started today, and he was supposed to return yesterday."

Julio cocked an eyebrow. "That's odd. Kaiden's a little lackadaisical, but he's not usually one to skip out on commitments. You'd think a gig like that wouldn't take him long."

"So you know about it, then?"

Julio gave him a look of ire. "You don't gotta do the coy interrogation thing with me, Commander. It wasn't some under the table thing." Julio leaned against the bar. "It's not side-gig or anything, but I am still set up as a gig agent. I get the occasional job request from time to time and deal them out to those I think would fit. It was a retrieval mission in the Amazon on a chain team. It didn't look like much and might have threatened a youngblood or runner, but it seemed like something Kaiden could do even without having gone to Nexus for a year and change."

"You seem to have a rather high opinion of him despite not knowing him very long," Sasha commented and sipped his drink.

"I could say the same. I may not see him much, but the fight on the day you took him in still sticks out. Plus, he had to deal with the occasional idiot who got too hotheaded or drunk for their own good while he worked with me along with a few successful missions he applied for and accomplished himself. I could tell he was looking for something a little bigger."

"Did he tell you why he's doing these gigs?"

Julio leaned back with a hand under his chin. "I don't think he ever said. I would assume spending money. He might want to hit things on occasion—you know, real things."

"The whole point of the Animus is to create experiences that the mind and body cannot differentiate from reality. If it is not enough for some of our students, perhaps I should take it up with the designer."

"I may have never used one myself, but you still know you're going in, right?" the bartender questioned. "For a guy like that, it's a feeling, right? No matter how much it 'feels like' the real thing, that edge is missing. You spent fifteen years in the military. Tell me you didn't feel that way during the real action."

"I was too preoccupied with my duties to take the time to consider such philosophy," Sasha retorted.

Julio smiled and snickered and a device in his ear began to glow. "Hold up a second," he asked and pressed the button to receive the call. "Hello? Well, speak of the devil—how are you, Kaiden?" Julio's smile widened, and he winked at the commander and leaned one hand on the bar. "You sound a little hoarse. Did you spend a night celebrating too hard?"

His smile faded and his lips pursed. He breathed sharp breaths through his nose. "Oh, Kaiden, man...I'm sorry." He nodded and was silent for another minute. "I see, that's...I can't believe it. I promise I would have never...I feel terrible. What? If I see... He's here, actually. You'll do it in person? I'll pass it along then. Get better, man. You've got a bottle or two waiting the next time you drop by. I'll be sure to screen the gigs more before...I guess you're right. I still feel like it's my fault, though. Okay, no, no, I get it. Thanks for letting me know. Get well, man." Julio clicked the button again and ended the call.

"That was Kaiden. You won't believe—"

"I heard," Sasha stated and pointed to the device around his head.

"Gin Sonny? He ran into a rev on his first out-of-state mission? And he almost died." Julio placed one hand on the bar and ran the other through his hair. "What are the chances?"

Sasha looked at the last of his lager and his fingers tapped the bar. "Almost too much."

CHAPTER TWENTY-TWO

As the hyperloop emerged from the water, the glass was greeted by more water as rain poured down from above. Kaiden leaned against the window and let the coolness calm him as he folded his arms across his chest, careful not to press too hard. The staff at the fixer station explained that they didn't have the tech to properly repair the wound and adapt the skin. The area was scarred and fragile but as he was in Los Angeles, there were plenty of options for further recovery.

He skipped out. The scar would remain. It was his reminder, now.

The pain wasn't as intense as it had been, and his body had recovered rather quickly thanks to the ultra-grade rejuv, but he still felt a dull throb now and then. He did wonder if he should have had it looked at by another surgeon but decided he would have Dr. Soni take a look if anything flared up again. He would visit her anyway to see if that blue stuff was back in stock.

The hyperloop finally arrived at the station. Kaiden

grabbed his case and prepared to disembark and look for a driver to take him to the Academy entrance. Instead, when he stepped into the line to leave and looked out the window, he saw Commander Sasha and Professor Laurie, both dressed in long black jackets. Sasha wore a white shirt and black slacks while Laurie had chosen a black silk shirt and slacks. They stood in the middle of the station and stared directly at him through the windows of the train.

He wondered if he should take in the sights of the next town.

Kaiden sighed, exited, and approached the men. Sasha remained his typical stoic self, his eyes hidden behind his oculars, but Laurie unnerved him. He had grown accustomed to the professor's jubilant demeanor and eccentric persona, but the look on his face was now as calm as Sasha's, although more dour and almost deadpan. A little paranoia surfaced, and he wondered if these were actually Doppel bots or something in disguise.

"Hey, Chief. Scan them and make sure they are real," he whispered.

"You got stabbed in the chest, Kaiden, not the head," he replied.

"Does Laurie look off to you?"

"Well, his prize science fair project almost died. I guess he's a little peeved."

He slid a hand into his jacket pocket and pulled out a card. "I have a note." He offered it weakly and hoped it would suffice.

Laurie approached first. Kaiden hadn't noticed before, but the man was rather tall—almost the same height as he was, which meant probably six feet three inches, and some change. He studied Kaiden silently for a moment. The ace wondered if he was angry and felt a slight chill. Was he angry enough to take Chief and his EI device away?

To his astonishment, Laurie hugged him and pulled him close. "It's good to see you standing, Kaiden," he said and released him almost as quickly as he had grabbed him, although a hand lingered on his shoulder. "You gave us quite a fright."

"Well, uh, Halloween is coming up and everything." He tried to jest but earned an annoyed look from the professor. "Sorry. I didn't think it would go down like that. I also didn't think you would bother or know that I left at all."

"A rather foolish assumption," Sasha said as he joined them. "Laurie gives you your autonomy, but if he has to, he can find your device, just as he can every student and faculty member of the Academy. And target acquisition was a specialty of mine."

"You should share more stories," Kaiden said in an effort to add a little humor to the situation. They didn't bite.

"Would you like a ride, Kaiden?" Sasha asked. He felt unnerved because it seemed like an uncomfortable ride. They obviously weren't there to be chauffeurs.

"It's all right. I can find a driver. I'm sure you guys have to—"

"Let's go to the car, Kaiden." Laurie walked away with Kaiden's case in his hand.

"Hey that's my—" Sasha stopped him, made a beckoning motion with his hand, and followed the professor. Kaiden sighed. Hopefully, this would be a quick drive.

God, it was agony. The ace shifted in the back seat of the car. Sasha and Laurie sat in front and faced away, even though it wasn't necessary as the front window was closed and the car was on autoride. The drive from the station to the academy usually only took around thirty-five minutes, but time had either slowed to a crawl or they decided to take the scenic route and said nothing the entire time. Was he in trouble? Granted, he hadn't read the agreement thoroughly when he'd joined the Academy, but if there was something against taking gigs, he was sure Chief would have said something. Speaking of Chief, he was oddly silent. He actually wished his EI would yammer on as usual and break the tension, but either he decided to keep to himself, or Laurie had remotely cut off his audio and visuals.

It wasn't like he'd expected it to go down like it had, and he wasn't exactly looking for sympathy when he got back. He simply wanted to play it off, and while he was sure they and his friends would have questions, he had prepared excuses for them. All he wanted was for things to go back to normal so he could find his feet again.

"How's the wound, Kaiden?" Sasha asked. The ace ran a hand unconsciously over his chest.

"It's…all right, I guess. I plan to have Dr. Soni look it over if it hurts too much or interferes with Animus training."

"A possibility," Laurie concurred. "Considering the circumstances and the purpose of the training, real-world injuries transfer over when you sync to the Animus."

"You've taken on another scar, I noticed," Sasha pointed out and gestured at his eye in the rearview mirror. "Is that some sort of macabre collection?"

"Tattoos are expensive," he responded to brush it off as he trailed a finger on the scar along his eye. "I guess these are too in their own way."

Silence fell again, but Kaiden didn't want it to drag on. "Am I in trouble or something?"

"There's no reason why that I can think of," Sasha said. "I was able to get your files from the fixer station, so you are clear on your missed days, but you'll probably have some work to make up."

"How did you manage that?"

"As a student at our Academy, we retain a certain guardianship over you. It took very little time for Councilor Mya to find the files and transfer them to me. She wishes you well and hopes you'll stop by soon."

Kaiden shifted in his chair again. "You haven't said it out loud, but you know what went down, right?"

"I got the details from Mr. Alverez," Sasha confirmed. "I am amazed you survived a run-in with someone on the Revenant List. It must have been terrifying."

"It wasn't something I was prepared for. The mutants are still kind of a new thing, but I've dealt with them. Even assassin's and hitmen and guys like that, but he was... something different."

"Try not to make it a habit if you would." Laurie turned his chair and smiled at him. "These luscious locks of mine are rather expensive to maintain. I wouldn't want to ruin them with grays."

Kaiden blinked in surprise before he nodded and responded with a small grin of his own.

Laurie leaned forward. "I know you will probably want to rest when we return but stop by as soon as possible. I need to scan Chief for any potential viruses and his records of the incident."

"What for?" the ace asked. "This wasn't academy business or anything."

"True, but Gin is wanted galaxy-wide. Even our alien allies all have reasons to pursue him. We don't have a lot of records on him, so this is the first time in a while that we've been able to get more than blurred pictures or snippets of video of him," Sasha explained as he turned to look at Kaiden.

"My guess is that he has some sort of interference device or uploads a virus to remove all but his choice traces of footage," Laurie suggested.

"It's a game to him," Sasha concurred.

"That seems like his thing—he's kind of a technophile." Kaiden shrugged. "At least, that's the image I got, plus what Magellan said."

"Magellan?" Laurie asked. "Which Magellan?"

The ace looked up with a slightly amused smile. "What circles do you move in that you have a group of Magellans to confuse?" He chuckled "A bounty hunter, Magellan Desperaux."

As he leaned back Laurie's gaze darted to Sasha, but he didn't return the look. A ringing sounded from the front of the car and the front screen opened to show the car driving up to the entrance of the academy. Sasha smiled. "It appears we're back."

Laurie left the two after they arrived. He returned to his office after he wished Kaiden well and reminded him to visit after he had recuperated. Sasha escorted the ace across the school grounds. It was still raining, and the plaza was eerily deserted save for a few students under arches or who ran across the grounds to reach a building.

Laurie had given Kaiden his umbrella and told him to return it to him when he came by. Both he and Sasha walked through the plaza. "You don't have to walk me to the dorms," he said. "It was nice enough that you drove me here."

"I have to go this way anyway. I'll see a staff member after this," the commander explained. "I can understand that you want some alone time, but I doubt you'll get that."

"Why would you say—"

"Hey, Kaiden!" someone shouted. He turned as Flynn, Amber, Marlo, Genos, Chiyo, Jaxon, Luke, and Silas ran from behind a building.

"Good Lord, are they a hive-mind?" he mumbled and waved.

"Where you been, mate?" Flynn asked. He and Amber were under an umbrella as was Chiyo. The others simply wore rain jackets with the exception of Jaxon and Genos, whose skin, Kaiden noted, had never looked as shiny as it did in the rain.

"I went out for a bit and went on a little bender," he said, which was technically true.

Sasha shook his head. "Adva Jericho went on a personal mission during his free time, during which he was attacked and nearly killed by the serial killer Gin Sonny."

Gasps and shocked stares issued from the group as well as Kaiden, although he looked at Sasha.

Dick! He clenched his teeth in frustration. "Why?" he groaned.

"You have a few lessons to make up," Sasha stated and turned away from him. "And as an ace, you should learn not to hide too many things from your comrades."

Kaiden sighed in annoyance. He'd known he wouldn't get off easy.

"I will depart now, Kaiden," the commander announced. "I'm sure your friends can escort you the rest of the way as you catch up."

The group was silent as he walked away and entered the main building. The ace looked at the expectant faces of his friends and twirled the umbrella for a moment, unable to hold their gazes. "I would have told y'all eventually."

"You almost died?" Flynn asked. "What happened?"

He filled them in quickly, although he left certain parts out at his discretion. They listened quietly and occasionally, their eyes widened, or a horrified look would cross their faces when he talked about certain fights and when he had confronted Gin. He finished with when he was stabbed and then woke up at the fixer station.

"Man…I mean… That's horrible," Marlo stammered.

"Before anyone asks, I didn't keep it a secret for any reason. I honestly didn't think it mattered," Kaiden added. "The gigs I've done up to this point weren't anything special, especially considering what we've gone through in the Animus. This should have been a cakewalk, all things considered. Shit happens, I guess."

"That is rotten luck," Flynn huffed. "I know that sounds like I'm making light of it, but I'm not. I wanna say something like you should have taken me with you, but I can't think that I would have been much help there."

"Honestly, it was probably better that none of you were there," he admitted and earned different reactions from the group. Some were confused and others worried or angry. He held up a hand. "I'm not saying I think you can't handle yourselves. But I almost died, and three others did die. If that had happened to any of you...I can't say I've been trained to have to deliver news like that yet."

"Yeah, I follow." Silas nodded and looked away for a moment. "I've trained since I was a kid, in prep academies and skirmishes and all that. Hearing about this, though, would it be ironic or corny to say it feels like what we're doing... It feels more real?"

"Probably both, but appropriate," Kaiden admitted.

"Friend Kaiden, might I see your wound?" Genos asked. Jaxon glared him, and he realized that what he'd asked might have been too forward.

"Yeah, that's fine, Genos." Kaiden lifted his shirt to reveal the scar. It ran vertically over his sternum and was about three and a half inches in length, and the rain falling onto it made it look darker.

"Damn," Luke muttered.

"That's so precise," Amber whispered almost inaudibly. "Surgical."

"I want to have your mom take a look," Kaiden said as

he lowered his shirt. "But later. Right now, I wanna rest a while."

"Oh, right." Flynn nodded and backed away. "Sure, mate."

"I'll let the others know," Jaxon said. "For now, you should get some rest and know that you're safe here."

"Thanks." Kaiden walked through the group and toward the soldier's dorms. As he drew nearer to the building, he heard the splash and tap of water behind him. He turned as Chiyo ran up to him.

"Hey, Chiyo." She stopped and simply looked at him. Her eyes…he had to admit to himself he had trouble reading her even under normal circumstances, but she seemed despondent. "What's up?" Her silence continued and Kaiden leaned back, a little uncomfortable. "I get that it's probably shocking and everything, but I'm all right. I'm sure that I'll be back to normal in a few days."

She nodded and stepped closer. "I know it's not your fault." She placed her hand over his wound. He looked down at her hand and then at her. "But please don't be so reckless."

"I…uh, I won't," he promised.

She nodded and moved her hand away. "Please mean it this time." With that, she turned and left. The rain slowed as Kaiden stood in front of the dorms. He placed his hand over his wound again; it felt unaccountably warm.

CHAPTER TWENTY-THREE

Wolfson grumbled curses to himself as he continued to clean the weights area after his last class. "Damn negligent idiots. You take care of the equipment as much as you do yourself." He removed the weights from one of the bench press bars and heard the door to his gym open. Kaiden walked in with a small black box. He tossed the weight aside and hurried forward to greet his student. "Well, look who's finally returned," he bellowed cheerfully. "You look a little glum there, Kaiden. Did the gig not pan out like you thought?"

The ace shut the door and looked at his instructor, his face pensive but curious. "You don't know?"

"How should I? You haven't reported back until now. It's been almost a week since you left. You've missed two classes and personal training." As he moved closer, he noticed the stoic look on Kaiden's face. "Is something wrong?"

The ace moved the box from one hand to the other,

opened his jacket, and pulled his shirt up. Wolfson looked at the scar, and his face fell. "What happened, boy?"

He sighed as he let his shirt drop. "I guess Sasha wanted me to fill you in myself, which I had planned to do anyway." He handed the man the box and slid his hands into his jacket pockets. "The gig didn't go as planned. We ran into a guy named Gin Sonny."

Wolfson's hands clamped down on the box so hard the corners at the top and bottom warped. "That killer? The one on the space station?"

"Among other hot spots, including the Amazon, apparently." Kaiden leaned against the wall and looked away. "This is the last time I give anyone the summary. It's now become a drag."

The instructor thought back. He had been in some rough situations during his time in the WCM, but he was typically in a unit with men to cover his back, strategies to consider, and a large battlefield in which to maneuver. He was at a loss, and while he could see Kaiden tried to keep a cool demeanor, he was obviously shaken.

"To cut a long story short, we finished the job, but three members of the team died at his hands. I almost died and would have without the help of two of the others. It's up there with my worst moments."

"I see," was all Wolfson could muster. He was usually good at rallying the troops when the need arose, but that was during times of do or die. When it came to the drop afterward, he wasn't as good without the assistance of liquor or a round of sparring, but Kaiden didn't look up to doing either. He opened the box and the recreation of

Debonair lay within, slightly scratched and scuffed but nothing he couldn't fix and shine in a few hours.

"I lost my Tempest and most of my armor, so I gotta replace it the next chance I have some free time. Fortunately, I got extra creds. The bounty hunter I was with gave me his cut—another thing to thank him for." Kaiden pushed off the wall and looked at the pistol. "It served me well. Thanks for getting it for me."

"It was your gift for training so hard and winning my scenario in the Alaskan wilderness," Wolfson muttered. "Raza sent a message while you were away. He wanted to know how you were doing. I should tell him and see how he deals with an angry Sauren warlord on his heels."

"Don't bother," Kaiden requested.

"You know that Sauren live for a good hunt, and he took a shine to you. He would hate it if someone killed you before he did."

"And I appreciate that particular brand of Sauren comradery," Kaiden assured him jokingly. "But he is a warlord, and that comes with certain responsibilities. I don't need him to run off on behalf of a human. Sauren relations are lukewarm and practical. If one of their leaders shows any more of a heart, I would imagine that's not a good look."

Wolfson thought about it for a moment and huffed. "I guess that's about right." He withdrew the pistol and retrieved the object wrapped in a dark cloth beneath it. "What's this?" he asked. The dark metal of Gin's Yokai pistol gleamed in the light.

"That was his gun or one of them at least," Kaiden explained. "Does it look familiar?"

"It's one of our development division's designs," the instructor muttered.

"I don't know how he got his hands on one. But apparently, he's known for taking experimental or high-grade technology from different labs and facilities." Kaiden shifted and removed a hand from his pocket to rub the back of his head. "Do you think he could have gotten in here at some point?"

Wolfson walked to his desk and placed the Yokai on top. He wondered for a moment if he should tell him but decided that it should be done later—he had enough to concern himself with now. "No, the development center here focuses on creating things for the Academy proper. The bigger facility in Seattle focuses on weapons, armor, and all that for council projects and graduate items. I don't think he got in there, no matter how good he is or how many doodads he might have. I am almost certain that we would have heard about such a break-in. My guess is that he stole it from a graduate or got it on the black market."

Kaiden stared at it for a moment before he nodded and headed to the door. "I can't keep it on me. I'll probably get expelled, and it's not my kind of weapon anyway. I already turned it down during initiation. You can keep it or give it to Sasha the next time you see him."

"Where are you headed, Kaiden?" Wolfson asked as the soldier opened the door.

"Out to clear my head. I have some stuff to make up, and I hear there's gonna be another test in a week so I gotta prep," he answered. "I'm still a bit sore. I'll come back for training in a couple of days. Later, Wolfson." With that, he left the room and shut the door softly behind him.

The instructor folded his arms and his fingers tapped against his elbow as he thought. He picked Debonair up and primed it. It still seemed in working order. He examined it for a few seconds before he turned it off and retrieved the holster from the box. Calmly, he slid the pistol into it and grabbed his coat.

Kaiden walked through the academy grounds and looked aimlessly around. It was almost lunchtime, but he didn't feel particularly hungry. He received a network notice from Flynn but ignored it and canceled the screen.

"That's the fifth invite you've declined in the last two days," Chief muttered. He retrieved his optic shades and put them on, and Chief's avatar appeared in the corner. *"They're worried, partner. Sure, some of them come from military families, but this is probably the first time they've really had to deal with something like this."*

"I know, but I can't deal with the questions and all that right now," Kaiden admitted and continued his walk. "I'll be fine. I ain't going to be worth much after I get out of here if I let one near-death experience rattle me, right? I'll probably have a few more of those come my way, at least."

"You've only gone to two workshops," the EI noted. *"It's your time and all, but if you miss exams and missions, that'll cost you in more ways than one."*

"I've already told you I'll prep for the test next week," he retorted and stopped in front of the Animus Center. He looked at it for a moment, and a small tremor of concern raced through him. It was quickly replaced by annoyance. "I think I'll start now."

Kaiden appeared in the middle of a circular cave with two tunnels on either side and platforms above him.

"You can begin the trial when ready," Chief informed him and appeared over his shoulder *"Are you sure you wanna run one of these?"*

"It's only a three-wave horde match," Kaiden responded. He opened the loadout screen, selected his saved option, and his weapons appeared—the Raptor in his hands and Debonair in its holster on his side. "It'll last fifteen minutes, tops. I gotta shake off the dust and stretch."

The EI studied him for a moment before he moved to Kaiden's HUD. *"Droids and explosions. It's good to be back to something normal,"* he quipped.

"Begin," the ace ordered. A loud alarm clanged, and words appeared on his visor.

Wave 1 Commencing

Several Security droids appeared. Kaiden spun and obliterated three before they could so much as take a step. Two others fired, but he dodged their slow shots and returned fire to blast one's head and drop the other with two rounds to the chest.

A few more spawned in, but he found his rhythm and eliminated each of them with a single shot before they had a chance to fire.

He vented his rifle and Chief scanned the room. *"Nothing poppin' but you have some hostiles approaching from the tunnel in front of you. By their readings, they look like Guardians."*

Kaiden took a shock grenade from the container and held the activator down. Three Guardian droids appeared, rolled along on their tracks, and took aim. He threw the shock, and the blast froze the droids as he ran closer and fired several shots at their weaker bottom halves. They toppled and disappeared.

Wave 1 Complete

"Maybe I made it too easy," the ace mulled to himself.

"This one's got Guardians, Brute droids, and those zippy Sentry bastards."

"Flying or ground?"

"Both."

Kaiden looked at the platforms above. "Then I should probably scale up a bit." He made a running jump against the cave wall and used that to launch himself higher. As two Guardian droids appeared below, he grabbed one of the floating platforms and hauled himself up. Quickly, he switched to ballistic rounds and fired at the treads of the oncoming enemy. The shots maimed them, and they immediately fell.

"Brutes at four." A trio of bipedal, red, stocky droids aimed their arm cannons at him. The ace leapt upward and fired at the top of the middle droid's cannon to knock it down as it fired. The mechanical was destroyed in the blast and the other two tumbled to the ground. As Kaiden landed, a stinging blast struck him in the shoulder and he glanced up. Sentries flew above him, and a few clung to the side of the cave wall.

He growled as he swapped his Raptor for Debonair,

leapt between the platforms, and focused his fire at the sentries on the wall. They were eliminated with ease and their stun shots missed, but another slug from a flying droid struck his shin and he almost tumbled from his platform. He spun quickly and shot the attacker out of the air, but two more circled above, dove toward him, and fired. Kaiden flung himself off the platform to one below and hurled a shock grenade above him. It exploded, and the droids lost control. They spiraled before one slammed into the platform Kaiden was on and another flew past and into the cave wall. He kicked the malfunctioning sentry off the platform, and it crumbled and disappeared.

Wave 2 Complete

"Nice shooting, Tex," Chief chirped.

"You know you haven't used that pun as much as I would like you to."

"I gotta keep it fresh, right?" the EI snickered

Wave 3 Commencing

"All right, this will have—" the EI's words cut off as the lights in the cave dimmed and darkened. Even with the visor's light enhancer, the ace could barely see in front of him.

"This ain't right. It's supposed to be another wave with some Havoc droids. What's with the blackout?"

"I don't see anything," Kaiden said. He hopped off the platform and landed on the ground below. "A glitch maybe? A special round?"

"Animus glitches are rare and even then, are usually visual," Chief stated. *"You might have met the conditions for a change-up. They did want you Advanced class guys to shake things up,*

but I don't see—Wait, someone's accessed the console. Someone with high clearance."

"Who did—wait, did you hear that?" The ace drew his Raptor and looked around. "Scan the cave." The white grid appeared but revealed nothing. "If something's wrong I would have de-synced by now. What the hell is going on?"

A brief, faint click sounded behind him, and Kaiden spun and fired. It didn't seem that he had hit anything but the wall, but he could have sworn he saw something in the light of the laser fire.

Without warning, he was tackled to the ground and he dropped his rifle. In a split second, a metal hand closed around his throat and held him in place. A droid with a skull-like head and burning red eyes stare down at him.

"Assassin droid! Reaper-class!" Chief cried. The mechanical continued to glare at him before it raised its other hand and a large, jagged blade emerged from the top of its wrist. It leaned back to strike. Kaiden raised his hand as the blade descended and it cut through his palm. He cried out in pain and struggled to keep the blade from advancing, but the droid was far stronger. The ace flicked his other wrist and his heat blade popped out. He activated it as he turned his head quickly to avoid the droid's strike. The blade plunged into the ground and twisted his arm back painfully.

Kaiden inhaled sharply and struck at the droid's bladed arm with his knife but managed to only cut into it and not through it. It seemed to be enough to stop his attacker from using the arm, but it tightened its grip around the ace's throat. He retaliated and swiped his blade toward the droid's head. It leaned back to avoid the attack, and he used the opportunity to slice into the arm around his throat. He had to saw into it, even with the heated blade, and the arm finally came off. It still clutched his neck, but he was able to roll away and used the blade to hack the hand away. The remains of the droid's arms ejected from its body. The sides of its chest opened, and two new arms unfolded to take their place.

"Dammit," the ace cursed and retrieved his last shock grenade along with debonair. The droid charged at him. He threw the grenade along the ground and fired at it to create an electrical explosion. The mechanical's advance slowed as it stumbled, but it recovered rapidly.

"Those kinds of droids are better protected from shocks. That won't do much."

Kaiden fired Debonair until it overheated. The blasts did little against the droid's barrier. He needed the ballistic rounds. The ace dove for his Raptor and grabbed it as he tumbled and managed to land on his knees and turned to fire. When he had the droid in his sights, it pointed its arm at him. He hesitated, and the mechanical fired a blade from its arm directly through his head.

Kaiden dragged in a shocked gasp of air as the Animus pod opened. He stumbled out and fell, his vision blurred, but he saw someone large standing over him.

"Wolfson?" he asked as his eyes adjusted.

The instructor observed him for a moment before he picked him up, steadied him, and looked at him once more.

The ace looked at the console that displayed a feed of his trial.

"You were watching?" he asked.

"Aye." Wolfson nodded. "Come with me, Kaiden. We have more to knock out of you than dust."

CHAPTER TWENTY-FOUR

A wave of déjà vu swept over Kaiden as he sat on a bench in Wolfson's dropship. His thoughts pulled him back, both to the Arctic and to a week before and the beginning of his gig. Fortunately, this time, Wolfson dragged him along somewhat willingly. He wasn't sure exactly what the man had in mind, but he had never seen the security head with such a determined or serious expression, even during their most intense spars. He stood and walked to the cockpit where Wolfson watched over the autopilot process. The view through the window revealed a mass of thin trees below.

"Where are we?" he asked.

The instructor glanced at him for a moment before he answered, "Ontario."

"Canada?" Kaiden questioned. "Are proper border protocols merely a silly myth to you?"

"Relax, idiot. I already took care of that before takeoff." He shushed him with a wave of his hand. "I thought I told you to put your armor on."

Kaiden looked at the black underlay suit he wore. "I told you, my armor is wrecked. You haven't told me what we're doing. Is this reconnaissance training or something?"

"I don't remember you being this yappy," Wolfson mumbled. "Think of it as an adventure for now."

"You make that sound more foreboding than enticing," He huffed and sat in the co-pilot's chair. He looked at the land below in a viewing screen as they passed over a large wall. "What's that?"

"A wall. It blocks things." Wolfson snickered.

Kaiden shook his head. "Funny. Why are we here, Wolfson? I told you I wasn't up to any training. I thought this was an errand or something until you slapped this underlay into my hands after we took off."

"And I didn't hear a peep out of you when I did," the large man pointed out. "But…I suppose I should fill you in and make sure you're at least a little ready."

"That is usually standard, yes." He folded his arms and looked expectantly at the head officer.

Wolfson was quiet as he considered the right words to say. "I haven't told you much about my past boy—some of it because it seems pointless, and other times, because I think it wouldn't really stick in that feeble mind of yours."

"Thanks. I wasn't using that bit of ego anyway," Kaiden snarked.

"But a lot of it is because there are things I'd rather not discuss and some I would prefer to be rid of all together. Seeing you back at the gym brought up a few of those moments when I was a commander and leader of a fine group of soldiers," he continued, his voice now quiet and solemn. Kaiden gave Wolfson his full attention in this rare moment of emotion.

"There were times where we lost good men or dealt with horrors that no sane man would willingly confront, let alone try to kill them. You grow strong and determined in the military, but it begins to compound after a while—all those instances of shock and revulsion, anger and helplessness. I saw good men become nothing more than husks as the years went on, their minds still in control but the will gone. I always see those men as my failures, not their own. I should have seen the change sooner and done something about it."

Kaiden was at a loss for words. He looked away for a moment to allow his companion to compose himself before he continued. "When I saw you and you told me what happened, I had that same sinking feeling. I'm sure you'll say I'm usually boisterous and brash, and yeah, sure I am. I'm not here to psychoanalyze you or whatever is the normal thing, but I want to believe there are different ways of dealing with trauma if you catch it before it truly takes hold."

"I'm not traumatized," Kaiden vowed and clenched a fist. "I lived, he's a killer, and he failed. I've proven I'm plenty strong."

"And I know that that's not always enough," Wolfson stated. "I watched your trial. You were fine when dealing with the normal trash bots like you always are. But when I sent in that top-class Assassin, you acted like you were a novice again."

"So that was you," Kaiden grunted. "Chief said he read someone tampering with the console."

"I wanted to see how you are. Fighting those children's toys won't prove anything except that you can still shoot well and you're smart enough to avoid getting hit." He looked at his student for a moment. "Which you did a couple times."

"They were sentries and the shots felt like mosquito bites," Kaiden said defensively before he lowered his shoulders and leaned back. "Although I suppose that's an excuse, isn't it?"

"It's good to see you haven't lost all your instincts." Wolfson nodded. "But you have the right idea. We gotta make sure you're back to par. That infuriating ego may be a pain to deal with when you're mouthing off, but it's also one of your most valuable assets. You've almost made it out to be some sort of superpower. I've seen guys like you charge into the fray and yell about how they will kill everyone before they die in a hail of laser fire. Yet you've avoided that, for the most part, and actually lived up to your boasts." Wolfson assumed control of the ship, banked toward the forest, and looked for a place to land. "I may complain, but I don't want to see that fire of yours go out."

Kaiden thought over the man's words for a time. "I… appreciate that, Wolfson." He tapped his fingers on his arm. "But why does that bring us here?"

"Like I said, it won't do much good if you simply run the basic stuff. Doubt is one of the first things that hobbles a soldier." The instructor finally spotted a clearing and took the dropship in slowly. "You told me before you left that your gig in the Amazon had mutants as potential hostiles, right?"

"They didn't turn out to be only potential," Kaiden remarked.

"But I bet you didn't have a problem with them, right? Did it feel good to go against something with grit?"

He mulled it over and cocked his head to one side. "I destroyed a few and things got a bit dicey here and there, but we mostly ran away."

"Don't talk like that, Kaiden," Wolfson snapped, and the ace jumped in his seat. "That's what I was talking about. Normally, you brag about your kill count and how it was a walk in the park for you. Even if you mentioned a retreat, it would be made out as a tactical decision or because you were bored. You can't focus on your failings. There's a thin line between humility and meekness, boy, and you've tripped and fallen onto the bad side."

"All right, all right, I getcha," he said in an annoyed tone. "What am I supposed to do, then?"

"There are mutants in this forest—Likan, which are essentially meaner and more vicious wolves," the instructor explained as he unlatched the belt of his seat. "This enclosure isn't to keep them in a safe area for themselves, it's to keep them away from the outside world. One of the changes was to their breeding patterns and visibility. They breed like rabbits. It's hunting season for them and any hunters and trackers with the balls to go after them come and collect heads and pelts for their bounty." He stood and headed to the back of the ship. Kaiden followed. "I want to show you—or rather, have you show yourself— that you can take these gigs, that your skills aren't suddenly crap because you fell into a bad situation."

"And you thought the best way to do this was to take

me into a forest filled with mutant wolves?" the ace asked.

"There's a cave nearby, and a pack always takes it over during the year. We'll go in there to not only take care of a few of them but you—" He spun and pointed a large finger at Kaiden. "You will go after the alpha."

"Specifically? Why?" he asked and clenched his fist slightly as another bubble of doubt grew in his stomach.

"You got the skills, weapons, and tech to deal with the runts and betas, but the alphas acquire their status by being the leader of the pack. They are the meanest and most cunning among them. Some even have mutations unique to themselves. I'll be with you, but I know you can take it out. You failed when confronted by an enemy with unique skills in the trial, but I want you to know that it won't stop you now."

Kaiden looked at the cockpit and out the window to observe the forest. Doubt still stirred, but it had dwindled between Wolfson's encouragement and a voice within himself that barked at him to man the hell up.

"You keep saying I have weapons and armor, but I told you I lost my machine gun and most of my armor, and I left Debonair at the Academy. There isn't a lot of room for mistakes with only an underlay."

"Nah, you got something." Wolfson withdrew a massive case from one of the compartments. He placed it horizontally on both benches and popped it open to reveal a set of silver and black armor and a round helmet with a curved visor. "I got this for you to celebrate your first successful high-level gig. You did succeed even if you don't feel that way." The large man took a rifle with a large barrel and metal frame from the compartment and tossed it to

Kaiden. The ace grabbed it and examined it. His fingers traced the outline of a small chamber on the bottom of the frame.

"It looks like this thing fires energy blasts," he noted and watched the glowing white energy that swirled around the tube. He stared curiously at Wolfson. "This doesn't seem like your style."

"I didn't get it for me," he replied with a smile. He handed Debonair to Kaiden. "So, what do you say?"

The ace rested the gun against his shoulder and glanced at the armor, then at Wolfson. "You said we'll get paid for this?"

"Five to seven thousand creds per Likan, twenty to thirty for an alpha," the instructor confirmed.

He closed his eyes for a moment, the trepidation faded, and he grinned. "It would be a waste to not give your gifts a quick test."

Kaiden approached the cave. No Likan were in evidence, but bones and rotting carcasses were scattered around the entrance. He looked at Wolfson, who was decked out in slightly worn heavy armor with a faded WCM logo on the chest. "Are you sure you're gonna be all right in that old stuff? You don't even have a helmet."

The large man nodded with a grin. "I'll be fine. This is about you, remember?" he declared as he pumped his shotgun

"At least I don't have to deal with the smell," Kaiden muttered. "Are we going in?"

"Let's." Wolfson charged ahead and Kaiden followed.

It didn't take long for them to encounter some of the Likan with the way Wolfson barreled into the cave. They had apparently awoken them from a nap, and the mutants were pissed. Kaiden stood his ground as one howled from a ledge above. He aimed and fired. Even with the dampeners, the shot knocked his weapon back a little, but the blast almost evaporated the front half of the creature.

This'll do just fine.

Wolfson hurtled into a leaping Likan and knocked it to the ground before he fired at another approaching beast. He pumped his gun quickly and slammed his boot down on the first creature's head. As he turned to fire at another one above, he yelled, "Stop stroking that thing and get to work."

"Give me a moment to admire the craftsmanship and whatnot," Kaiden retorted. He spun quickly away from a swipe by one of the runts and shoved the butt of his gun into it. The Likan staggered, and he whipped Debonair out to finish it off with a few quick shots. He turned and fired his rifle behind him. The blast shredded two flanking wolves.

"Are packs usually this big?" he asked as a trio appeared from farther in the tunnel. "How are there so many?"

"I can give you the facts of nature when we're done here," Wolfson snarked. He grabbed one mutant by the throat and smashed it into the ground before he tossed it into the wall. "Focus on taking them out. Gah! Get off me, *jävlar!*" The large man roared as two Likan had landed on the back of his armor and their strong fangs bit through the metal.

"Wolfson!" Kaiden turned but froze at a frenzied bark behind him. The new mutant seemed stronger and better fed than the others. The ace fired a blast from the rifle, but the beast managed to avoid it and continued its attack as the blast exploded behind it. Kaiden rolled as it leapt at him, flipped a switch on his rifle, and fired at its stomach as it sailed overhead. The rifle shot a wave of energy that catapulted the Likan forward to impact another creature that Wolfson had thrown. The instructor jumped back and crushed the other attacker on his back into the cave wall. He grabbed the dazed mutant by its tail and hurled it into the ground before he threw it aside.

"You know, with your name, I would have thought you'd show more kinship with these things. You are kind of a mutant yourself," Kaiden jested.

"Hilarious," Wolfson muttered, dusted himself off, and retrieved his shotgun. "All right, deeper into the cave we go. That alpha has to be here somewhere."

"How far in do you think we gotta go?"

The large man shrugged, stepped over the corpses, and proceeded. "This is a pretty big place, and he could be in deep. Alphas usually only go on big hunts and let everyone else take care of the small stuff. It's probably lounging somewhere... Aye?" A cracking sound echoed as Wolfson walked to one side of the cave followed by a rumble and rush of rock and dirt as he disappeared.

"Wolfson!" Kaiden shouted and ran forward. He readied his rifle, but when he looked down, he didn't know whether he should be worry or laugh.

The Security head had fallen down a hole.

CHAPTER TWENTY-FIVE

K aiden peered down into the hole to locate his companion, but it was too dark. "Wolfson?" he called. "Wolfson, are you alive?"

"Aye, though the embarrassment makes me wish I wasn't." His low, gravelly response sounded unamused.

"How far down are you? I can't see you."

"Do I look like a damn geologist?"

"I'm not sure what that has to do with anything. I think you confused your jobs. Do you need me to come down?"

"Well, I would think... Actually, no, this could work out," Wolfson said thoughtfully.

"What are you yackin' on about?" Kaiden asked. "Did you hit your head on the way down?"

"Maybe, but that ain't a problem." A small light appeared below. Wolfson had fallen a significant distance.

Kaiden snickered. "Maybe not."

"I didn't know there was another level down here. You can run through the top level, and I'll run down here. The first one to find the alpha will radio the other—" He was cut off by the sounds of snarls and barks.

"Are you sure you're gonna be all right?"

"Might I remind you which one of us hasn't lost during our little skirmishes? These little beasties won't do anything but give me a little more grief than a warm-up," Wolfson bragged. "I'll be fine. Get your ass in gear and find that big bastard." Shotgun fire and more rabid barks issued from the lower level.

"Stay alive, Wolfson," the ace muttered. "I'll keep my end of the bargain if you do that." He stood and ran through the cave in search of his mutated monster of a prey.

"Did you find anything yet, Chief?" Kaiden asked as he examined the dark dens of rock and dust.

"Nada. I would usually complain about you not getting upgrades, but I'm gonna say this once that I'm glad you haven't gotten the scanner upgrade for scents," Chief mused. *"It would probably be a big fog of musk and scat."*

"That's why I watch my footing even though we're on flat ground." He occasionally heard rocks fall, drips from stalactites, and paws running along the floor, but they hadn't encountered even one more Likan on their journey through the cave.

"I wonder how Wolfson is doing."

"I don't think we need to worry about him. I felt sorrier for the mutants when he batted them around like that," the EI said before he rolled his eye. *"Although that wasn't a great plan,*

telling us to call him when we found the alpha. He doesn't have a comm on that old junk armor of his. Not one I can link to, anyway. Does he not update his equipment?"

"I'm sure he at least has a tracker." Kaiden looked up, and in the enhanced vision on his visor he saw a new path in the distance. "It might be old, but it's still military equipment and was top-of-the-line when he got it. It'll have that as standard."

"Yeah, top-of-the-line two decades ago. Even if he got your gear off the discount rack, it still smokes his."

The ace glanced at his armor through his HUD. "This stuff is almost as good as the suit I use in the Animus. He probably spent a hefty cred or two on it."

"Nice of him, for sure. But he also can't beat you up if you're already crippled when you get back from missions," Chief pointed out. *"I have to say that it is nice to see you getting your groove back. I was a little worried that all this had put that idea out of your head for good."*

Kaiden stopped for a moment and rested his rifle against his chest. "I'm not gonna lie, I thought that for a little while too. But I'm starting to understand what Magellan meant when he said to not let Gin haunt me." His teeth clenched and his heart raced a little faster. "I won't let him get to me. I won't let him beat me when he isn't even here."

"Or he could be right behind you right now," Chief quipped and earned a glare that was more annoyed than angry. *"Sorry, stupid joke."*

The ace sighed but quickly followed it with a chuckle. "It's good to see you back to your old self, even if the sense of humor still needs work."

"I guess I'll also admit to being a little shook up for a few days there."

"It felt pretty close to death, huh?"

The EI looked away as he responded. *"That wasn't my primary concern."*

Kaiden scoffed, but his grin remained. "Thanks, partner." He continued down the path. "Now, let's see if we can find that big beastie, as Wolfson would put it."

"Sure thing, but my guess is that if it's hiding out, then there's a better chance that Wolfson will— Kaiden, to your left. I'm picking up a heartbeat."

He moved to the cave wall, flattened himself against it, and slid toward a hole in the rock. Cautiously, he leaned into the cavern. A large shape rested atop a pile of some kind at the far end.

"That is big," he whispered. "Ten gets you twenty that's the alpha."

"I ain't taking no fool's bet," Chief retorted. *"Besides, you haven't given me my allowance for the month."*

Kaiden rolled his eyes as he crept inside. He inched closer to the beast, alert for any other Likan, but it seemed this one liked its solitude. At only about ten yards away, he paused and studied his target. It was massive and even in it's curled, sleeping state it seemed bigger than the soldier. He zoomed in his vision to study the gray fur with black and white patches. Deep claw marks scarred its face, snout, and front legs. This thing had seen some fierce fights.

"Most mutants have accelerated healing, but even then, it has scars," Kaiden said quietly. "You think we should wait for Wolfson?"

"*It looks like you got a good chance to take it down without a fight.*"

"I kind of feel bad taking it out while it's sleeping but—"

"*You'll feel worse when those fangs and claws dig into you, trust me,*" Chief warned. "*Take it out, and if you need more reason, look at what it's sleeping on.*"

Kaiden raised his rifle and peered through the scope. A pile of corpses constituted the alpha Likan's bed—different animals and other, smaller wolves, potentially previous challengers for its rank. But then he saw human body parts strewn among them as well.

His sympathy evaporated as he flipped the switch on his rifle to return it to firing shots. The mutant's ears twitched for a moment, but it was too late. The ace depressed the trigger and fired. Instantly, the alpha scrambled to its feet, snatched one of the bodies from the pile, and threw it up. The shot collided with the corpse and scattered the remains.

"*This thing is smart.*"

"And quick, dammit!" Kaiden cursed, jumped back, and prepared for the attack. The Likan slid off its bed and stared at the intruder with red eyes as if it to figure out if he was worth its time.

There was something familiar about that look like it mentally tossed a coin on whether this was a threat or a plaything.

The soldier growled and fired two more shots at the beast, which evaded them easily and dashed toward him with its bloodstained fangs visible. Kaiden prepared to fire another shot, but the wolf was on him faster than he'd thought possible. It lashed at him and forced him back. He lifted his rifle and moved his arms back. His finger hit the trigger and sent a blast at the ceiling.

The roof of the cavern erupted, and rocks and stalactites fell from above. Both he and the wolf scrambled back to avoid getting crushed. Kaiden recovered quickly and scanned the cavern for the alpha. The mutant was difficult to see in the low light and dust, but a skitter of rock to his left alerted him and he turned quickly. The Likan stood on top of the debris and stared balefully at him. It was no longer curious but furious and crouched and snarled as it prepared to attack.

"Don't let it get you," Chief shouted. Kaiden wanted to snark at what was an obvious order, but the wolf barreled down too quickly. He flipped the switch back rapidly to the force shot and aimed to his left. As he fired, he jumped, and the force knocked him away as the mutant snapped at the air where he'd stood a second before. He had to manage his shots carefully, he realized, or the gun would overheat soon and he couldn't risk venting with this thing on the offensive.

He landed hard and slid back. The wolf bucked and twisted and found its feet with a deafening howl. If he shot directly, it would simply juke the shots. Instead, he should aim for the ground in its path once it charged. Perhaps that could knock it back or down to give him a better shot. The beast growled and hurtled forward once again. Kaiden toggled the switch and fired only a few feet ahead.

The wolf attempted to evade and almost succeeded, but the force of the blast pushed it farther and bowled Kaiden over. He landed with a thud and ignored the jarring pain in his chest from the impact. He flipped as the wolf clambered to its feet—a good opportunity. He fired and a warning signal lit up on the back of the rifle to warn that it had begun to overheat. The shot blazed toward the alpha. The Likan turned at the last second and tried to twist aside, but the blast connected and struck the beast's back.

"Yes!" he shouted as the alpha was driven back. It didn't disintegrate but fur smoldered and its flesh charred. It howled in anger and pain as it skidded along the cave floor. He glanced back to check for reinforcements, but nothing appeared.

Kaiden vented the rifle. "What is this thing made of?" he wondered aloud as he drew Debonair and approached the mutant wolf slowly. The blast seemed to have shattered most of its left leg, which would significantly hinder its ability and speed.

Or so he thought.

The Likan's eyes shot open and it used its good legs to launch itself at him. The ace fired and a shot penetrated its eye, but it remained determined. He threw himself aside, but the mutant snatched his leg. The armor cracked and the teeth ground into his leg, barely short of biting through it.

Despite the threat of losing a limb, Kaiden remained calm. He wouldn't lose, not again and not to a beast. He dropped his rifle, placed Debonair along the gumline of the wolf's mouth, and fired. The Likan yelped and released him. He snatched his rifle, slammed the vent shut, and took a cue from the wolf to use his good leg to thrust forward. Without hesitation, he pressed the barrel to its stomach and fired.

The ace was instantly coated in blood and the alpha's

final howl faded into a quiet growl as it slumped over. It raised a claw to swipe feebly at him, but the gesture was futile and short-lived.

Kaiden swayed on his feet. The wound on his leg was deep, but he could support himself. *"Activating wraps,"* Chief said as the bandages snaked down his leg. *"Congrats, partner. You took him out."*

"Yeah, I did." He let that sink in for a moment, rested his rifle against his shoulder, and rolled his free hand around in a dismissive gesture. "That wasn't such a chore."

"You know it."

Loud clapping startled him, and he turned to see a bright light at the entrance of the cavern. He held up a hand to block the glare and dimmed his visor. "Wolfson? Is that you?"

"Indeed, boy! Look at you. You took that thing down all by your lonesome. How do you feel now?" the giant bellowed. He turned the light on the shoulders of his armor off, and moved toward his student.

"I could use a drink and a meal. I'm suddenly famished," Kaiden admitted and rested a hand on his stomach. "What do you think?"

"I think it's a fine catch," Wolfson said and turned his attention to the alpha. "It's a big one too. You'll probably get a bonus for this one." He knelt and opened the wolf's jaw. "Ah, yeah, see the curvature of the fangs? That will slice through steel." He looked at Kaiden's leg and the crushed armor. "By God, boy. I just gave you that."

"I guess I was lucky it only got me with its back teeth. Otherwise, I would have a sliced leg instead of crushed armor." The ace sighed with relief. "So do we gotta carry this thing back?"

"Nah, we take the head. It's not like you can eat mutant meat—at least, you aren't supposed to," Wolfson said as he drew a large knife.

"Wait. The head? I thought it was usually pelts or something." Kaiden thought back and cursed. "Man, either way, I vaporized a few of the Likan at the entrance to the cave. Those aren't worth jack now, are they?"

"Don't worry yourself about the small fry." The instructor focused on his gory task. "We'll grab the ones we can and turn them in. You deserve a feast, and I happen to know a great steakhouse in Hamilton."

"I'll take you up on that." He took a few steps on his leg and winced. "Do you have some rejuv back on the ship?"

"I'll patch you up, but you gotta get yourself back there. I ain't carrying your ass," Wolfson stated as he slid the blade back into its sheath and lifted the alpha's head. He walked to Kaiden and placed an arm around his shoulder. "Do you feel that fire again. Kaiden?"

He draped an arm around the giant's back to steady himself as he limped along. "Yeah, burning bright." He nodded as they left the cavern and turned toward the exit. "Like I said, I had to knock off a bit of dust."

Wolfson laughed. The boy had done well, very well. Taking down an alpha like that was no easy feat. He felt that he didn't have to worry that Kaiden would be lost.

He even felt good enough that he wouldn't tell him that he took care of the dominus Likan below which was probably twice the size of the alpha. He might bring it up when he graduated, though.

CHAPTER TWENTY-SIX

Chiyo sat at a table in the library with multiple tablets, holoscreens, scrolls, and even a few very old books strewn about. She hated moments like this when she felt she was looking for something too vague to condense and create a proper path to follow. She shifted her focus from screen to screen. Each held various snippets of information and topics on several different people, places, and events. She issued commands to a holoscreen and attempted to look for anything in the Academy's files and database—tracers, fraudulent checks, and suspicious or odd activity. Once again, she found nothing.

The infiltrator leaned back. A few of the screens turned off and darkened the area around her. She clasped her hands together, folded them in, and took some time to breathe and focus herself.

"Pardon me, madame," Kaitō interjected. *"I've done as you asked, but I could find nothing in the student profiles or identification center. There seems to have been no one looking through*

those areas besides academy students, faculty, or the family members of certain students."

"Still nothing." She sighed. "I suppose it was too much to hope that I could stumble upon something obvious like a virus or spy in the systems."

"Forgive me, but might I ask why we are looking at this once more?" Kaitō asked. *"I feel the need to remind you that this is rather unscrupulous and against Academy protocol. I know we've done this before, but that was for an end goal. Doing this for rather tangential reasons is a huge risk, especially as you exhaust yourself which could lead to mistakes."*

"I know, Kaitō," Chiyo said and straightened. "I'm doing this for personal reasons. I haven't explained myself simply because I don't yet know what I'll do once I find what I'm looking for. But..." She looked out the window in the direction of the soldier's dorm. "I don't want to sit back and do nothing."

"Do nothing? Is this a mission or a personal request?" the EI asked.

Chiyo shook her head. "Never mind, Kaitō. Please scan through the net pages on the World Council and anything you might find on the gray net about the Revenant List. I want more information."

"It is rather late, madame."

"I know. This is my last order for the night. Once you're done, I'll turn in. Until then, I'll keep going."

"As you wish, madame." The wire-frame fox bowed his head. *"I shall finish my orders as quickly as possible."* With that, he disappeared from her lenses.

Chiyo swiped one of the holoscreens and read an article that was translated from Portuguese about a 'horror in the jungle' and how three bodies were found in an Axiom dome lab in the Amazon along with various eaten remains. It said that most of the bodies were attacked and eaten by the mutants in the area, but two of them had wounds inflicted by blades and spikes. One was partially destroyed in a blast. The police had nothing to report, but they were contacting different hunter guilds and gig ports to find out more information.

"Will you return to space soon?" Sasha asked the man on his screen.

"No, not for a while," he responded and shook his head. "Not as long as he's still running loose. They didn't find his body. The obvious conclusion is that he's still kicking. I'll return to the jungle to comb for clues, but I doubt he's still there."

"There are constant dangers in the world," Sasha muttered and folded his hands on his desk. "But it is always shrouded in happenstance. I do admit that it is more unnerving when you know the specifics. What exactly is out there looking for you?"

"I'll try to minimize that," the man assured him. "I owe it to a lot of people."

"A noble sentiment, but don't let that blind you. I've seen that turn to rage and single-mindedness a number of times, and that only creates a different problem."

"Are you really worried I'll lose it at this point?" He chuckled darkly. "Come on, Commander. By now, I'm rather hardened."

"No doubt, Magellan, but I have read the story of Moby Dick. There are some parallels and I can tell you that the story doesn't end well for the obsessed hunter."

"I promise I'll keep my wits about me." His face showed sign of concern, "How's Kaiden?"

"He was rather despondent for a few days. I worried about his mental health more than his physical," Sasha admitted. "But it seems Wolfson has taken precautions to ensure he doesn't fall into a funk."

"That's good," the bounty hunter said with obvious relief. "It's nice to see he has good people looking after him. He seemed a prickly sort, but he's a good man."

"A great soldier as well." Sasha unlatched his hands and tapped a finger on his desk. "I'm glad I sent you along. I'm also glad you were able to get me that information about the Arbiter Organization."

"It wasn't much. For a while there, I wondered if you had me going on a snipe hunt," Magellan confessed. "I'm not even sure if that has anything to do with the organization proper, but the files weren't marked to the WC or Nexus and it talked a fair amount about the professor's inventions, particularly Kaiden's EI and its device. It didn't seem like something that was really common knowledge."

"It's not. Even most of the staff don't know much about it. I think most simply believe it's a new EI mod," Sasha explained. "Right now, it has no purpose outside the Academy's regimen. I can't see a reason they have such an interest in it. But considering everything that has happened, they targeted Kaiden by proxy. A mission where he was on the far side of the world seemed like a potential time to strike." Sasha huffed as he scratched his head. "I'll admit, I was also worried that I was simply paranoid. It is something of a relief that my fears didn't manifest into mad ramblings, but I never could have guessed that they would be so severe."

"Do you think there's a link between the two?" Magellan questioned. "I would think, if anything, that they potentially set the gig up and expected him to die during the fighting."

"I don't think that would have been a smart plan. Unless they were waiting to scoop his corpse up, there would have been a good chance one of the mutants would have simply eaten him," Sasha countered. "My guess is that, like myself, they don't tend to rely on coincidence that much."

"Gin said he was there to meet someone. I wanted to believe it was merely a bluff. How could anyone get hold of him? Why would they even if they could?" Magellan growled. "While he's still alive and here on Earth, Kaiden shouldn't take any gigs that are too far away from the Academy."

"We'll keep an eye on him, and I made sure his agent wouldn't give him anything too extreme, but I won't barricade him. It would possibly cause a commotion among the student body if there were rumors that a member of the Revenant List could be stalking the grounds. Plus, I doubt Kaiden would stand for it once he gets his mind back together."

The bounty hunter frowned. The commander's explanation did not sit well. "I guess I follow but still don't like it. There's only one notable survivor who crossed Gin, a military man who lost an arm to him. My guess is that Gin hasn't returned because he's now stationed on a military vessel and has a Gatling gun for an arm. But he doesn't like leaving witnesses."

"We already have Kaiden's account and his EI's recordings. I'm sure he is aware of that. And considering that Kaiden has tests coming up and a fair amount of work to make up for, he will be here for at least several weeks before he'll have the time to attempt another excursion." Sasha removed his oculars and folded his hands once again. "You have no need to worry, Magellan. We'll protect him as much as we can."

"Good to know," he acknowledged but grew quiet and avoided the other man's gaze.

"Is something wrong?" Sasha asked.

"Yeah, it was something Gin said before I left." He glanced at the commander. "He said he used to go to Nexus. Do you know if that's true?"

Sasha' lips pursed and his eyelids lowered in anger. "It is." He nodded, and Magellan's eyes widened in shock. "He attended the Academy for three years before he simply vanished. When I began my tenure here, he was in the master class." He scowled. "But he didn't use the name Gin Sonny at the time."

"I'm telling you that I won't take any more of your gigs," Julio fumed over the line at the man dressed in a dark business suit and with combed-back brown hair. "The first one you sent me nearly got my guy killed!"

"Yes, we have learned about the unfortunate incident," he replied in calm, collected voice. "We do apologize and are always sure to create a proper list of the known dangers and identify the threat level properly. I assure you we had no idea that such a madman would be on the grounds. From the news reports, he wasn't even on Earth when we created the listing."

"Dios, you suits always gotta go to the charts and stats when things blow up in your face," the bartender and gig agent chided. "It doesn't change my mind. No amount of creds will get you back on my list."

"I understand. Thank you for at least having the decency to call and tell me directly instead of simply delisting the company."

"Pah, I only did that so I could give you a piece of my mind. I hope you feel at least a little terrible as you sleep on your king-size bed made of ivory and sweatshop tears," he spat before ending the call.

"What an annoying little gnat," he muttered and spun his chair slowly to face his desk. "But he played his part well enough."

"I like him." His visitor grinned. "He has pizzazz. I might pay him a visit sometime."

"You don't seem to have much discretion with your targets, do you?"

The man's smile widened, and he placed his two artificial hands on the desk. "I don't usually have to—whatever catches my fancy and all that. But don't worry, I'll save it for my free time, Mr. Zubaz."

"Zub*anz*, Mr. Sonny," he corrected. He pressed a button on his desk and a glass bottle of whiskey appeared from a compartment below. "But thank you for trying. I guess that your time alone has weakened your interpersonal skills slightly."

"Honestly? It was never my strong suit to begin with." The chairman offered Gin one of the glasses. He took it in his new arm and tilted it so that Zubanz could pour the liquor. "I must say, I was impressed that you were able to get hold of me. When that handsome face of yours popped on the screen at that lab I was ransacking, I thought you were gonna be another one of those proud military guys hacking in to tell me I was surrounded and that there was no escape or something."

"You were quite difficult to contact. But that was to be expected. If it were easy, we would have pursued another potential agent," he explained as he poured his own glass. "For what we wish for you to accomplish, it would be better if you worked alone and couldn't be traced, and you fit both criteria well—along with your other talents."

"I have many." The killer held the glass up in a toast. "I've always said that if you do something you love, you'll never work a day in your life."

"A nice philosophy. I can't say I enjoy all facets of my profession." He looked at the liquid in his glass before taking a small sip. "But you find ways to cope."

"So, about the job." Gin crossed his legs and leaned back in the chair. "You said you wanted that thing in the kid's noggin, right?"

"I suppose I should have laid that out before you came to Earth. But in the circumstances, I hope you'll forgive me for being vague."

"I've already forgiven you for trying to make me do your dirty work before getting paid," Gin admitted. He sipped slowly and smiled with satisfaction. "I was pissed, at first, once I realized what was going on, but you know, I can't stay mad at a face like yours. Plus, the creds and toys you've promised me are rather enticing. Assuming that's still viable."

"Indeed, you will have whatever items and funds you need to complete the task however you see fit. Once completed, you can look through our inventory for whatever you can carry out with you and you will be paid sixty-five million credits—the worth of your bounty I believe."

"Third from the top for solo artists like me. That Anakis chick always beats me somehow, and also that other guy...I don't know his name."

"No one does. It's part of the reason he's on the list. They merely call him 'The Dybbuk Man.'"

"What the hell is a dybbuk?" Gin mused. "I've never met him, although I did meet the woman. We had a grand old time on one of the colonies. I'm kinda surprised you didn't go for her."

"Would you believe that you seemed more agreeable?" the man asked.

"I have a way about me. My charm makes up for the lack of 'interpersonal skill,'" he said and made air quotes with his fingers. "As for what I need, I can actually say I won't take much from this little fund you're giving me, mostly because for what I have in mind, I'll have to get what I need myself."

"So you have a plan already?" Zubanz asked. "Please do keep in mind that we would prefer discretion and that you'll have to find a way to lure him to you unless you want to deal with an entire Academy coming after you."

Gin flicked a finger at him. "That's the thing. I will get him while he's at the Academy, but it won't be graphic. They won't even know I'm there."

The chairman looked questioningly at him. "What do you have in mind?"

"Ah, ah, ah." He wagged his finger. "A killer's rule is similar to a magician's—don't give away the secrets. You'll have to trust me. It's not like I won't kill him. I have a reputation to think about." He finished his drink and placed the glass on the table. "The rest is a bonus." He extended a hand to the chairman and the silver mesh wrapped around it hid the electronic components within. "But we can shake on it if you want."

The man looked at him for a moment but took the killer's hand. He had to remind himself this was to the benefit of the organization and that he had made plenty of shady deals on less certain terms. And yet, as the vice-like grip of Gin's hand shook his, he felt this was the closest he had come to shaking hands with the devil.

He wondered if he would regret it.

AUTHOR NOTES

DECEMBER 13, 2018

THANK YOU for not only reading this story but these *Author Notes* as well.

(I think I've been good with always opening with "thank you." If not, I need to edit the other *Author Notes!*)

RANDOM (*sometimes*) THOUGHTS?
DAMN YOU, GIN!

Ok, I have to admit that when working with Joshua, it can occasionally be frustrating. Why?

He likes bad guys. I'm a "good guy who wears a black hat" sort of person. I like the protagonist who bends the rules but gets the jobs done. Joshua loves to create complex bad guys.

For once, I think I have a bad guy in a story that I can at least enjoy. Gin is so over-the-top about himself that I can't even get upset about his choices. He is delicious in his efforts, and while I know it sucks for our side, he is a worthy antagonist.

=== Excerpt from Chapter 1 ===

(*unedited*)

(Gin is in a black market area, talking to an older man, a hacker...)

"Except for the stooges, I would think." Gin said, looking back at the door.

"If they give you any trouble, feel free to do what you must."

Gin raised an eyebrow. "Not too attached, huh?"

"Customer service. Can't have them making one of my new customers think this is a place that would allow such idiocy," Vinci reasoned, moving the screen to show it to Gin. "Here are the schematics and functions of the cracked EI you requested."

Gin leaned in more, looking at the screen and whistled. "That's a lot of coding. You did all this in two weeks?"

"Would you believe this is one of the longest projects I've had in almost five years?" Vinci chuckled. "Most of the time it takes hours or a couple days at most. You gave me something to really get my fingers tapping."

"Glad you enjoyed it," Gin chirped. "What do I owe you?"

"One million even," Vinci stated.

Gin tapped a finger on his chin, "From our initial conversation, I was expecting more than triple that amount."

Vinci offer Gin his tablet, "It's a discount for giving me

such an interesting bit of work and for being such a nice man to work with."

"Guess a little kindness goes a long way, huh?" Gin took the tablet and transferred the money to the older hacker. "This will work wonderfully."

"Don't do anything too naughty with it," Vinci said in a knowing, playful tone as he unlocked a domed device, the two side splitting open to reveal a chip. He placed it into a box and handed it to Gin.

"You should know that someone like me can't promise that," Gin said as he stood up. "I mean, otherwise, why would I order it?"

Vinci laughed as he made his way to the door. "Good point!" He opened the door and nodded at Gin as he made to depart.

Gin grabbed his tablet and put it in his jacket as he made his way to the guards. "It's finished, boys. I'll be taking back my things now."

"We don't think so," the lead guard growled, earning a curious look from Gin and a sigh from Vinci.

"What the hell are you doing?" the hacker complained, "He's paid and done nothing suspicious. Do you lot want me to report you?"

"This guy isn't on the up and up, Vinci!" another guard declared, holding up the omni-blade. "Look at this thing! There's no way he could just *have* something like this! You can't even get one on the black market! It's way more advanced than anything I've ever seen."

"I'm sure that your knowledge is vast." Gin muttered, "If you must know, I stole it from a tactical and security division tech development facility. Ironically, it was not that well secured."

"Tac-Sec? You broke into a Tac-Sec facility by yourself? Bullshit." The leader scoffed, "We were thinking…"

"Congratulations."

"Shut up!" the guard snapped, grabbing Gin's neck, "You're a spook, aren't you?!"

"I assure you he isn't. He's…" Vinci started to warn them, but stopped as Gin held up a hand.

"I suppose I never did properly introduce myself to you. My bad." Gin took off his glasses and the guards were unnerved by his eyes, "Perhaps I could give it another go so that we can become properly acquainted?"

"This guy is a damn idiot," one gasped. "Boss, we can't have a guy like him with our tech! What if it gets traced back to us?"

"You think I'm that sloppy?" Vinci barked. "Don't besmirch *me* because *you* are a bunch of paranoid idiots."

"Still, best to be rid of him. We got the money, right?" the guard said with a smirk, holding up Gin's knife to his face. "Wonder what people will think when it gets around that I took out a guy like Gin Sonny?"

"You are really committed to this, aren't you?" Gin groused, looking at both him and the blade in boredom.

"If you hadn't pissed me off, like you're doing now, I might have let you walk out of here," he stated. "Like I said, outsiders don't get the same treatment in the bazaar. You gotta be a killer to even set foot in a place like this and expect to leave."

"Oh, the irony." Gin snickered, then leaned back, tilting his head and looking at Vinci, "You can go ahead and tell them if you want; see if it makes any difference. If not, I think I'll take you up on your offer."

The guards looked at Vinci, who had indifference on his face. "I hope the *next* batch they send me aren't so stubborn.

=== End excerpt ===

It is a bad guy like this who stops me from hating him all the way through...

HOW TO MARKET FOR BOOKS YOU LOVE

We are able to support our efforts with you reading our books, and we appreciate you doing this!

If you enjoyed this or ANY book by any author, especially Indie-published, we always appreciate if you make the time to review a book, since it lets other readers who might be on the fence to take a chance on it as well.

AROUND THE WORLD IN 80 DAYS

One of the interesting (at least to me) aspects of my life is the ability to work from anywhere and at any time. In the future, I hope to re-read my own *Author Notes* and remember my life as a diary entry.

Dec 13th, 2018

I'm at my desk in the Vegas Condo typing my little hands off at the moment. I just had a full day of working with Kevin McLaughlin (another author) as we plan out a new series. (Urban Fantasy - Dragons - new world.)

We had breakfast this morning with the Las Vegas Indie Writer community at a crepes place near Henderson.

What is it with this town and crepes? This is the second coffee / crepes place I've been to in the last couple of weeks, when I had not been to a single one in the first fifty years of my life.

Think pancakes, I've been told. Yes, they are kinda like a flat pancake without the airy goodness. They have a slightly different flavor than what I'm used to with pancakes, but it might be me imagining things. Further, you shouldn't stick your breakfast inside a crepe (or pancake.)

That's just wrong!

So, I asked them to separate my stuffing (eggs, Italian sausage, and cheese) and the crepe. If I want to eat a pancake (flat as it is) I think I need syrup on that bad boy. I can't eat syrup with my eggs.

<SIGH>

I'm getting old, aren't I? I'm the food equivalent of the old gray-haired man next door telling the kids to get off his lawn.

Damn, I am going to have to become more open-minded about crepes.

(*Editor's note: And vegetables, Michael! Possibly crepes with vegetables.*)

FML.

FAN PRICING

If you would like to find out what LMBPN is doing and the books we will be publishing, just sign up at http://lmbpn.com/email/. When you sign up, we notify you of books coming out for the week, any new posts of interest in the books and pop culture arena, and the fan pricing on Saturday.

Ad Aeternitatem,

Michael Anderle

BOOKS BY MICHAEL ANDERLE

For a complete list of books by Michael Anderle, please visit

www.lmbpn.com/ma-books/

All LMBPN Audiobooks are Available at Audible.com and iTunes. For a complete list of audiobooks visit:

www.lmbpn.com/audible

CONNECT WITH THE AUTHORS

Michael Anderle Social
Website:
http://lmbpn.com

Email List:
http://lmbpn.com/email/

Facebook Here:
https://www.facebook.com/OriceranUniverse/
https://www.
facebook.com/TheKurtherianGambitBooks/
https://www.facebook.com/groups/
320172985053521/ (Protected by the Damned Facebook
Group)

Made in the USA
Columbia, SC
19 November 2020